FRAULEIN
FRANKENSTEIN

By the Author

Novels

THROUGH VIOLET EYES

WITH RED HANDS

IN GOLDEN BLOOD

FROM BLACK ROOMS

Short Story Collections

A CARNIVAL OF CHIMERAS
-FORTHCOMING-

STEPHEN WOODWORTH

FRAULEIN
FRANKENSTEIN

SHADOWRIDGE PRESS

FRAULEIN FRANKENSTEIN
First print edition published February 2017
by Shadowridge Press

This work was previously published in
digital form by Kindle Press, 2016

Book layout and design by Robert Barr
Cover illustration by Deranged Doctor Designs

ISBN: 978-1-946808-19-6

shadowridgepress.com

ACKNOWLEDGEMENTS

To give proper thanks to everyone who helped jolt this book to life would require a whole book in itself, but I want to give special mention to the following: my wife, Kelly Dunn, for her advice, comfort, commiseration, and unflagging faith in me; my father, Harry Woodworth, who supported me during the difficult period in which the novel was gestating and sadly passed away before seeing it published; my friends and first readers Peter Atkins, Wendy Rathbone, and Beth and Jim Sturges for reassuring me that, yes, it was actually a pretty good book; the crew at Deranged Doctor Design for creating such a wonderful cover for the novel; the good people at Kindle Scout for selecting the book and helping me prepare it for publication; and all the family, friends, *Through Violet Eyes* fans, and complete strangers who nominated the book and encouraged their acquaintances to do the same. Each of you contributed a crucial piece to the creation that is *FRAULEIN FRANKENSTEIN!*

This book is dedicated to-
PETER ATKINS
and
WENDY RATHBONE
my fearless laboratory assistants;

to
KELLY DUNN,
my monster mate;

and most especially to my
favorite mad scientist,
my father,
HARRY WOODWORTH
1929-2016

FRAULEIN
FRANKENSTEIN

CHAPTER 1

BIRTH PAINS

I was born in horror, my first speech a scream.

Consciousness came as I convulsed upon a slab, thick leather straps binding me to a plank of wood as iron manacles funneled lightning into my body and brain. I shrieked in birth agony, as if mother and child in one, and the strangeness of my own voice frightened me. Through a thin veil of gauze over my eyes, I could see the blue fire of electricity flare around me.

Then everything went dark. My fingers and feet tingled, either from the residue of static or from the blood that began to course through my extremities.

My throat raw, I gasped and hiccoughed, unused to the chore of breathing. I heard the scuffing of footsteps and felt brusque hands tear open the rough smock that covered my chest. A circle of polished wood—the bell of an ear trumpet—pressed down upon the cleft between my breasts.

"The heart beats." A voice, clipped and frigid, dripping with disappointment and disgust. "Your mate lives."

"Let me see her!" another voice demanded, deeper and cruder

11

than the first. I thrashed to free myself from my bonds as heavy, thudding steps approached.

"She's not ready," the first voice protested.

"Show her *now*!"

I heard a scuffling, and the first voice cried out, "Very well, very well! Now unhand me . . ."

He panted with panic. I strained to hear what they might do next.

Then the cool blade of a pair of shears slid underneath the gauze at my neck and snipped away the bandages that wrapped my face like funereal cerements. As the strips of cloth fell away and my eyelids flicked open, the terrible new wonder of vision assaulted my unformed mind.

Beside me stood a man, though I did not yet understand that his sex differed from mine. All I knew was that he was a being like myself. His thoughts were inscrutable to me, yet he clearly had me at his mercy. Attired in a fine—if somewhat severe—black frock coat, he possessed a high, cerebral forehead made more prominent by a receding shock of reddish-brown hair. The gravity of his expression etched deep lines in his youthful face, and he peered down at me with eyes that each contained a smaller, screaming face. Those tiny faces were actually my own, reflected in the oval lenses of his spectacles.

"There," he said, and I recognized at once the brusque, clinical tone. "I trust you are satisfied—"

"Release her." I strained to see the source of that other, harsher voice, but it remained just outside the periphery of my vision, as if deliberately shying away from me.

The man clenched the fist that held his shears, as if tempted to use them as a weapon. "I tell you, she's not ready yet."

"I want her to come to me."

The man's frown deepened, and he cast aside the shears. "As you wish."

He took a metal ring from a peg on the adjacent wall. An odd, square metal key dangled from the ring, and he used this key to unscrew the manacles at my ankles and wrists. When I wriggled to worm my limbs from the leather straps that still held them, he flinched away.

"Be still now," he murmured, as if calming a captive animal.

He unfastened the circlet of iron that encompassed my forehead and pried it off. Charred skin clung to the metal points that had fired sparks into my temples.

I watched, chest heaving, as he undid the leather bindings on my upper legs and midriff. My fear had no patience, so before he could free my right arm I yanked it loose, ripping the thick animal hide in two as easily as if tearing fine lace. The man staggered back in fright.

Sensing I now had the advantage, I sprang forward, snarling. But I had no mastery over my body, and when I levered my feet off the wooden plank my legs folded beneath me and I fell to my knees on the hard stone floor. I yelped in pain and grabbed the edge of the slab to pull myself back up, the strip of torn leather still hanging from my right wrist.

The man shot a panicked glance into the darkness that lay at the far end of the room. There, outside the circle of yellow light cast by the oil lamp above us, I saw a hulking form hunched in the shadows. It appeared to be almost as tall as the man and twice as broad.

Then it stood up.

Its head nearly brushed the ceiling timbers. Its face was blotted by darkness, but I could see the figure possessed a misshapen, distorted quality, a fearful asymmetry. Lightning from the ongoing storm outside flashed through one of the chamber's narrow windows, so that the silhouette appeared to emanate a flickering aura of unearthly silver-white energy. The stone floor seemed to quake under the giant's tread, amplified by the reverberation of thunder. It reached for me with arms that were too long and too large for its frayed peasant's coat, its splayed hands the size of a bear's claws.

As the creature stooped down into the lamplight, its head emerged from eclipse like a baleful moon. Lank black hair drooped in unctuous tangles around an unfinished face. Yellow skin stretched like a distended lamb's bladder over sharp bone, its translucence revealing a web of gangrenous purple veins. It leered at me, black pupils in jaundiced eyes, and bared tarnished teeth in the crooked semblance of a smile.

Yet it was not the creature's hideous aspect that repulsed me. Innocent as an infant, I had no aesthetic prejudice by which to judge it ugly. Rather, I instinctively feared the desperate desire that trembled through every fiber of the monster's massive frame—an all-consuming possessiveness gathered into the single word it spoke as it came for me.

"*Mine.*"

Shrieking, I dropped on all fours and scuttled away from its grasping hands. To my surprise, the thing did not attempt to seize me but instead retreated into the dark end of the chamber as though *I* had frightened *it*. It wrapped its arms over its head in abject shame and wailed.

"Damn you, Frankenstein! You made her *pretty*."

The well-dressed man regarded me with scorn. "That is easily fixed."

The man called Frankenstein snatched a scalpel from a tray of surgical implements beside the slab and stalked toward me, raising the blade. I barely dodged the knife as he slashed it in an arc toward my cheek.

Scrabbling away across the floor, I realized I could never escape him by crawling. I clutched at the corner of a dissection table opposite the slab where I had lain and hauled myself up to a standing position, willing myself to walk as my pursuer did. As I gripped the table's edge, my fingers slipped through a slick, viscous liquid, and my nose filled with a heavy iron odor. I raised myself above the level of the tabletop and saw the nude form of a woman in repose upon the marble, her figure statuesque, her skin as pale and unblemished as alabaster. A ragged gash punctured her chest just below the breastbone, and her swanlike neck ended in a stump of sawn meat and bone. Dark burgundy fluid drained into a gutter chiseled into the table's stone surface.

I recoiled from the headless corpse and nearly collided with Frankenstein, whose knife I suddenly dreaded more than ever. He grabbed a fold of my loose smock and dragged me toward him, the blade scything toward my face.

"*No!*"

The creature seized Frankenstein's arm in its enormous fist. The man cried out in pain and dropped the knife, and I tugged my smock free of his other hand.

"Are you mad?" Frankenstein shouted at the monster. "Do you want her or not?"

Indecision rippled the beast's expression. He released his grip on the man, who surged toward me.

Tottering like a newborn calf, I lunged for the first weapon I could lay hands upon. Wooden shelves laden with glass containers lined the walls of the room, and in each jar gelatinous organs floated in a murk of alcohol and blood. I hurled these flasks at my pursuer, and a stink like pickled pig's feet erupted as the jars burst and splashed entrails on the floor. The lid of one container came off in midair, showering Frankenstein with plasma solution as two raw kidneys stained his waistcoat.

While he wiped the scum from his spectacles and spat dripping blood, I frantically pawed the perimeter of the square chamber, seeking an exit. Reaching a gap between two sets of shelves, I beat at the heavy oaken door I found there but succeeded only in rattling its cast-iron hinges.

A shadow engulfed me, and I gasped. The creature had come up behind me. I trembled in terror, certain it would crush me in its embrace. When I gazed up into its yellowed eyes, though, I saw such an aching sadness there that my fear dissolved into pity for the monster. Rather than seizing me, it slid back the door's iron bolt, lifted the latch, and pulled the portal open.

I had neither time to wonder why the giant had shown me such mercy nor words to express my gratitude to it, for I heard the blood-drenched man behind me give an angry yell. I leaped through the door's open archway and nearly tumbled down a flight of stone steps. Clinging to the side of the unlit stairwell, I felt my way blindly down its incline, bare toes feeling for each step. As I came to the first corner in the descent, the dim amber rays of a lantern fell on the stairs behind me, but I shrank from its searching beams as it approached.

Spurred by the rapid patter of leather-soled footsteps behind me, I hurried down the stairs and around the next right-angle turn. My pace quickened as I learned to use my legs, and two more flights of steps brought me to the bottom of the staircase. Feeling my way forward, I touched the rough grain of another heavy wooden door. I battered it with my fists, threw my entire weight against it. The door shuddered, but it would not open.

Lantern light bloomed in the stairwell behind me, the footfalls growing louder. Frantic, I remembered how the creature had opened the previous door. I pawed the wood until my fingertips brushed cold iron fittings. I shot back the bolt and rattled the latch until it clattered open, falling through the archway as the door swung open into the room beyond.

I slumped onto the smooth marble floor of this new chamber. A faint, guttering glow illuminated furnishings of richly carved mahogany and walnut and gilt-framed portraits of glowering ancestors. I shrieked when I saw what appeared to be a silver man with a spear standing over me, then realized it was merely a hollow suit of armor with a pike held in its empty gauntlet.

I was not alone, however. The light in the room emanated from three tapers in a candelabrum held by an old man in a nightshirt who gaped down at me in wide-eyed astonishment.

I sprang to my feet again and skittered away from him. As I did so, Frankenstein burst through the open doorway from the stairwell. "Hans, you fool!" he shouted at the old man. "Stop her!"

Seeing both men come toward me, I darted glances around the room, seeking escape. Lightning flashed in a window to my left, and I understood that the storm raged *outside* this place where I was trapped.

The incandescent flicker also revealed a pair of doors beside the window. Unlike the other doors, these were smooth and polished, with handles and hinges of fine brass instead of rough iron. I charged toward them, but Frankenstein caught me around the waist. Without thinking, I roughly shoved him away, and to my surprise, the force of the blow sent him reeling back against his elderly manservant.

I tore one of the double doors open, hesitating only an instant as another thunderbolt cracked the darkness ahead of me. Then I dashed out into the night, preferring to take my chances with the storm and the unknown world beyond.

CHAPTER 2

SANCTUARY

Raindrops pelted me as I raced down a dozen stone steps and barreled into the black wilderness beyond. A crack of thunder startled me, and, panicked, I looked back over my shoulder. A blindingly bright lightning bolt struck a rod atop one of the two square towers that rose from the castle I'd fled. As thunder rent the air, an enormous silhouette filled the tower's narrow upper window.

I knew the strange figure could not be Frankenstein. I could see my well-dressed pursuer in the lightning's silver glare as he burst forth from the castle's entrance. Wearing a tall, broad-brimmed hat to shield his eyes from the rain, Frankenstein still carried the lantern in his left hand but now cradled what appeared to be a long metal tube in the crook of his right arm.

Although I could not begin to understand the danger I was in, I ran as if I did, colliding with the cragged trunks of trees that seemed to materialize in front of me with every flicker of lightning. Every time I glanced over my shoulder, I saw the lantern's amber glow bobbing after me like a relentless revenant.

Rainwater matted my hair until the locks dripped right into

my eyes. My bare feet sank to the ankle in an ooze of mud and sodden leaves with every stride. The ground sloped downward unexpectedly, and I slipped in the muck, water sluicing around me as I slid along the incline. I scratched at the hillside, sinking my fingers into the silt to halt my descent. As I lifted myself, drenched and shivering, from the slime, I saw Frankenstein stop only a short distance behind me. He set the lantern on the ground beside him and lifted the metal tube to shoulder-level, sighting along its length as he pointed it at me.

I mistook the loud report that followed for another thunderclap. But I could see the puff of smoke from the barrel and the flare of sparks from the gunpowder, which he had kept dry by bracing the gun's stock under the sleeve of his frockcoat. A musket ball whistled past my ear and chipped bark from a tree behind me.

I wheezed with fright, and Frankenstein cursed when he saw he'd missed. With no time to muzzle-load the weapon, he threw down the musket, reached beneath his coat, and drew a dueling pistol from the waist of his breeches.

I scampered off, darting and weaving among the trees as he tried to aim. He must have snatched up the lantern again, for a shaft of sickly yellow light glinted through the branches around me as I ran. Another crack, then a pistol ball nipped off the bristle of a pine right above my head.

The slope leveled off and the woods thinned. I panicked as the fringe of the forest gave way to an open clearing, for without the protection of the trees, I would have no place to hide. I turned back toward the woods but found the lantern hovering mere steps behind me, the hunter at my heels.

Another flicker of the storm revealed a rutted dirt road to my left, the canals of its wagon tracks flooded with rainwater. The road curved toward a cluster of slant-roofed buildings, dark and sleeping in the depths of the night. With no other shelter available to me, I sprinted toward the town.

I reached the largest of the structures—a big, drafty stable. Its doors were closed to me, however, and I did not see the sort of bolts and latches I knew how to open. Frenzied with frustration, I pounded at the entrance with such force that the whole stable rattled and the thick oaken beam that barred the doors groaned and nearly buckled. Startled by my assault, the horses within bucked and whinnied, ready to bolt.

Lantern light bathed the right side of my face, and I looked over to see Frankenstein standing near the corner of the stable, panting with exertion. Lightning illumined the dark face beneath the brim of his hat, revealing the cold determination of his expression. He pulled a second dueling pistol from beneath his coat—the twin of the one he'd already fired—and cocked the hammer, leveling the barrel at the circle of light he had centered on my gaping eyes.

At that moment a second lantern swung into view, emerging from a cottage of timber and brick adjacent to the barn. "Settle down, you stupid beasts!" an uncouth voice yelled as the horses continued to stamp and neigh. "Great God, but it's only a bit of thunder."

My pursuer lowered his weapon, cloaked his own lantern with the tail of his coat, and hastily retreated around the stable's corner, out of sight. Since I did not know what I might have to fear from this unexpected stranger, I, too, shied away, flattening myself in the shadows far to the left of the stable's entrance.

A bow-legged peasant waddled up to the doors, his shirttail only half-tucked into his breeches. "Keep whining like that," he muttered to the unsettled animals, "and I'll give you something to whine about."

Mopping rain from his brow with his sleeve, the peasant hung his lantern on a hook to the right, levered the bar up to one side, and pulled one of the two doors open just enough to sidle through the gap. When he retrieved his lantern and entered, I crept in after him. Although I could not be sure what harm the peasant might do me, I could tell that as long as I was in the stranger's presence, Frankenstein would not dare to come near.

I kept well outside the aura of the stable hand's lantern as he moved from stall to stall, alternately soothing and berating the horses for their noise. The animals must have sensed my presence, however, for their agitation only increased. Fortunately, the peasant dismissed their restlessness as a reaction to the storm outside.

21

"Devil take you all!" he grumbled when both coos and threats had failed to calm them. I crouched behind a pile of hay as he trudged out, only exhaling when he barred the barn door.

Penned in darkness with the horses, I buried myself in the straw to conceal my body from both human sight and animal scent. The horses quieted as they gradually forgot about me, and this impromptu nest lulled me with such a sense of warmth and security that I succumbed to the oblivion of sleep.

I then had what may have been a dream.

The clatter of hooves awakened me. The horses brayed with anxiety again, and I was certain that I'd been discovered. I peered out through a small hole in the hay but could see no one. Cautiously, I raised my head. Doves that were roosting in the rafters above me suddenly scattered, the frantic flutter of their wings causing me to look up.

Through the square windows near the roof, the storm's glimmer played upon a shape. It hunched at the edge of the loft like a gargoyle. Rain had pasted its black hair to its livid brow. Ebon eyes peered, unblinking, down upon me. Watching me . . . or, perhaps, watching *over* me, a sentinel to defend me from Frankenstein and any other hostile humans.

Whatever its motives, the creature remained as motionless as statuary. I fixed my gaze on the loft even as the stable went dark again, every muscle tensed for flight in case the giant should come for me.

When lightning next shimmered in the barn windows, the loft was vacant.

I stifled a cry and kept utterly still, straining to catch any glimpse or sound of the thing. I stayed that way until the storm ended, until the dreary gray sunlight of an overcast dawn seeped into the loft.

The creature was not there. Perhaps it had never been there.

Although the immediate menace of Frankenstein was gone, the morning brought no comfort. Having slept little the previous night, I felt the vigor of fright give way to the dull disease of exhaustion. I sprawled in the hay in a stupor, leaden weariness weighting my limbs. The grassy smell of straw and manure that had made the stable seem so snug during the storm now sickened me. And I was still lost and alone among beings I did not understand and could not trust.

I wanted to leave the stable before the peasant returned, but to my dismay I discovered that the barred doors could only be opened from outside. The horses grew restive as soon as I revealed myself. The noise would rouse their master before long. In search of another exit, I cast my eyes upward—to the loft. If I had, in fact, seen the creature perched there, it must have climbed in through one of the open upper windows. But they were all so high above me . . .

I was so preoccupied with finding a way to reach those windows that I was still standing dumbly in the center of the barn when I heard the peasant lifting the bar from the doors. With no chance to burrow back into the hay, I hurried to press myself against the wall to the left of the barn's entrance. I held my breath and hoped he wouldn't notice me.

The right door creaked outward, flooding the barn with daylight, and the irascible stable hand shuffled inside. Again, the restlessness of the horses worked in my favor, for their clamor irked him, drawing his attention.

"Be still, you miserable nags, or I'll whip the lot of you! Come now, Gretchen—time for work."

As he went to the mare's stall and began fitting her with a bridle, I scurried through the open door.

Still wary that Frankenstein might be lurking in the woods behind me, I meandered onward, deeper into the forbidding maze of civilization. White cliffs of buildings three stories high walled me in on either side, studded with windows trimmed in red. The gray dawn awakened the town, compounding the risk of discovery. Many times I had to scuttle into the narrow alleys off the main thoroughfare in order to avoid the street vendors with their pushcarts and the shopkeepers who were setting out their wares.

With no object other than self-preservation, I wandered the jagged avenues in a kind of delirium, stupefied by my new surroundings yet driven by a need I could not name. An agonizing emptiness cramped my stomach and dizzied my head, until I reeled from weakness. Only

23

when I caught the warm gravy scent of stewed rabbit on the air did I learn the craving that compelled me.

Hunger.

All caution departed as my yearning body staggered toward the source of the smell. I tottered from a dim passageway between two boardinghouses into a small plaza. In the plaza's center was a baroque structure of reddish stone whose spire dominated the cityscape—the town's Stadtkirche, or city church. A mass of beggars and cripples had congregated around the octagonal chapel at the near end of the building. There, a balding man in a black cassock and a matron in a drab gray dress ladled stew from an iron pot into bowls fashioned from loaves of bread. The indigents ranged in age from children barely able to toddle to shriveled crones propped on walking sticks, but each accepted the offered food with a humble bow. Some wore rags as frayed as my smock, many were missing limbs or were disfigured by pox, and all stank of filth. Yet, as I lurched into view, ravening like an animal, the paupers scattered, so terror-struck they even abandoned the meal they'd come to beg.

Only the minister and the matron remained, aghast at my bestial appearance. The woman dropped the ladle and grabbed the silver cross that hung on a chain around her neck, kissing the symbol and whispering under her breath. The pastor merely whispered "My God!" as I ripped a stew-saturated loaf from his hands and tore into it with my teeth, gagging as I tried to swallow without chewing.

"Child, who are you?" He bent over me as I squatted on the ground and gorged myself. "Where is your family?"

Even if I had understood him, I would not have answered, so intent was I on stuffing my mouth with bread and meat.

"She must be mute," he concluded. "Perhaps even deaf. We must tend to her."

The matron regarded me with a fretful look, the cross still at her lips. "Georg, are you sure . . . ?"

"Birgit!" he admonished her. "She is a child of God!"

Little did he know that he and I did not share the same Creator.

Unconvinced, Birgit continued to worry at her cross while I wolfed my bread. Although I would have eaten three more loaves like it, Birgit reluctantly took my hand and pulled me upright.

"We must get you inside." Casting embarrassed glances up and down the street to see who might be watching, she tugged my smock closed over my exposed bosom and hurried me across the square to the townhouse that served as the parsonage. Too dazed and weary to resist, I allowed myself to be led like a docile cow. These people had given me food, and that was reason enough to stay with them.

Once we were inside the sparsely furnished abode, Birgit shut the curtains on the front windows, muttering her thoughts aloud. "I suppose we shall put you in Gerta's old room. There might even be a dress to fit you. But not until you're clean."

She herded me down a hall of lacquered wood and into a barren room that contained little more than a cot, a stool, and a wardrobe. After forcing me onto the stool, she bustled out the door, holding the hand that had touched me away from her as if it were tainted. Several minutes later, she returned with a chamber pot of water and a scrap of stained linen.

"Can't have you looking like you sleep in a sty." She soaked the cloth and swabbed my face with it, washing the smeared gravy from my mouth and the dirt from my brow. Though she believed me deaf and dumb, she kept chattering to me in an indulgent way, as if pampering a pet.

"*There!*" she chimed with a final, triumphant swipe. "You look almost human now."

To have me admire her handiwork, she led me to a framed pane of silvered glass. Other than a crucifix hanging on the opposite wall, it was the room's only ornamentation. It was positioned so you could see the cross in the mirror's reflection—spirituality and vanity in perpetual confrontation.

"See what a pretty girl you are!" Birgit said as I gaped at an image I did not understand was my own.

I put out my hand, half expecting to touch the soft cheek of the woman who reached toward me. Though the glass stopped my fingertips, I pressed them against the fall of blonde hair, still damp and tangled from Birgit's cleaning. It amazed me when the head in the mirror cocked in tandem with mine, for I felt peculiarly detached from the form I wore, as if I were merely manipulating a marionette. I did not know what Birgit meant by "pretty" and neither liked nor disliked the features of the woman before me: large, almond-shaped azure eyes; a straight, slightly upturned nose; prominent cheekbones; and a strong chin. Framed by the flaxen mane, the face possessed a vaguely leonine appearance.

"You'll have plenty of time to preen later," Birgit chided as I gazed at myself. "First, we must get you into some decent clothes."

She peeled the wretched smock off my shoulders. Unschooled in modesty, I let the garment fall to the floor without objection.

"*Oh* . . . oh, my." Birgit backed away from me, mouth bobbing as she hyperventilated. She gawped at me with such horror that I wondered if my appearance were truly that repulsive. "Georg! *Georg!*"

She ran from the room to fetch the pastor, leaving me to contemplate my own nakedness. The body I examined was trim and well-proportioned, the ivory skin still grimy from my escape but otherwise unblemished. Yet one thing did mar its purity: at my shoulders and hips, the red lips of puckering scars had been cinched together with rag-doll stitches. Another such seam formed a circlet around my throat.

I leaned toward the mirror, traced the black tracks of the stitches all the way around the nape of my neck and back to my windpipe. My skin stippled with gooseflesh, for I needed no lessons in anatomy or medicine to know that no living thing should survive having its head severed.

At that moment, I realized I was a monster.

CHAPTER
3

FIRST WORD

Pastor Georg blanched when he first saw my wounds, his mouth quivering as speech failed him.

"The cuts must not be deep," he said at last, refusing to believe what could not be possible. "The girl was obviously savaged by bandits, then treated by a physician." The minister nodded, convinced by his own argument. "A miracle she survived, truly. Clothe her, Birgit. Providence has consigned her to our care while she heals."

The woman's face plumped in a grimace as the clergyman again assigned responsibility for me to her. Nevertheless, she dutifully attempted to drape a dress over me, but I kicked and batted her away every time she moved to throw the bunched cloth over my head.

"Oh, you cur!" she cried when I boxed her ear. "You want to be treated like a dog, eh? Very well!"

Birgit shoved the dress under her arm and huffed out of the bedchamber. She returned some minutes later with a wily look, the dress in one fist, a stew-drenched loaf in the other. As I leaped for the food, she yanked it from my reach.

"No, you don't! First this . . ." She brandished the dress. "*Then* this." Once more, she tantalized me with the bread.

My gaze flicked between her hands, from requirement to reward. When Birgit next presented the dress, I remained still, permitting her to pull it over my head and to maneuver my arms into its puffy sleeves. The garment, which had evidently belonged to the "Gerta" who once occupied this room, did not really fit me. The skirts barely reached my knees, and I chafed at the tight tailoring beneath my breasts. I pouted at Birgit, glaring toward the loaf she'd set aside while dressing me.

"Fair enough." She handed me the bread. "You've earned it."

Still famished, I seized the loaf, but something stopped me from eating. This woman's kindness had stirred a sense of civility in me. I wasn't sure how to behave. I recalled the supplicants outside the church and mimicked them, bowing my head in gratitude.

Birgit's eyes widened. *"You understand."*

I then stuffed the heel of the loaf into my mouth, gobbling in an abandon of appetite.

Birgit sighed and stroked my hair. "Poor dear. We really must find something to call you," she mused. "Georg says you are a child of God. From now on, you shall be Liesl."

I continued to glut myself, unaware that I had been christened. I felt as detached from this strange name—this label placed upon me—as I did from the unfamiliar reflection I saw in the mirror.

Therefore, I was perplexed and unsettled when, as I later joined them for a humble dinner, both Birgit and Pastor Georg applied the name to me with every sentence they spoke, the way one does when domesticating an animal. "We are so pleased to have you with us, Liesl." "Would you like more sausage, Liesl?" "Liesl! Do not stick your fingers in the soup." And, like an animal, I found myself responding to the name, reflexively turning my head to whoever spoke it.

"You see, Georg?" Birgit said. "She hears."

The minister nodded, peering intently at me across the table. "So she does. Perhaps she listens as well."

I averted my eyes, for he seemed to stare straight into my mind. Would I be as welcome in their home, I wondered, if he could see my true history?

When the time came for sleep, Birgit had to lie on the cot in Gerta's room and pretend to doze in order to demonstrate the bed's purpose to me. Having only slept on a barn floor during my short life, I had difficulty accepting that I could be given such comfort. I lay stiffly between the goose-feather mattress and linen sheets. Despite their enveloping softness and the crushing fatigue I felt, I found it hard to keep my eyes closed, even when Birgit took away the candle that provided the room's only light. The bed made me uneasy for a reason I could not grasp.

Only when I slipped into a fitful slumber did I learn why the act of lying on the cot bothered me so, for I dreamed I was shackled to a slab instead, wrapped in gauze rather than linen. Lightning seemed to sear through me and I jolted awake, screaming.

Chest heaving, I sprang upright in bed, relieved yet perplexed to find the room awash in daylight. The night, which had seemed endless while I lay awake, had dissolved into nightmare.

Birgit blustered into the room, wiping flour from her hands onto her apron. "Good Lord, child, what is it?"

She sat beside me on the cot, patting my back to calm me. I sobbed and made shapeless vocal slurs. I wanted so badly to communicate everything to her—about my unnatural conception and the well-dressed man and the malformed giant in the laboratory—but the subtle art of speech eluded me, and I snarled in frustration.

"It's all right," Birgit cooed, rubbing my shoulder. "Don't be afraid, Liesl. You're safe here."

The name, which I had greeted with suspicion the night before, now pacified me—made me feel like I *belonged*. My sobs quieted to a soft mewling.

"That's better. Now let us get you some breakfast."

Birgit took my hand to lead me to the kitchen, but as we neared the home's foyer, I overheard a voice that made me wonder if I had awakened from one nightmare into another.

"A scullery maid of mine. She had a jealous lover who did frightful violence to her with a knife."

Pastor Georg stood with the front door ajar, conversing with a visitor on the stoop outside. I couldn't see the stranger—and didn't need to. I knew the cold, clipped tones of that voice better than my own.

Birgit regarded me with alarm as I staggered back against the wall, shuddering. "Liesl?"

I didn't answer but glared instead at the open door as the unseen speaker went on.

"I sewed up her wounds," he said with professional nonchalance, "but the girl ran off, fearing the lover would come back for her. I'm afraid she might perish without medical attention, and I thought she might have fled to town. Have you seen her by any chance?"

The minister's lips parted to answer and he eased the door open a bit as if about to invite the visitor inside. Then, out of the corner of his eye, he caught sight of me, pallid and trembling.

"I'm sorry, Baron Frankenstein," he said firmly to the man on the doorstep. "I have seen no one such as you describe. Now, if you'll excuse me, I must bid you good day."

He shut the door before the visitor could make any objection.

The pastor's protectiveness ought to have reassured me, but the mention of that name—the first I'd ever heard—only made my heart beat faster.

Damn you, Frankenstein! the giant had moaned. *You made her pretty . . .*

"F-frahnk . . ." I bellowed my lungs to push the sound out, my mouth squirming to mold vowels and consonants. "Frahnk . . . en . . . shh-hhteiiiiiin!"

Pastor Georg looked ashen as he came down the hallway toward me. "Birgit, we must teach this girl to speak," he said hoarsely. "She must tell us what he did to her."

CHAPTER 4

FRANKENSTEIN'S BRIDE

For the first two months I stayed with them, Pastor Georg and Birgit did not let me leave their house, lest the Baron or any of his confidants should see me. I did not object to my confinement, however, for I had a world of things to learn.

Poor Birgit had not a moment of peace, for whether she was cleaning, cooking, sewing, or praying, I pressed her to teach me the words to describe what she did. I would point at a pot, a thimble, a blanket, a Bible, and bleat plaintively until she told me the name for the object. I proved an extraordinarily apt pupil, picking up the language as easily as if the vocabulary were already embroidered in the fabric of my brain. Perhaps it was.

Whatever unnatural advantages I possessed in my education, I was speaking rudimentary German and demanding lessons in reading and writing from my hosts within a fortnight. But they taught me far more than simple school lessons—far more than they intended.

Although I could see the most obvious differences in appearance and dress between men and women, it did not occur to my child's mind that the sexes were distinct beings or that they interacted in any way other than the commonplace acts of eating, sleeping, working, or conversing. I certainly did not think a female anatomy that I did not even choose would ultimately determine my destiny.

Yet I noticed a closeness between Birgit and Pastor Georg that they didn't exhibit with their parishioners. When I first began staying with them, they maintained a stiff, self-conscious propriety in my presence, but as they became accustomed to me they touched hands frequently, exchanged secretive smiles, and whispered endearments.

One morning, just before Pastor Georg left for the church, he pressed his mouth to Birgit's with a disgusting slurping sound, as if trying to chew the lips from her face. I watched, nauseated, from the hallway. As soon as he'd gone out the door, I rushed forward to tug at Birgit's elbow.

"What is? What is?" I imitated the repulsive sucking noise.

Birgit glance from my face to where Pastor Georg had just stood and back again, either unsure what I was asking or unable to believe I did not already know the answer. Then she let out a laugh.

"Why, that's a *kiss*, of course! It's how Georg shows his love for me." She stared, expecting some sign of comprehension from me. "Haven't you ever been kissed, Liesl? Liesl?"

I ran back to my room and slammed the door. My head reeled from a mixture of confusion and a blistering new emotion for which I had no word: embarrassment.

I stood before the mirror and made the squidlike pucker of a "kiss" to my reflection. How could one possibly want such a thing? But Birgit had spoken of a kiss as if it were a delight, seemed to pity me for never having had one. She said it was a sign of something else I did not have, another word whose meaning was unfathomable to me.

Love.

Before long, I received an even more vulgar—and less welcome— demonstration of "love."

Having gone to bed early one evening, I again squirmed in the clutches of a nightmare, a confabulation of real memory and horrible imagining. The Goliath from the laboratory reached for my naked body with cold, greedy hands.

Mine, it said.

Its obsidian eyes fixed on me in a covetous stare, its bluish lips bunching to claim a kiss. As the simian arms enfolded me, the massive mouth swelled in my vision until it seemed a bottomless gullet that would swallow me whole. I shrieked and levered upright in bed, panting and perspiring.

Now awake, I heard more shrieks, as if the dream were still ringing in my ears. But no . . . Birgit's voice shrilled, not mine.

I thought there must have been a real horror going on in the house.

I rose and padded to the kitchen on tiptoe, stifling exclamations of surprise and pain as I banged into furniture in the dark. Fumbling to locate the candlestick on the table, I lit the taper with a spill I ignited from the smoldering coals in the cooking fire, as I had seen Birgit do. She was still squealing like a sow impaled on a spit as I grabbed a poker from the hearth as a weapon and crept to the bedchamber upstairs.

The sounds from within the room grew worse—a sickening slapping of flesh, punctuated by Birgit's yelps and a rough, porcine snorting.

She's being beaten, I thought.

Choking up my grip on the poker, I pressed the door's latch down with my knuckles and pushed the door open with my foot. As I thrust the candle into the room, the taper sloshed yellow light over the hairy flabbiness of an aging man's bare back, buttocks, and flanks. As I raised the poker to strike, the man on the bed rolled to one side and looked back at me, puffing, his cheeks red from either exertion or humiliation.

It was Pastor Georg.

Beneath him lay Birgit, equally nude, equally mortified. She had stopped squealing and now only wheezed, aghast. I took little notice of her, however, for I could not tear my gaze from the pastor. It was the first time I had seen him without his clerical vestments, the first time I had seen *any* man unclothed.

"Liesl? What . . . what . . . " Stammering, he withdrew from Birgit, and his . . . his *appendage* drooped in sorry defeat.

I dropped the poker and backed out into the hall. Hobbling out of bed, Pastor Georg flustered into the first garment he could get hold of—his cassock, which he shrugged on without buttoning. The robe still afforded glimpses of the profane beneath the sacred, and the minister reeked of sweat and secretion as he came after me.

"Liesl!" he cried, commanding, pleading. "It is not what you think. We are Lutherans. Birgit is my wife."

He must have misinterpreted my disgust as Catholic indignation at the sins of an uncelibate priest. I had little conception of God, much less the differences in doctrine between Christian sects, so his explanations made no sense to me.

A nightshirt now wrapped around her, Birgit timidly emerged from the bedchamber to stand behind the minister.

I glared at the two of them. "What is? What is?"

Pastor Georg put his arm around Birgit, placed a hand on her breastbone. "Wife. My wife." He moved the hand to his own chest. "Husband. I'm her husband."

I waved the candle in Birgit's direction, accusing. "You—you *hurt.*"

The minister shook his head and smiled. "No, no, she is not hurt. See?"

He gestured to his wife, who smiled sheepishly in affirmation.

"Love between man and woman is a gift from God." The pastor chuckled. "Even for a man of the cloth."

He extended a paternal hand toward me but relented when I flinched away. "Someday, you will understand," he promised.

I nodded only so that I could get away from him and go back to my room. *My* wife. Something about those words brought back the memory of the monster's huge hands, its needy grasping as it moved toward me. I shuddered. In reality, I understood nothing of man and woman, husband and wife. I did not think I ever would.

After my wounds had scabbed and sealed, Birgit took a pair of delicate sewing scissors and snipped each of my stitches. "I may not be much of a surgeon," she remarked, gently tugging loose threads free from my skin, "but I'm as good a seamstress as you're likely to find."

As the black scabs flaked away, they left thick, whitish scars that slithered around my joints and throat like nightcrawlers. Birgit insisted that I keep them covered at all times, required me to wear either scarves or high-collared dresses to hide my neck. I also learned to tolerate the perpetual constriction of shoes and cumbersome layers of undergarments.

When I had mastered enough manners and speech not to arouse unwanted attention, Pastor Georg deemed me proper enough to work with them in the Stadtkirche as a charwoman. There, in the church, I received yet another lesson in the ritual mysteries of marriage, and from a most unexpected source.

The well-dressed man named Frankenstein lurked constantly in the shadowed corridors of my dreams, but during my waking hours I'd had little cause or desire to dwell on him. Only a few times after I learned to speak did Pastor Georg awkwardly attempt to broach the subject.

"Liesl," he would begin after much hemming and hawing, "if there's anything you wish to tell us about the night you came to us . . . anything about Baron Frankenstein . . ."

As soon as he mentioned the name, I trembled so piteously that he abandoned the topic at once. My fear, while well-founded, was not entirely genuine. I could not have said why I dissembled in order to protect a man who'd tried to kill me, except that Baron Frankenstein was the only person who knew the truth of my existence. I sensed somehow that, if I bore witness against him, I might never have the opportunity to ask him who I was or how I came to be.

The chance that I would ever get such an opportunity seemed slight at best. I was nothing but a housemaid, he a reclusive nobleman who hadn't visited the city in more than a month. I had no reason to hope our paths would ever cross again, much less to think that we would meet again in the very church where I now swept the nave.

One afternoon, I was whisking my broom in the octagonal chapel when Frankenstein opened the front door, removing his hat as he leaned inside. Recognizing him at once, I spun around and swept up the center aisle in the opposite direction so he would not see my face.

Fortunately, the Baron did not seem to recognize me now that I no longer wore stitches and bandages. "You there!" he called. "Where is the minister?"

I kept at my cleaning, pretending not to hear.

"Girl! Are you deaf? Where is your master?"

Pastor Georg hurried forward to intercede. "I am here. How may I help you, Baron?"

Curiosity compelled me to look, and I maneuvered between the pews so that I could watch from the corner of my eye. My stomach knotted, for I was convinced he'd returned for me.

Frankenstein had other business, however. He had not come alone. He held the door for his companion—a slim, prim-looking young woman in a fashionable-yet-modest gown, her dark hair bound in a bun but for ringlets that fell over her ears. She had a round, pleasant face and a faint smile that shone with good-natured amusement.

Frankenstein, by contrast, bore a funereal frown, even in such charming company. "May I present my fiancée Elizabeth Lavenza?" he announced to the pastor with impatient formality. "We must have our wedding here in the Stadtkirche, immediately. Every moment we delay may part us forever."

CHAPTER
5

WEDDING NIGHT

I could almost feel the tension in Pastor Georg's neck muscles as he strained to avoid glancing in my direction. "Are you certain, Baron?" he asked, nonplussed. "So soon after your mother—"

"My family's misfortunes are nothing to you," Frankenstein replied.

I would later learn that Victor Frankenstein had lost several of his closest relations and friends in tragic and mysterious circumstances over the past few weeks.

Pastor Georg became flustered, sought to placate the nobleman. "We would be honored, of course. But such a distinguished event will require preparation. If you could give us a few weeks—"

The Baron remained adamant. "It must be no later than tomorrow."

Elizabeth nudged her groom-to-be in gentle remonstrance. "Victor, have patience! Surely we can wait . . ."

"No. *I* cannot." He took her hand in his in the first gesture of real tenderness I had ever seen him display. "The only thing left that I want from this life is to be wed to you. Please . . . don't deny me that."

Behind their spectacles, his eyes deepened with such desolation that I almost pitied the man. *What,* I wondered, *could have caused the stone of his heart to crumble so?*

Elizabeth's smile faded. "You know there is nothing I want more than to marry you," she assured him. "Tomorrow it shall be, then."

He kissed her hand, holding it to his lips as if afraid it might disappear.

The intensity of the moment discomfited Pastor Georg. "Well . . . I suppose I'd better get to work. Will four o'clock in the afternoon be acceptable for the ceremony?"

Victor Frankenstein recovered himself somewhat, although his gaze remained glassy. "Oh . . . yes. That will be fine. Thank you."

The Baron and his intended took their leave of the pastor, who strode off to seek Birgit's help for the preparations. I hastened to the front door of the church in order to peek out at Frankenstein as he helped Elizabeth into a carriage that waited for them in the plaza. He darted a glance over his shoulder, and for a moment I was afraid he might have seen me.

He continued to scan the square, as if wary of being spied upon. He was about to enter the coach himself when he spotted something atop a house across the square that made him freeze.

I traced the trajectory of his gaze up to a dormer window on the roof of a three-story home. The sun had set behind the building, reddening the sky and blurring details of the slanted shingles into a single black plane of shadow. But there seemed to be an irregular figure that straddled the peak of the dormer—a splotch of silhouette with bunched shoulders and a massive, misshapen head.

Then the figure crouched lower and blended into the rooftop's dusky penumbra . . . if, in fact, it had been there at all. None of the townspeople who traipsed across the sparsely populated square had noticed it. Only Victor Frankenstein and I saw its lurking presence.

The Baron's posture drooped as he climbed into the carriage beside his fiancée. I nearly ran after the coach as it trundled off toward the castle on the hill outside town. If that prowling shadow got to Frankenstein before I did, I'd never get the answers I so desperately wanted.

Tomorrow, I thought. *He'll be back tomorrow . . . and then I'll make him tell me who I am.*

Even for a peasant, the wedding the following day would have been considered modest. For a nobleman like Baron Victor Frankenstein, it must have seemed a social fiasco. On such short notice, hardly any of the couple's immediate family or friends were able to reach the city in time. All but the first few pews in the Stadtkirche remained empty. To help fill the seats, Frankenstein had cajoled the town's pear-shaped burgomaster and a few of the more sycophantic businessmen into attending the ceremony. The sole groomsman was the old servant, Hans, who'd tried to help his master prevent my escape from the castle.

Frankenstein's servants festooned the altar and apse with a scant supply of fresh flowers they had purchased in town.

"Not enough," I heard Frankenstein mutter as he inspected their handiwork prior to the ceremony. He gestured to some handsome flower arrangements that the domestics had put aside while they placed the new flowers. The blossoms were all white, draped with night-black crepe.

"Not those, Master!" gasped Hans.

"Yes, those," Frankenstein snapped. "And quickly!"

From a distance, I watched as the servants hastily removed the black ribbons and refurbished the bouquets with white lace. I heard Birgit clucking her tongue behind me. "To think that the Baron would use his own mother's funeral flowers at his wedding!"

"Hush, Birgit," said Pastor Georg. "We have much to do."

I knew an important event had occurred in the church a few days before, but I'd had no opportunity to ask what had brought all the townsfolk to church on a weekday, or so darkly dressed. Birgit had assigned me the task of cleaning the house, as she always did when there was any chance I might attract too much attention. I did not know the word "funeral." And I couldn't have guessed just how soon I would discover what it really meant.

Unable to procure a full choir to sing the wedding liturgy on

39

a day when most of his parishioners were tending their shops or plowing their fields, Pastor Georg settled for only two choristers— one a young boy, the other an elderly widow. Their thin, high voices wavered, hollow and forlorn, in the cavernous Stadtkirche as the wedding began.

Hiding behind one of the pillars in the transept, I watched the ritual unfold. Though the paltry congregation feigned gaiety as Elizabeth walked down the aisle toward her groom, I sensed their superstitious dread. Elizabeth wore white, her waist encircled by a wide, black velvet sash. The costume reminded me of the pallid flowers with their streamers of black crepe. The bride's face looked pale, yet serene.

Victor Frankenstein himself appeared distant, distracted. He mumbled his vows, his gaze wandering from the bride to scan the empty benches at the back of the church, as if expecting to find an uninvited guest seated there—perhaps a looming, leering shadow like the one perched on the rooftop the previous day.

The sole glimmer of joy in the service came from Elizabeth. Despite Frankenstein's dolor, she clasped his hand in both of hers and smiled. "I take you, Victor, to be my husband from this day forward," she recited with fervid passion. "To join with you, and to share all that is to come. And I promise to be faithful to you as long as we both shall live."

She glowed with such rapture that I found myself envying her, even though she was marrying a man I loathed and feared. I suddenly felt bereft, a void gaping within me where none had been a moment before. Was this that intangible ideal state called "love"?

Little in the way of celebration followed the ceremony. The baron apologized to his guests for not providing a dinner and vowed to host them all for a proper feast at a future date. The newlyweds accepted tepid congratulations from the townsfolk, then departed for Castle Frankenstein, attended by Elizabeth's lady's maid and Hans.

As I watched the wedding party's carriages rattle up the road that led out of the city, my gaze flicked again to the roof of the house across the square. No shadow straddled the dormer's peak.

Its absence did not calm the sense of urgency that agitated me.

Quite the opposite. If the monster was not at the wedding, where was it . . . and what might it do next?

I wanted to go after the baron immediately but could not find a way to abscond unnoticed from Birgit and Pastor Georg. I lost a precious hour sweeping up rose petals strewn like dead butterflies along the church's center aisle, fretting every moment that the creature might deprive me forever of my chance to confront Frankenstein.

It was dinnertime before I finally finished my chores at the Stadtkirche. Though famished, I told Birgit that I wasn't hungry and wanted to go to bed early.

"It's the baron, isn't it?" She nodded knowingly, and I was afraid she'd guessed my true intention. Then she patted my shoulder and walked me to my room. "It must have upset you terribly to have him around. I hope you know that if he weren't a nobleman, we would never have allowed him in our church. It was sweet of you not to say anything to spoil the wedding. Go and rest now—you won't ever have to see him again. I promise."

Birgit left me alone in the bedchamber with this maternal vow, unaware that I intended to seek out Victor Frankenstein the moment she was gone. Under the blanket of my cot, I heaped some clothes in the shape of a sleeping figure in case anyone glanced into the darkened bedchamber. Then I donned a black cloak I'd borrowed from Birgit's wardrobe upstairs and blew out the candle on my dresser. Unlatching the sole window in my room, I pushed myself up onto the sill and jumped down into the cramped lane that ran behind the townhouse.

With the cloak's hood raised to hide my face, I skulked back to the Stadtkirche to recover a bouquet I'd hidden behind a flap of ivy that draped one of the graveyard walls. The rest of the wedding flowers I'd taken to the church's refuse heap, where they'd either be scavenged by paupers or left to rot into compost. Although the bouquet's crimson petals had blackened like drying scabs as the day wore on, this one dainty bunch of roses had remained fresher than the others. I chose to use it as my pretext to enter Castle Frankenstein.

Everyone in town knew the spiraling road that led up the hill to the ancient fortress, yet I elected to take the less conspicuous path through the forest—a trail I remembered well from the night Victor Frankenstein had tracked me through thunder and rain. I had not counted on how much more troublesome it would be to traverse the woods in a petticoat and skirts, branches and undergrowth pricking at the muslin like a harpist's fingernails. Snarling at each snag, I longed to tear my dress off and run through the trees half-naked, as I had before. Such wildness would hardly suit my plan, however, so I steadied myself by rehearsing the lines I intended to say as best I could in the limited German I possessed.

At least the weather favored me. The rains had let up over the past month, and the night was clear, if chilly. I carried no candle or lantern, but a gibbous moon sifted white beams through the lattice of branches to light my way. It was still early evening when I emerged from the trees to see the peaked caps of Castle Frankenstein's towers rising before me. Tonight, the ominous edifice presented a more welcoming face than when I had last seen it. All the windows in the great stone structure glowed with warm, dancing lamplight.

All, that is, but the topmost window in the right-hand tower. It remained dark, as if the castle's occupants were trying to forget its existence.

My feet grew heavy with trepidation as I ascended the steps to the front entrance. I was taking a terrible chance, and for what reward? Victor Frankenstein might simply kill or imprison me without ever revealing where I came from. Yet the thought of continuing life as a nonentity with no past or personality seemed far worse. If I could only get the baron in my power for a short while, I thought, perhaps I could wring enough of the truth from him to relieve the unbearable enigma of my existence.

Standing before the massive double doors, I lowered my hood, nestled the bouquet in the crook of my arm, and mouthed the words I'd practiced. Reflexively, I checked my scarf to make sure that it covered the grotesque white circlet of scar around my throat. Then I took hold of one of the door's polished brass knockers and rapped it loudly.

No one responded at first. As I reached to knock again, the door swung away from my hand and I found myself almost nose-to-nose with the servant, Hans. The old man peered at me with his protuberant gray eyes in the same fashion as the night he'd first seen me, and I became tongue-tied with anxiety, certain that he'd recognized me.

"Yes?" he snapped. "What do you want?"

When he showed no sign of familiarity, I moistened my numb lips and tongue.

"I . . . from wedding," I stammered, snatching at all the phrases I'd practiced as they flew around in my head like birds in a cage. "Need see . . . Elizabeth."

"Impossible. The baron has insisted that they not be disturbed this evening." Hans straightened himself to board stiffness and moved to slam the door.

Flustered, I nearly forgot the bouquet I'd brought. I thrust it toward the servant. "Elizabeth . . . she want flowers. Be very angry if she not get them."

Hans motioned impatiently with his hand. "Give them to me. I'll make sure the mistress gets them."

I shook my head, pulled the bouquet from his reach. "No . . . I must give to Elizabeth. Have message for her."

Grumbling something about ignorant Hungarian scullery maids, Hans stepped back and permitted me to enter.

"Follow me," he said as he shut the door, "and make it quick."

The old manservant led me up the castle's grand central staircase, where the harsh stone steps of the medieval fortress had been softened by a cascade of florid carpeting held fast by black cast-iron rods. Souvenirs of the fortress's violent past lined the walls. Swords fanned out in a semicircle above a shield bearing the Frankenstein coat of arms—a helmet adorned with the wings of a swan above a battle-ax whose double blades had been stained red. Maces and flails had been bracketed to the stone in an attitude of attack, their chains and spiked balls frozen in lethal flight. And in the center of all, the chiseled bas-relief of a sixteenth-century Baron Frankenstein in full plate mail, a war hammer braced upon his shoulder, his right foot stamping upon the carcass of a slain dragon. Evidently, the family had a long history of combating monsters.

Hans and I reached the top of the stairs and entered a dim hall lit only by sconces. The tapers barely illuminated the Black Forest linden of the wall paneling. Although the corridor had many doors, only one at the end stood ajar, a slice of light cleaved from the darkness. I knew this must be our destination—even before I heard the shriek that knifed down the hallway toward us.

Hans forgot about me in an instant. In his haste to propel himself toward the noise, the old man nearly blustered into his master, who burst forth from a washroom halfway down the hall. Victor Frankenstein wore only a red satin dressing gown and slippers; he exuded the heady fragrance of rose-water cologne.

The baron was too agitated—or perhaps simply too nearsighted without his spectacles—to take note of me. "Hans! What the devil was that?"

"I . . . I don't . . ." The aged servant made a helpless gesture toward the open door at the end of the corridor and shook his head, as if already denying responsibility for whatever disaster had occurred there.

"*Elizabeth.*" Shoving the servant aside, Victor Frankenstein sprinted down the hall and through the open door. The scream had ceased. Dreadful silence followed.

Although I was as anxious as the baron to learn what had happened, I lagged behind Hans as he waddled forward, for I didn't want to remind him of my presence. He hesitated in the open doorway, wanting to aid his master yet too afraid to enter. Since I stood almost a half foot taller than the stooped old man, I had no difficulty peering over his shoulder into the bedchamber beyond.

Victor Frankenstein had halted between the door and the plush marriage bed with its tasseled burgundy canopy. He stared, aghast, at the consummation of an unholy matrimony: Elizabeth trembled on the down mattress, clad in a thin, virgin-white shift in anticipation of the first night with her husband, the neck pulled aside to expose a ripe nipple. Still clothed in its shabby peasant's suit, the monster embraced the bride with a fierce passion. With one gorilla-like arm enveloping her midriff and one outsize hand encircling her throat, it forced the terrified woman to look up at her impotent groom.

When she kicked and thrashed, the creature pinched the thumb and fingers around her neck a little tighter until she became still, barely a rattle of breath escaping her gasping mouth.

Frankenstein snarled and tensed to spring but stopped as the creature jabbed Elizabeth in the side, allowing her enough air to let out a squeal. It stared straight at its creator with its dark, dead eyes.

"I told you I would be with you on your wedding night," it said.

Frankenstein's gaze darted about the chamber in an apoplectic rage, but this seemed to be the only room in the castle that did not have weapons mounted on the walls. He seized one of the chest-high candelabra that lit the room, dashed its guttering tapers against the stone wall, and stabbed the wrought-iron stand toward the creature as if wielding a lance. "*Leave her alone!* It's *me* you should kill."

The monster tightened the pincers of its fingers again, until Elizabeth hacked out a cough that made Frankenstein jerk back the candelabrum's pronged bar. "Oh, but you're wrong, cursed creator," the beast muttered, yellow teeth bared. "You failed to give me a mate who could love me, so you, too, shall spend your miserable life alone."

And it squeezed its enormous hand closed around Elizabeth's skinny neck as if cinching shut the mouth of a sack. The throat stretched grotesquely with a crunching of crushed vertebrae, and the bride's eyes bulged past their lids, red tears leaking from the burst blood vessels in the sockets. Her lips fluttered in a parody of speech, but all that came out was an appalling gurgle and a swollen, purpled tongue. Then her head flopped to one side, dangling from nothing more than the rubbery bundle of skin and sinew clutched in the creature's fist.

Victor Frankenstein wailed in blind grief and, heedless of his wife's corpse, charged at her murderer. The creature batted the candelabrum from the baron's hands as if it were a matchstick, then hurled Frankenstein against the carved cherubim on the bed's headboard. The baron fell back onto the bed, facedown, stunned, and semiconscious. His arm fell across the cast-aside cadaver of his betrothed, embracing her at last.

Hans scampered back down the hall, wheezing and clutching at his chest. Even I cried out and dropped the bouquet of dead roses I held, aghast at how easily the thing had squashed the life from Elizabeth.

Only one individual heard my screech. Its head brushing the underside of the canopy as it stood, the monster rose from the bed and lumbered toward the open door. I should have fled, for it could have ripped me apart. But it had left me unharmed before, and perhaps that's why I did not fear it—despite the slaughter I'd just seen.

Indeed, as soon as it spotted me outside the bedchamber, its entire demeanor changed. My face must have shown my revulsion, for the creature's remorseless cruelty crumbled into abject shame. It backed away from me, blubbering, crossing its arms in front of its face as if it could not bear the judgment of my gaze. And although I could have done nothing to stop it, the beast reacted as if I were an impassable barrier. It hurled itself toward the window on the far side of the room.

"No!" I surged forward, too late, to catch it.

The glass exploded outward as the monster crashed through the leaded panes. I rushed to the sill and looked down even before the last of the glittering shards had sprinkled to the battlements below.

The castle's nearest rampart was not as far down as I had feared. Less than ten feet beneath me, I saw a dark, irregular oval on the walkway. I wondered whether the monster had shattered its giant body on the flagstones. But no—like a cat, it had landed on all fours. As I watched, it lifted its face to me in a kind of supplication. Did it want empathy? Understanding? Forgiveness? In the darkness, it was impossible to tell.

A groan from behind made me turn my head. Victor Frankenstein had rolled over on the bed and was shaking off his stupor with groggy resolve. A few seconds more and the sight of his limp bride, her unmoored head dangling upside-down upon her breast, would remind him of his need for vengeance.

Meanwhile, a fusillade of footsteps approached in the hall. Hans must have recruited reinforcements among the servants, for

I could hear him shush the nervous jabber of many voices. They would no doubt demand to know who I was and why I had chosen to come on the night their new mistress was murdered.

I pivoted back toward the broken window. Sticking my head outside again, I saw that only a haphazard mosaic of glass fragments remained on the rampart below. The creature was gone. If *it* could survive the drop . . .

With only a heartbeat's hesitation, I climbed over the sill and hung from it until I'd lowered myself to arm's length against the outside wall. Swaying about six feet above the battlement beneath me, I let go of the window ledge.

The shock of the landing shuddered up from the soles of my feet all the way to my hips, but my legs folded to absorb most of the impact. Like the creature, I also dropped forward onto my hands to break the fall. I scraped my palms on broken glass in the process.

Recalling how the monster had crouched where I now squatted, I glanced up and down the length of the castle wall in hopes of tracking it as it fled. Maybe *it* could give me the answers that I would never get from Victor Frankenstein.

But the fugitive was nowhere to be seen. A hue and cry blared forth from the ruined window above, frantic silhouettes already clustering to gaze down at me from the jagged hole. It would be only a matter of minutes before Frankenstein and his forces commenced their manhunt.

Shards of glass splintering beneath my boots, I ran to the nearest flight of stone steps that would lead me down the battlements and away from Castle Frankenstein.

CHAPTER
6

GRAVEDIGGER'S DELIGHT

It was past three in the morning when I lifted myself through the window of Pastor Georg's house and into my own bedchamber again; I knew I would have to act thoroughly rested and refreshed when Birgit roused me at dawn a few hours later.

I brushed off my dusty boots as best I could and hid my dirty skirts in the wardrobe to wash later. When Birgit arrived, I kept my hands folded so she wouldn't see the scratches from broken glass on my palms.

I also had to feign ignorance of the sensational scandal, the gossip of which had swept through the city before the rising sun had cleared the horizon.

"Baroness Frankenstein was strangled in her bridal bed!" Hedda, the butcher's wife, told Birgit when we went to fetch a loin of pork for dinner. She leaned far across the chopping block to whisper in confidence, gesturing with her cleaver for emphasis. "The baron claims it was an intruder, of course—some vagrant from the woods. You ask me, it sounds like the work of a brutish husband."

Birgit shook her head sadly. "I can't believe he would do such a thing. If you had seen the way he looked at her during the wedding yesterday . . . he had such love for her."

"Love!" Hedda snorted. "Love's killed more good women than the pox, you ask me."

I said nothing, merely held Birgit's breadbasket and tried to seem shocked by the news. Only I knew how close the butcher's wife had come to the truth. Jealousy *had* been the motive for Elizabeth's murder. The monster had envied Frankenstein's happiness.

Is love such a treasure that men will kill to possess it . . . or to deprive others of it out of spite?

"I hear the baron may have had another woman," Hedda went on, relishing the sordid rumor. "They say some girl no one had ever seen before showed up at the castle last night just before the baroness was killed, then disappeared before anyone could find out who she was. You ask me, *she* was the one who put him up to it."

I felt the blood throb faster in my veins and hoped the telltale flush did not show in my face. Fortunately, neither Hedda nor Birgit came close to imagining that I was the supposed Jezebel. I think I hardly breathed until the conversation ended and we left the shop.

For the rest of the morning, I made sure to keep my hood up and my head bowed while out in public, lest anyone identify me as the mysterious visitor to Castle Frankenstein. After that I kept to my room as much as possible, complaining of chills every time Birgit asked me to help her with chores outside. Alas, I could not play ill for more than a day without causing Birgit to call in the local doctor—who happened to be a personal friend and colleague of fellow physician Victor Frankenstein. And so I found myself unable to avoid the most perilous occasion of all: Elizabeth's funeral.

As with the wedding, I helped Birgit tidy the nave of the Stadtkirche for the service. Again, I observed the rites from behind a column near the back of the church. But for the somber clothing and the dirgelike drear of the music, the two sacraments appeared nearly identical. The same singers, the same congregants, even flowers like those I had seen before Frankenstein's wedding: white blooms with black bows.

Victor Frankenstein had chosen to bury his virgin wife in her lace wedding gown; its high collar hid the crushed putty of her neck. The baron had reportedly employed his arcane anatomical skills to embalm her himself rather than entrusting her to the dubious talents of the local mortician. He'd truly outdone himself, for her face looked as perfect and placid in repose in her casket as it had when she'd spoken her marriage vows, the maiden blush still upon her cheeks. While I arranged the floral accents around the bier before the service, however, I caught the pungent chemical tang of alcohol solution contaminating the oversweet fragrance of the garlands, and it galled me with memories of the laboratory and the vats of preserved viscera on the shelves.

To see Victor Frankenstein enter the Stadtkirche that morning, one could not imagine that he had possessed the presence of mind to serve as such an artful undertaker. He looked more like an ambulatory corpse himself—his eyes glazed, his expression utterly blank—as he shuffled up the church's aisle, supported at one elbow by Hans and at another by his footman, as if he might collapse without support. They lowered him onto a pew in the front row, where he vegetated, catatonic, through most of the service.

Only at the end, when it came time for him to step up to the bier for a final look at his intended wife, did Frankenstein display any comprehension of her death. As he bowed his head to gaze at her somnolent visage, he abruptly let out a yowl of fury so fearsome that the entire congregation paled and husbands shielded their wives in case the man went berserk with madness. The baron fell to his knees before the coffin and beat his head with his fists as if he were, in fact, her murderer. When Hans and the footman went to his aid, he waved away their attempts to lift him to his feet. Then he stalked out of the Stadtkirche in such a tearful rage that he passed by me without a glance.

He did not rejoin the mourners for the interment at the churchyard. His absence left the rest of the congregants in the awkward position of paying tribute to a woman most of them barely knew. I waited at the rear of the procession, head bowed, hoping the attitude of reverence would keep anyone from noticing me. When Pastor Georg finished the burial rites, I was supposed to arrange the funeral bouquets around the headstone. As the solemn recessional filed away, I moved quickly to place the flowers, eager to return to the safe seclusion of my room in the minister's house.

Thinking myself alone, I lowered my hood to keep it from falling over my eyes as I bent over the grave marker. Then I heard the snake hiss of fervent whispering. I glanced up to find two laborers in soil-stained linen shirts and breeches standing near the foot of the grave. I recognized them as the same men who'd used a crude rope sling to lower Elizabeth's coffin into its rectangular hole.

The thinner and more industrious of the two now scraped sod into the pit from the mound of freshly turned earth beside him. But the other leaned on his spade and gawked at me with eyes as round as if he'd seen me climb out of the grave instead of walk around it. A fat, unshaven fellow whose double chin and reddish complexion indicated a fondness for drink, he nudged his companion and spoke in a secretive hush, jerking his head toward me to urge his comrade to look my way. The latter grunted in annoyance and kept shoveling.

I turned my back on them and hastened to finish my chore, but I could feel the slovenly gravedigger's avid gaze tracing my every movement.

Could it be that wretch saw me at Castle Frankenstein? Why do I not remember him?

My anxiety eased when the men remained at their work as I left the cemetery. An hour later, though, I found the fat gravedigger standing outside the Stadtkirche, spade on his shoulder, when I emerged after tidying the sanctuary. His expectant attitude suggested that he had been waiting for me.

"Who is man?" I asked Pastor Georg as he joined me on the front steps of the church.

The clergyman cast an unconcerned glance toward the gravedigger. "Meyer? He is only our groundskeeper."

He even waved at the fellow, who raised a hand in response. Meyer grinned at me as well, the sickle of his mouth serrated with the gaps of missing teeth.

Although he evidently had no knowledge of my connection to

Victor Frankenstein, I didn't like the way this man Meyer leered at me and was grateful when Pastor Georg chaperoned me back to the house.

I remained tense for the rest of the week, cloistering myself in the pastor's house as much as possible and watching for Meyer whenever I had to go to the Stadtkirche. I caught sight of him from a distance a few times as he trimmed the hedges in front of the church or hauled wheelbarrows of refuse to the rubbish heap, but he seemed not to notice me. Believing the man had lost interest, I soon forgot about him.

I'd put Meyer so far from my mind that I did not even think of him when, in the dark of my bedchamber one night, someone roughly grabbed me as I slept and shackled my arms behind my back.

Ripped from slumber, I tried to yell, but my captor's accomplice stuffed a musty-tasting rag in my mouth. Before my eyes could make out the faces of the two intruders, one of them threw a sack over my head, smothering me with the smell of burlap and old potatoes. I kicked blindly, felt my foot contact a soft and yielding paunch, and heard one of the men thump to the floor with an *oof* and a string of grumbled profanities.

The floorboards of the room above us creaked. The noise had roused the pastor and his wife.

Despite my rolling and flailing, the two brutes managed to clap leg irons around my ankles. Heavy steps clumped down the wooden stairs out in the hall. "Liesl?" Pastor Georg called.

Slinging my wriggling body between them like a bag of seed, my captors hastily shoved me out the open window of my bedchamber. I thudded onto what felt like a mat of straw that waited in the alley outside. As Pastor Georg rapped furiously on the door of my room, calling my name, I heard the two villains blunder around me. A horse neighed, hooves clattered on cobblestones, and with a jostling rattle of cartwheels, we sped away from the only home I'd ever known.

I naturally assumed my abductors were Victor Frankenstein's henchmen, sent to reclaim me for the sinister physician. The chains and manacles reminded me of how the baron had bound me to the slab the night of my birth, and as the horse cart bumped along, I floundered in helpless terror, certain we were headed back to Castle Frankenstein so that he could complete whatever horrid plan he had for me.

Perhaps I will end up like that pitiful corpse on the dissection table—a headless and naked victim of Frankenstein's unholy lust.

The cart clattered on for what seemed like hours—far longer, I was sure, than it should have taken to traverse the few miles to the castle. I never felt the wagon tilt upward to commence the steep ascent of the hill to the ancient fortress. We bounced over ruts in a road, but with my head still wrapped in sackcloth, I could not be sure of anything else about our surroundings.

When I began to wonder if our journey would ever end, the wagon at last rocked to a stop. I heard the two villains fumbling about, bickering about which of them should carry me. Wherever we were, they must have felt secure in their treachery, for they made no attempt to lower or disguise their loutish voices. Fat hands grabbed me about the waist and hefted me onto a beefy shoulder so that my top half lay upside-down on the man's back. I twisted and writhed as much as my bonds would let me until the man swatted my flanks as if I were a temperamental mare.

"Behave yourself, pretty one," he warned, "or I'll do far worse."

"I'll do far worse to *you* if you've damaged her, simpleton," a new voice cut in. A woman's, harsh and graveled with age. "Now bring her in here."

Sensing this unfamiliar woman would defend me from harm, I did not struggle when the man carried me as she commanded, not even when he banged my shin while lugging me through a doorway. Warmth told me we were now indoors. I heard a latch click shut, a key turn in a lock. I was finally set upright in a cushioned chair, although no one yet dared to unfasten the fetters at my wrists or ankles.

"Well, let's see her," the woman snapped.

"You won't be disappointed, Frau Hauptmann," the churlish man promised with unctuous servility. "She's worth every pfennig."

"I'll be the judge of that. Remove the sack."

The sheath of burlap sloughed off my face, and I pinched my

eyes shut against the abrupt flood of light. When they had adjusted enough for me to open my lids without flinching, I saw I was sitting in a large bedchamber that rivaled Baron Frankenstein's in the richness and elegance of its walnut furnishings and brocaded draperies. However, the dainty intricacy of lace scarves on the dresser and fireplace mantel and the flowery palette of pink and rose hues of the bedclothes and wall hangings lent the room softness and delicacy—qualities I would soon learn were prized as "feminine."

Against this cheerful, sweetly colored background, the black-gowned dowager who stood before me resembled a crow in a flock of flamingoes. The tightness of the bun that trussed her tarnished-sterling hair gave her face an uncomfortably stretched appearance, and the severity of her black brows made her look permanently cross. This had to be the woman who'd sounded so severe and commanding a moment ago, but she now peered at me dumbstruck and palsied with emotion—whether fear or elation, I could not say.

"Did I not tell you?" boasted the man beside her, whom I now recognized as Meyer. "The very image of her, isn't she?"

"No . . . it *is* her." The old woman's imperiousness returned as she recovered herself. "For God's sake, man, get that thing out of her mouth!"

Meyer gave her a dubious look. "And the shackles?"

Uncertainty flickered in Frau Hauptmann's eyes as she assessed my hostile glare. "Leave them."

Meyer nodded, yanked the rag from my mouth. My tongue tasted of mildew and dust, and I gagged when swallowing my spit.

"Where am I?" I demanded.

Frau Hauptmann seemed genuinely surprised by the question. "You're home, Katarina."

"My name is *Liesl*. They *stole* me from home." I sneered at Meyer and his thin grave-digging partner, who idled near the bedchamber door, shifting his weight from foot to foot as if anxious to leave.

"Your name is not Liesl," the old woman said, a schoolmistress drilling a student in her catechism. "You are Katarina von Kemp."

Before I could argue, she strode to the hearth of the room's fireplace. Above the mantel hung a picture, its ornate gilt frame almost entirely obscured by a shroud of black lace that had been draped over it. Frau Hauptmann lifted the veil and hooked the cloth over one corner of the painting to hold it aside. It depicted a young woman of aristocratic mien, clad in a gown of glossy pink silk that highlighted her ample bosom. The ringlets of her golden hair held in place by a bejeweled diadem, she regarded the viewer with a cool hauteur, yet fiery passion flashed in her sapphire eyes.

The face was mine.

CHAPTER 7

BECOMING KATARINA

I stared at the woman in the portrait the way I'd first contemplated my reflection in Birgit's mirror. I shook my head, unable to connect the creature I saw with whom I felt myself to be. "That—that not me," I stammered.

"It *is*." Frau Hauptmann touched my cheek in maternal sympathy, but her eyes remained keen, calculating. "You've suffered so, you don't remember, poor thing. But you will soon be yourself again."

I gazed at the face in the painting. *My* face.

These people seem to know me . . . could I really be this Katarina of whom they speak?

It made sense that I had some existence before waking up on Victor Frankenstein's slab. *If that's so, why can I remember nothing of my previous life?*

Frau Hauptmann seized upon my weakening defiance. "Won't you let us help you?" she implored.

I had to agree. If this old woman really had known me before tonight, then I could learn from her the truth about my past.

As soon as I nodded, Frau Hauptmann motioned Meyer toward me. "Release her."

He held out his hand, palm upward, and coughed.

She grimaced with contempt and fetched a small leather pouch off the dresser, which she thrust into his hand. He gauged its weight, sniffed with satisfaction, and pocketed the bag before unlocking my fetters.

As I rubbed circulation back into my numb arms and chafed wrists, the instinct for freedom nearly overpowered me. I wanted to claw Meyer's eyes out and flee from this "home" that I could not recall and for which I felt nothing.

At that very moment, a mournful wail gusted into the room like a cold draft from the floor above.

I glanced up toward the ceiling. "What is?"

"Your husband." Frau Hauptmann looked pained as another sob racked the house. "You hear how he weeps for you."

Husband? I pictured Elizabeth in her white dress at the Stadtkirche altar, radiant with joy as she spoke her undying vows to Victor Frankenstein. It seemed inconceivable that I could feel such love for a man when I did not even know what love was. The thought that I might already have a husband brought no joy with it, only the queasy dread that I was somehow chained to that unseen, moaning phantom in the room above.

Yet if this was indeed the life I had before Frankenstein took it from me, I wanted it back.

"I . . . Katarina . . . von Kemp." I said the name slowly, trying it on for size as if fitting a new dress.

An incongruous smile spread over Frau Hauptmann's sour face.

Meyer and his partner scuttled off, fast as rats that had nabbed the cheese from a trap. Once we were alone, the old woman told me that she served as housekeeper to Herr von Kemp. My husband.

Frau Hauptmann asked if I needed any assistance readying myself for sleep. In response, I pointed to the nightclothes I had been wearing when I was stolen from my bed. Stung, she curtly excused herself without any further questions. I heard a key turn in the lock as soon as she shut the chamber door.

Imprisoned, I surveyed the room I had been told was mine. Accustomed to the narrow cot and bare walls of my room in Pastor Georg's house, I found the excess of luxury around me intimidating, as if I were stranded in a museum where I was not permitted to touch anything. Jewellike bottles of amber liquid clustered before the looking glass of a vanity. A set of bone-handled combs and brushes lay in a neat row on the table, and when I pinched the bristles of the largest brush, I pulled out fine tufts of blonde hair the exact shade of my own.

In sudden affright, I glanced up at my reflection in the mirror, wan in the light of the oil lamp beside me. The resemblance to the woman in the painting became so overwhelming that I felt as if she were staring back at me . . . *into* me. I turned toward her picture and again felt those blue eyes boring into my head.

Unable to stand her any longer, I pulled the black lace curtain back down over that frozen face. Then I extinguished the lamp and buried myself in the downy snowdrift of the massive canopied bed. The weeping from upstairs dripped relentlessly into my ears, and I had to wrap a pillow around my head to get to sleep.

I awoke late in the day to the strange sky of satin and lace above me. As soon as I stirred, I discovered Frau Hauptmann had already entered my room and stood waiting beside the bed in her black gown.

"Good afternoon, Katarina." She indicated a little table set up near the fire. "It is time to begin our lessons."

I sat up. At a nod from Frau Hauptmann, a young maid stepped forward, her arms filled with the length of a silk gown. "Bettina will help you dress."

"But my . . . husband?" The man's anguished cries still echoed in my mind. I struggled to express myself as correctly as possible with my limited language skills. "He must . . . want me, yes?"

"You will see him soon, my dear. When you are ready."

I hadn't noticed Bettina's maneuverings until my nightgown fell to the floor and the maid squealed, backing away as she pointed to my body.

I looked down. *Am I hurt?* But I only saw what had always been there: creamy white skin puckered and laced with raw, ridged scars.

59

Where Birgit and Pastor Georg had shown pity, however, this maid expressed only horror. An awful feeling gripped me, as if I had done something terribly wrong. I wanted to hide, to cover myself, but could only stand there while the maid gawped at me.

Frau Hauptmann's lips compressed into a thin line. "You may go, Bettina."

The maid fled, her hand over her mouth. Frau Hauptmann picked up the discarded gown and helped me into the skirt. I gasped as she tightened the lacing on the too-small bodice. She arranged my chemise until I was covered modestly enough for her satisfaction.

"Not a perfect fit, but we will remedy that." She led me to the table. "Come sit here, Katarina."

On the table waited a pot of coffee and a pitcher of hot milk, fresh bread, cheese, and fruit. I reached for the food only to have the dour woman slap my fingers hard enough for them to tingle.

"There is plenty of time for that. First we will talk. You must sit up straight and tall, like so." She put one hand on my back and one on my shoulders, showing me how to stretch my spine, lengthening my torso and thrusting out my chest. It felt strange, but I did not resist. I had to find out what she knew about me—or, rather, about whom I had been.

The woman settled herself opposite me at the table. "Now, do you remember the last time you saw Herr von Kemp, your husband? Take a moment and try."

I did try. *Was it possible I had gone through a wedding ceremony, as Frankenstein had with his Elizabeth? Had I once been held and treasured, as she had been?* But all I could remember before arriving at the Stadtkirche was the cold slab, my birth-scream, the terrified flight from Victor Frankenstein and my monstrous suitor.

"No. I not . . . remember."

"Hmph! Say, 'No, Frau Hauptmann,'" she muttered. When I repeated the phrase she continued her interrogation. "But you *do* remember your beautiful life here in this house, don't you? You mustn't forget Herr von Kemp's goodness to you."

Fearful of disappointing her, I nevertheless shook my head. "No, Frau Hauptmann."

"Well. We must help you remember then, eh? Let us bless our meal."

I folded my hands and closed my eyes, pleased that I could perform the task as Pastor Georg had taught me.

"Our Father, we thank you for restoring Katarina to the home of her loving and devoted husband. May she be truly grateful, and learn to conduct herself as a good wife should. Amen. Now let us enjoy a fine luncheon."

Hunger prompting me, I picked up a piece of bread, preparing to stuff it into my mouth.

"Not like that." In response to my confusion, she explained. "Here, we do not behave like the peasants at the Stadtkirche. We break our bread, you see? I will pour your coffee. Let us see how you hold your cup . . ."

I blundered through the meal, Frau Hauptmann correcting every breach of etiquette. Though I did not understand why the endless list of rules seemed so important to her, I did my best to imitate the housekeeper's precise movements. I took tiny bites of bread and cheese, and sipped from the china coffee cup exactly the way the housekeeper did. Finally, she nodded approval.

"Good. Very good. Herr von Kemp will like you better so."

I wondered how he had liked me before, but Frau Hauptmann had a way about her that made me afraid to ask too many questions. I could not picture myself following her about, babbling childishly, the way I had with Birgit.

"You did very well," Frau Hauptmann told me. To my surprise she led me back to bed, showing me that she wished for me to lie down. "We will have more lessons soon. I will leave you to rest, Katarina."

Taking away the silver breakfast tray, she departed, locking the door behind her.

Given how little I'd slept the previous night, I really wanted to rest. When I lay down, though, a niggling agitation disturbed me, and I got up and paced the room. I knew immediately what I wanted to do but fought the urge until I couldn't bear it any longer.

I threw aside the black lace that covered the portrait above the fireplace and gazed long at the painted face.

There could be no doubt: that visage belonged to me. But what about the rest? The woman in the portrait wore a low-necked gown. Her lovely throat bore no scar, as mine did. And her eyes expressed a complacency that I had never felt and could not share.

I grew melancholy as I thought of the maid's shriek of revulsion, the housekeeper's grunt of disgust, the sobs of a husband whose face I could not recall. Even here, at "home," I was a stranger. But I thought when I saw my husband, perhaps I would finally recollect myself. Until then, I would be a woman living under an assumed identity.

CHAPTER
8

THE ONCE AND FUTURE HUSBAND

From then on, Frau Hauptmann devoted every waking moment to my education. She drilled me on my elocution until I became fluent in German. Not content that I should speak only my native tongue, she tutored me in French, Italian, and English as well. Overwhelmed by the chore of learning even one language, I asked her what sort of people used these other strange words and why I would ever want to speak with them. She actually cackled at that, the only time I ever heard her laugh.

"Because you are a fine lady, Katarina," she reminded me, "and your knowledge should reflect your breeding."

When she taught me to write, she was not satisfied with the crude block letters that Birgit had shown me, nor even with the spiky cursive scrawl I struggled to practice with unaccustomed fingers. Rather, she spread the yellowed leaves of an old letter before me and insisted that I replicate its elegant, florid calligraphy, right down to the flamboyant curlicue that crossed the "t" in the signature "Katarina." I learned to mimic the other woman's script so well that it became habit, an unintentional exercise in forgery.

In the same fashion, Frau Hauptmann sought to mold every

aspect of my being as if shaping wet clay. How I sat, how I walked, how I held my head, how I held my fork—no detail or mannerism was too fine to escape her notice. As tedious and exasperating as her constant criticism could be, I absorbed the lessons eagerly, thrilled that I was actually *becoming* someone.

There were other aspects of my schooling, however, that I did not like.

Although Bettina overcame her initial revulsion at my appearance and proved a polite and dutiful servant, she remained stiff and timid around me. It saddened me to think I caused the mousy young girl such anxiety, and I strove to put her at her ease. I dressed and undressed myself in private so my grotesque scars would never upset her again, and she soon seemed to forget about them, even began to smile in my presence.

Then, one morning before Frau Hauptmann came to tutor me, Bettina entered with a small bunch of fresh peonies and shyly presented them to me. "They're the first of the season," she explained when I stared, uncomprehending, at the flowers. "The mistress—I mean, *you*—always liked to put them in your hair."

Sensing a chance to befriend the girl, I smiled broadly. "That is . . . very kind of you, Bettina," I said, taking care to use the proper German grammar I'd learned. "Would you show me how to do it?"

She smiled and curtsied. "Of course."

As I sat before the vanity mirror, the maid took strands of my blonde hair in her thin, nimble fingers and wove the stems of the flowers into a ropelike braid that twined across my scalp like a floral tiara. The pink petals brought out the luster of the gold of my hair and the blue of my eyes, and for the first time I felt a tickling pleasure in my appearance.

When Bettina had finished, I laughed gaily and snatched up the rest of the scattered blossoms. "But look how many blooms are left! It would be a shame to waste them." I stood from my stool. "Here—let me put the rest on you."

The maid blushed and shook her head. "Oh, no, Frau von Kemp. I couldn't."

I encouraged her to take the stool. "Please."

64

Bettina let out a nervous giggle and seated herself. "Well . . . if you *insist* . . . "

She removed her maid's cap and permitted me to thread a flower into her wispy brown hair. Although not as adept as she was, I did my best to imitate her skill. Bettina chuckled and teased me as I fumbled, but with her instruction, I soon had a blossom woven into the locks above her left ear. We took turns admiring each other, mincing and preening before the looking glass and laughing. I realized I had never felt such kinship with another being before, a camaraderie of equals. If I had known what such a thing was, I would have called Bettina my friend.

Then the razor of Frau Hauptmann's voice severed the two of us. "Bettina! What are you doing?"

The maid jumped to her feet. "Nothing, Frau Hauptmann. I—"

The housekeeper pointed to the open bedchamber door behind her. "Get back to your duties. And take that *thing* off your head."

"Yes, Frau Hauptmann." Bettina winced as she tugged the flower from the tangle of her hair. She put her maid's cap back on and scurried from the room, her manner again fretful and withdrawn.

Mortified, I glared at Frau Hauptmann. "Why were you so harsh with her?"

She frowned. "Why were *you* so indulgent?"

"She did nothing wrong," I protested.

"It is beneath you to be so familiar with the servants, Katarina. You are a fine lady—wife of one of the wealthiest landowners in Bavaria—and you must remember your place."

I bristled. For me to disdain Bettina because of her social class seemed as cruel and unjust as Frankenstein reviling the monster simply for its ugliness.

My expression hardened into one of cold condescension. "These servants you speak of . . . would they include you, my housekeeper?"

The old woman seemed taken aback. "Yes," she answered.

"In that case, you are dismissed, Frau Hauptmann."

The housekeeper stood quivering a moment, as if mortally offended. Then a chilling calm of satisfaction smoothed her scowl and she bowed deeply. "As you wish, Frau von Kemp."

After she departed, I turned to the mirror. The face there was so prideful, so aloof, so like that in the painting above the mantel, that I covered it with my hands, wanted to claw it off like a hideous mask. If this was what it meant to be Katarina von Kemp, I wanted nothing to do with her.

At such times, I longed to return to the simple affections of Birgit and Pastor Georg. I sat at my bedchamber window and sighed, watching the sunset and wondering if my adoptive parents prayed for the return of their Liesl. If they were searching, I doubted they would find me, for even I did not know where I was.

I briefly considered escape on several occasions. Although I was confined to my apartments—bedchamber, parlor, and library—it would have been an easy thing to overpower Frau Hauptmann and take her keys. But there was still so much I didn't know about my history in that house—elusive secrets that taunted me at night as I lay awake, listening to the keening cries from the room upstairs.

After weeks of incarceration, I could stand it no longer. I begged Frau Hauptmann to let me go outside before I went mad from confinement. She finally acquiesced, on two conditions: she would choose the time, and she would remain at my side from the moment I left my rooms until I returned.

Her hovering presence nettled me, but I ceased to care as soon as we stepped out into the soothing warmth of a late-spring morning. The estate included a breathtaking manicured garden, with islands of sculpted shrubs rising from dazzling seas of flowers. As we strolled along one of the pebbled paths that crisscrossed the grounds, ranks of tulips in yellow, red, and orange stood in regiments at either side of us like uniformed troops for review. The misty scent of morning dew still freshened the air, and the mélange of jasmine and orange blossom scents from the surrounding trees created a perfume that smelled far sweeter to me than the bottled odors of the colognes on my vanity table. I inhaled deeply and lifted my face to the sun to bask in its radiance.

"Here, use this." Frau Hauptmann handed me a parasol. "Too much sunlight will ruin your porcelain skin."

She was not looking up at the sun as she said this, however, but instead glanced back toward the house, eyeing a darkened window on the third floor.

The housekeeper walked at my elbow, dressed in black as ever and carried a parasol of her own to keep herself in shadow. "Herr von Kemp put in this garden after your trip to Paris, you know," she mentioned idly, never missing an opportunity to indoctrinate me in the details of my life as Katarina. "He saw how much you enjoyed the grounds of the Tuileries and wanted to surround you with the same sort of beauty. Oh, how in love you were!" She gave a rhapsodic sigh.

The mention of my still-faceless husband clouded the glorious day.

"How did I meet him?" I tried to make the question sound eager rather than anxious.

"Your late father introduced you, of course," the housekeeper replied. "Herr von Kemp had noticed you in the salons of Frankfurt and the two of them agreed that you would be a splendid match." She sniffed with an oddly rueful expression and glanced again toward the grand house behind us.

"When shall I see him?" I asked, my attention drawn in the same direction.

"Soon," Frau Hauptmann replied tonelessly. "Very soon."

She stared at a window on the third floor of the black-timbered Bavarian manse. A hand held aside one of the burgundy drapes, as if a theater performer were evaluating his prospective audience before the curtains parted. I could not distinguish the hand's owner in the dimness of the room beyond the window, and as soon as I glanced up, it let the drape fall back into place.

Frau Hauptmann never specified when I was to be reunited with Herr von Kemp, but I gathered the time must be drawing nigh from the way she redoubled her efforts to prepare me. More and more, she insinuated memories of Katarina into our conversations, memories I was expected to absorb and parrot as my own.

"This was always your favorite aria," she murmured on one

occasion as she played a few measures from one of Susanna's solos in *Le Nozze di Figaro* on the pianoforte in my parlor. "Won't it be wonderful to go to the Staatsoper again, Katarina?"

I did not even know what opera was—my only experience with music was what I had heard in the Stadtkirche—but the melody pleased me. I readily accepted it as my favorite aria . . . whatever an aria might be.

"Not too much rouge on your cheeks, dear," she said at another time as she instructed me in the mysterious art of cosmetics. "You know how Joseph hates that."

I knew no such thing, yet I apologized and said I'd simply forgotten his preference.

So my husband's name is Joseph, I thought, wondering why Frau Hauptmann had never told me his Christian name before and why she spoke of him so intimately now. She seemed to realize her *faux pas* and reverted to calling him "Herr von Kemp" for the rest of the day.

Finally, after supper one evening, the housekeeper came to my bedchamber bearing a lavish gown trimmed with ribbons and lace. "Come, Katarina," she said, "put on your lovely new dress."

I shivered with apprehension. "That's not a new dress."

She smiled, amused. "No. It's not."

It was, in fact, the dress worn by the woman in the painting above my mantelpiece. Frau Hauptmann did not need to tell me why I was to wear it that night.

My heart fluttered as I put on the gown. When I'd first tried it on a week earlier, it had been too snug in places, too loose in others, as if tailored for another woman, but since then it had been altered and now fit perfectly.

"Remember how to greet him."

"Yes, Frau Hauptmann."

"There is no need to be afraid. Remember, he worships you. And I will be there with you."

At her signal, I followed her upstairs to the bedchamber directly above mine—toward the wellspring of muffled weeping that I could hear even now, through the closed door. As we entered the room I smelled the heavy scent of cologne, and, under that, a dry, papery, stale smell—the odor of an old man.

He sat at the far end of the room, before a crackling fire in the grate. The high-backed chair was angled toward the fireplace, and I could only see the forearm that rested on the right side of the chair. An arthritic hand freckled with liver spots gripped the silver knob of a walking stick. A gold wedding band encircled the hand's third finger.

Frau Hauptmann motioned for me to wait.

"She is here," the housekeeper announced.

The lamentations abruptly ceased. The man in the chair became flustered, sniffing and coughing to clear his throat. Leaning heavily on the cane, he pushed himself to his feet. I noticed his hair first—a long white mane that fell past his shoulders. Old-fashioned knee britches and stockings covered legs that looked stick-thin. He did not face me immediately but instead wiped his cheeks with his free hand and drew his skeletal frame up to its full height. The ramrod stiffness of his posture suggested the bearing of a former military officer. Then he turned to regard me with rheumy brown eyes.

"Katarina?" He hobbled toward me, extended his trembling hand. "Can it really be you?"

"Good evening, dear husband." I genuflected as I had been taught.

To my shock, he dropped the walking stick and fell on his knees before me, his fists clutching the silk of my gown as he bowed to kiss its hem. I recoiled from those grasping hands, and in my mind I heard the monster's needy, possessive rasp. *Mine.*

"No, no, my dearest! Do not fear me!" Joseph von Kemp looked up at me, tears rolling down his withered face. "Don't you see? God has brought you back to me. If *He* can forgive, then surely *you . . .*"

"She has forgotten all that," Frau Hauptmann interjected. "There is no need to speak of it."

As I stood in awkward discomfiture the housekeeper stepped between us, reached down to help von Kemp stand. Taking her arm, he struggled to his feet, propping himself on the cane he'd recovered.

"You are right, Frau Hauptmann." His crooked fingers quavered as he brought his hand up to stroke my face. Only pity kept me from flinching away. His eyes roamed lower, first to the lace ribbon that concealed the scar around my neck, then to my bosom and waist. Von Kemp moistened his lips, his eyes glazing over. "If you would leave us alone . . ."

"I do not think that would be wise."

Von Kemp started. "Not wise? Why not wise?"

"She needs time, Herr von Kemp. Time to reacquaint herself with her former life. Time to get . . . accustomed to you again." When he opened his mouth to object, she fixed him with a piercing glance. "*Before* you can be alone. You want everything to be perfect for dear Katarina, do you not?"

My husband shuddered with frustrated longing, but to my relief he nodded. "Yes. It is for the best." He took my hand. "You will permit me to dine with you tomorrow evening, won't you, my dear?"

I looked to Frau Hauptmann for guidance. Almost imperceptibly, she inclined her head. In turn, I nodded to von Kemp. He bowed, and, to my surprise, placed his lips upon the back of my hand, making that slurping sound I had heard before.

I had just received my first "kiss." I still couldn't understand why anyone would desire one.

CHAPTER
9

THE RIVAL

The following morning, Joseph von Kemp began a halting, almost adolescent courtship of me, his supposed wife. I awoke to find an enormous bouquet of fresh-cut roses on my dressing table along with an embossed card inscribed,"For my Heart's Treasure. Your Abject Servant—J."

Despite this written expression of ardor, in person he remained as shy and skittish as a schoolboy. He forbade me to visit him until our scheduled supper, as if afraid to let me see his withered countenance in the unforgiving light of day.

When I arrived in the dining room that evening, I saw he had tied his white hair back with a black ribbon, as if it were a powdered wig of the last century, and wore a frock coat whose fit flattered his trim frame, making him appear less frail than before. In the subdued light of the room's candelabra, I could easily imagine the dashing figure he must have cut in his youth. Yet his manner still wavered between yearning and shame; he stared wistfully at me when my face was turned yet averted his eyes whenever I looked at him directly.

"You see that I have had chef prepare all your favorites, my dear." He made a grand gesture toward the repast on the long dining table, using the excuse to look at the food rather than my eyes. "Braised stag, pheasant eggs, sautéed truffles, and, of course, a mince strudel for dessert."

He smiled at me for a moment, then lowered his head as though I were some goddess upon whom he was not permitted to gaze.

I surveyed the delectable array of dishes laid out on the sterling service before me, none of which I could recall ever tasting before. The mingled aromas of sweet and savory spices smelled delicious, and I knew I would accept these foods as my favorites as readily as I had adopted Mozart as my composer of choice.

"How thoughtful!" I exclaimed, genuinely touched by his desire to please. "But you shouldn't have gone to such trouble, Herr—" Frau Hauptmann admonished me with a look, and I corrected myself. "*Dear* Joseph."

The endearment felt stilted, as if I were speaking lines in a play written for someone else. My awkwardness didn't bother Herr von Kemp, who beamed as I called him by his given name. With charming gallantry, he pulled my chair from the table so that I could seat myself.

The dinner was exquisite, although the conversation consisted mostly of nostalgia from Herr von Kemp and polite nods from me as I pretended to share his recollections.

"Ah!" he sighed in one instance, raising his cut-crystal goblet to admire the garnet-hued fluid within. "We brought this wine back from our first visit to Burgundy."

"Oh, yes!" I chimed in. "The vineyards were so lovely."

Frau Hauptmann, who stood to one side of the table with folded hands, smiled at my improvisation.

Although I took pains to commit every scrap of this trivia to memory, such ephemera failed to clear the mist from my past. Whenever our talk veered too close to uncomfortable revelations, Frau Hauptmann steered it back toward banality.

"We must call on your family again," Herr von Kemp suggested. "I know your father has fretted himself ill over you . . ."

"I am sure Herr Bauer will not mind if we wait until she regains her health," the housekeeper interrupted. "I think the journey to Frankfurt would be far too taxing for our Katarina, don't you? Now, let's clear these plates for dessert."

The subsequent clamor of china and cutlery obliterated any further discussion of the family I did not know I had.

The meal passed pleasantly enough. When Herr von Kemp rose to bid me goodnight, he gave a courtly bow rather than prostrating himself in front of me.

"It was lovely, Joseph," I said. "Thank you so much."

"It is I who should thank you, dear lady." He looked me in the eye for the first time that evening, and feverish heat poured off his palm as he took my hand in his. "You *have* forgiven me, haven't you?" he asked in a barely audible croak.

I could not think what to say. I tried to withdraw my hand, but he did not let go of it. Instead, he moistened his lips and leaned forward.

"Joseph!"

He glowered at Frau Hauptmann's intrusion.

"I'm sure Katarina must be very tired," the housekeeper said.

Herr von Kemp glared at her defiantly and bent even closer, until I could almost taste the hot gust of his breath in my mouth. Then he lightly touched his lips to my left cheek. The scrape of his whiskers and papery lips caused me to shiver.

"Until tomorrow, my love." He stepped back and released my hand.

Choked with clashing emotions, I could not respond and so merely curtsied and excused myself. I returned to the seclusion of my room and sprawled on the bed, uncertain how I should feel. The old man had been kind and seemed genuinely fond of me. Yet his words and his kiss both implied dark expectations that I had no idea how to fulfill.

Until tomorrow, my love . . .

For how many tomorrows would I have to remain imprisoned in a life that did not seem to belong to me? And how long would Joseph von Kemp wait for me to become the love I did not know how to be?

I extinguished the lights in my bedchamber but still couldn't sleep. For the first time since my arrival, no wails of grief disturbed the night.

We carried on this chaste affair for three weeks, gradually increasing the time we spent together without ever approaching physical intimacy. In addition to dining together, Joseph began to accompany me on my strolls through the garden, Frau Hauptmann shadowing us as our silent chaperone. Though I could see the desire sharpening in his eyes every time he looked at me, Joseph remained a perfect gentleman, contenting himself with nothing more than the touch of a hand or a peck on the cheek. His theatrical chivalry made me quite fond of him, although my affection was more daughterly than spousal. Ignorant of the animal aspects of passion, I might have believed it an ideal marriage. My husband seemed a gentle and generous benefactor who showered me with all the comforts and kindnesses I could want.

Things went so well, in fact, that the apparent harmony between us prompted Joseph to make the act of hubris that led to his undoing.

We had just embarked upon our daily promenade one morning when he glanced up at the cloudless sky of periwinkle blue and inhaled the fresh air as if relishing the bouquet of a fine brandy.

"What a glorious day!" he exclaimed. "Bettina, have Franz and the boys hitch a team to the carriage. It is time my wife and I rode into town."

The maid, who had stepped outside to hand Joseph his cane and me my parasol, blanched and cast a timorous glance at Frau Hauptmann, who lurked beside us, as always.

"I think that would be most unwise, Herr von Kemp," the housekeeper demurred in syllables as clipped as a pair of shears snapping shut. "People in the village do not know that Katarina has recovered from her recent . . . illness."

"They do not concern me. All they need to see is that my lovely wife has been restored to me and that the von Kemps are again a happy couple." With his walking stick in hand, he offered me his free arm.

"But Herr von Kemp, what if *he*—"

"Bettina, I gave you an order. My wife and I are going to town." He cautioned Frau Hauptmann with a look. "Alone."

Bettina curtsied hastily and hurried off. Frau Hauptmann grew sullen but did not dare to object, and the three of us waited in silence until a landau pulled by a pair of chestnut-colored horses stuttered around the corner of the house and clicked to a stop in front of us. Attired in immaculate gray livery and a top hat, Franz, the stoic coachman, hopped down from the driver's perch and, without a word, helped both me and Joseph climb into the rear passenger seat of the carriage. A moment later we were off, leaving the black wraith of Frau Hauptmann behind us.

Although I hadn't said as much, I secretly rejoiced to be away from the house and its housekeeper, both of which I found stifling. We rode with the landau's top down, enjoying the play of sunshine on the barley fields and hop yards on either side of us.

"All our tenants, my dear," Joseph said with a devil-may-care grin, indicating the acres of farms. "No one lifts a stein in these parts without tasting a bit of von Kemp!" He grew so bold as to put his arm around my shoulder, which I did not resist. Seated there so close to him, with the breeze of freedom caressing my face, I could imagine this life as truly my own.

After about forty minutes, we arrived in the village of Liebeheim. Smaller and quainter than the city of Darmstadt, where I had lived with Pastor Georg and Birgit, it consisted of a mere handful of half-timbered, peaked-roof buildings along one central street. The few inhabitants who listlessly meandered in the lane gawped at the approach of our carriage as if the very chariot of Helios had descended upon them. Upon sighting me, two plump peasant women whispered to each other with shocked expressions; it was all I could do to keep from glaring at them.

Indeed, the whole community seemed to stop and peer at us as we alighted from the landau in front of a small hofbräu— apparently the town's only dining establishment. The proprietor, a bald man with a prodigious mustache, emerged from the restaurant to greet us warmly, but even his joviality carried an edge of unease.

"Herr von Kemp!" He spread his hands in welcome. "It has been too long since you privileged us with your presence." The barkeep smiled at me but studied my face as if unable to believe the evidence of his eyes. "And you, Frau von Kemp . . . you are quite well?"

"She is in excellent health, Dieter," Joseph answered for me. "Her sojourn abroad has done wonders for her illness and she has made a complete recovery, as I knew she would. We are here to celebrate her return. The best of everything!"

"Of course, sir." Dieter bowed and gestured for us to precede him into the hofbräu.

The beerhall was small yet cheerful, with gaily painted stencils of leaves and flowers on the coved ceiling and overhead beams. The barmaid assigned to guide us to our table dampened our mood considerably, however, when she paled as Dieter announced us.

"Frau von Kemp? But I thought—" Dieter gave a subtle shake of his head, and she broke off. "Please . . . follow me."

The establishment truly gave us the best it had to offer—plump sausages, boiled cabbage, fresh cheese and grapes, white wine from the Rhineland—but I could hardly enjoy the food due to the constant stares of all the patrons around us. Unwilling to acknowledge their rudeness, Joseph and I dined in silence, with our heads bowed over our plates.

If we had left the village right after our disconcerting luncheon, I might have dismissed the locals' bizarre leeriness as class prejudice. But as we waited outside the restaurant for Franz to fetch our carriage, a young man in the loose linen shirt and leather knee breeches of a stable boy came sprinting up the street toward us.

Joseph's hand tightened on mine, clenching the knuckles until I almost cried out in pain.

"Trina! *Trina!*"

The name the youth shouted meant nothing to me, and I looked around to see whether he might actually be calling to someone else. He skidded to a stop right in front of me, gazed into my face with eyes as blue and pure as glacial ice.

"I couldn't believe it when I heard you were here." He grinned

76

and reached as if to take me in his arms. When I flinched away, he cast an insolent look at Joseph. "They said you were deathly ill, and I feared the worst."

"I . . . I am quite well, thank you." I thought it best to act as if I knew the boy, although I was certain I'd never seen him before. If I had, he would have been seared into my memory like a brand.

He couldn't have been older than one-and-twenty, with a smooth, well-defined jaw that had barely sprouted its first stubble of beard, yet he stood several inches taller than Joseph. Thick blond hair tossed in waves about a face browned by days of labor in the sun, gold on bronze. He'd left his shirt carelessly open at the neck to relieve the heat, revealing a broad, firm chest bedewed with sweat from fieldwork. His classically male physique reminded me of sculptured Greek heroes in the history texts Frau Hauptmann had shown me during our lessons—Perseus, perhaps—and by that time, I had learned to appreciate the shapes and symmetries of human beauty.

What captivated me far more than his appearance, however, was the way he *looked* at me—as if no one had ever looked at me before. His gaze held desire, yes, but not simply the base hunger and grasping possessiveness of the monster in Victor Frankenstein's laboratory. There was a warmth in those eyes, a joy that both reached out to me and invited me in. He regarded me with the same blissful reverence that Frankenstein had shown for Elizabeth.

It could only be love.

"I thought I might never see you again," he said, desolation dimming his radiance. Then he smiled again and the sun itself seemed to brighten. "But now that you're here, nothing shall keep us apart."

I was so dumbfounded I couldn't speak. I didn't realize that Joseph had let go of my hand until I heard the slice of sliding metal. With the fluidity of a practiced swordsman, the old man drew a rapier from the wooden sheath of his walking stick and thrust the point up against the youth's Adam's apple. Again, I could see the formidable soldier Joseph had once been. This time he seemed not cavalier, however, but coldly lethal.

"Leave us be, Stefan," he hissed.

The boy snarled, tried to dodge away. Joseph nudged the blade's tip deeper into the skin of Stefan's throat.

"Let the lady speak for herself!" the youth demanded.

Both of them turned to me, as did the mass of spectators that had coalesced around us. Stefan's face glowed with naïve hope; Joseph's withered with contempt. I knew he would not hesitate to slay Stefan where he stood.

"I'm afraid I don't know you, sir," I told Stefan in a hoarse voice. It was not only the truth—I knew that phrase would spare his life.

The boy grimaced as if *I* had stabbed him. His full lips curled in the same sneer he'd given Joseph. "Don't know me? Or don't *want* to know me because I'm not rich enough? That's always how it was with you, wasn't it?"

I couldn't bear the accusation of betrayal that blazed in those blue eyes, so I looked toward the landau that Franz had pulled up beside us.

Joseph laughed and slid his sword back into the cane. "You heard the lady, stable boy. Be on your way."

With a jaunty air, he offered me his arm, and we climbed into the carriage together. I opened my parasol to hide my face, but I could still hear Stefan calling after me, wounded and plaintive.

"Trade me for his jewels if you want, Trina! But you know I have the real treasure!"

Joseph harrumphed derisively and rapped his cane on the coachman's seat to signal Franz to drive away. As the carriage rolled off, I angled my parasol to dart a discreet glance back at the golden-haired boy behind us. He still waited there, as loyal and forlorn as an abandoned spaniel. It became clear to me then that Joseph would only ever tell me about the woman he wanted me to be, but Stefan could reveal the woman I had actually been.

For that reason—but not only that reason—I knew I had to see him again.

CHAPTER 10

AN ASSIGNATION

"Well, what did you expect?" Frau Hauptmann commented that evening as Joseph fumed over the encounter with Stefan. "Honestly . . . I tried to warn you."

"The insolence of the whelp!" Joseph limped the length of the parlor floor, flailed his cane as if lunging the rapier at the youth's heart. "I should have finished him then and there."

"It is good that you didn't." I placed a hand on his back to soothe him. "After all, he is nothing to you. To any of us."

My blithe tone mollified him, and the tightness in his shoulders eased. My counterfeit smile became genuine. I had my own reasons for reassuring him that I cared nothing for the fair-haired peasant boy.

Joseph chuckled. "You are right, of course, my sweet. I shan't waste another thought on him." He cradled my cheek in one knobby hand, eyes rheumy with sentiment. "Do you think . . . tonight . . . you might . . . ?"

"I think you've exerted yourself quite enough for one day," Frau Hauptmann huffed.

His face fell.

"She's right," I agreed. "Not tonight. But soon." And I softly touched my lips to his weathered cheek.

The old man closed his eyes in a kind of reverie. I regretted the cruelty of that kiss and the false hope it gave him.

Frau Hauptmann and I left him in his apartments and returned to mine. "So who is he? This . . . what was his name?" I asked casually, although I remembered perfectly well.

"Stefan." The housekeeper winced as if it tasted foul on her tongue. "And he is best forgotten, as you yourself said. I think God, in His infinite wisdom, effaced your memory simply to wipe your mind clean of that boy."

"All right, then. Who *was* he?" I wheedled as she helped me undress. I tried to sound playful and teasing so she wouldn't guess how serious I was.

"Your groom, if you must know. Stefan tended Lorelei, your mare, and gave you riding lessons," she explained, helping me into my nightgown. "But he was a rude and lazy servant so your husband dismissed him." She stressed the words *your husband*.

So Joseph had not simply been condescending when he'd called Stefan a stable boy! Yet the bitter way he'd hurled the insult told me that the young swain had been much more than a slothful servant.

"We are well rid of him, then," I said with an affected, jaded yawn.

Frau Hauptmann smiled. "Very sensible of you, Frau von Kemp."

"I think I shall require a new groom, however," I added as I started to brush out the hair I'd just let down. "I must learn to ride all over again."

The housekeeper bowed, her mouth crimping into a frown.

For the next several days, I made no reference to Stefan whatsoever, did not even breathe his name although he haunted my thoughts constantly. I was a sweeter, more attentive wife to Joseph during that brief period than at any other time in our acquaintance. He was so happy that he did not object when I continued to refuse his romantic advances. He didn't know that I was spending the entire time plotting a rendezvous with the rival he despised.

Every Sunday, Bettina received leave from her duties to go into the village to attend church and to spend the evening with her family. One week, I implored her to let me go in her place. In exchange for being my accomplice, I offered her a silver brooch from my jewelry box that she could sell to supplement the meager wages Joseph paid her. With two aging parents to support, she reluctantly agreed, extracting a promise from me that I would shield her from the wrath of Frau Hauptmann and the master if our scheme unraveled.

On the appointed day, I awoke complaining of extreme fatigue and claimed I could not even lift my head from the pillow. When Frau Hauptmann asked if she should send for the doctor, I insisted that all I needed was rest. I suggested that Bettina bring me a bit of bread and broth, and that I should spend the rest of the day in bed, during which time I was not to be disturbed. The housekeeper expressed concern from my health but did not seem to suspect any deception.

Once we were in private, Bettina and I disrobed and exchanged clothes. Tailored to a slight figure, her dress made for a tight fit on my taller, more buxom frame, but we were similar enough in stature that only a careful eye would spot the difference. At my request, she had also brought a dark riding cloak with a hood that I could use to hide my face and blonde hair.

In turn, Bettina put on my nightgown and promised to remain in the bedchamber with the door locked until I returned. If Frau Hauptmann tried to enter with her key, Bettina was to jump into bed, pull the sheets over her brown hair, and groan loudly.

"Oh! And one more thing," I said as I cloaked my head with the hood. "How do I find—"

"He lives at the blacksmith's." She didn't need to hear his name, nor did she need to say it. "He apprenticed there after the master dismissed him."

Her troubled look almost made me abandon our plan. Almost.

"Thank you," I said softly.

She shook her head. "Don't thank me. I only tell you because I know you'd find him anyway. What happens now is entirely your doing."

I nodded and left, anxiety tying my stomach in knots. Whatever I'd done with Stefan in my previous life had evidently led to disaster, but I needed to find out what the catastrophe had been—even if it meant repeating it.

My head bowed and covered, I descended the cramped back staircase intended for the maids. I emerged in the kitchen and managed to pass the chef without distracting him from the pot of soup he was stirring on the cast-iron stove.

"Bettina!"

I'd forgotten that I was supposed to answer to that name and was halfway out the servants' exit when Frau Hauptmann called again.

"Bettina!"

I paused in the doorframe, half turned, and prayed that I would not have to speak or show my face.

"You will return in time to give your mistress tomorrow's breakfast, will you not?"

I bobbed my hooded head.

"See that you do. I know how you dawdle." The housekeeper swept away to scrutinize the rest of the staff.

Franz waited outside in the landau to take me—that is, Bettina—to town. If he noticed that I was not really his appointed passenger, he made no sign of it. An ideal servant, the coachman kept his eyes fixed on the road ahead and his nose out of others' business.

Without a word, he delivered me to a small cottage on the outskirts of Liebeheim, which I presumed to be Bettina's family home. I descended from the carriage and pretended to fumble with the latch on the garden gate until Franz drove off. Then I set off on foot toward the heart of the village.

No hammer clanged on the anvil as I arrived at the blacksmith's shop, and the incandescent orange coals of its forge had gone cold and black.

Of course, I thought. *It's the Sabbath.*

Neither the smith nor Stefan would be working that day. I cursed myself for my stupidity and despaired that my whole errand had been in vain.

Unwilling to give up, I circled around the shop and approached the modest house behind it. Because the gossips of the village all seemed to know my face, I did not dare to knock on the front door and ask the smith where I could find his apprentice. Instead, I skulked around the side of the house and tried to peer through the paned windows.

The house sat on a raised foundation, which meant I had to stand on tiptoes to peep over the sill and so could only catch brief glimpses of the home's occupants. A trim, plain woman in the kitchen pulled a steaming pie from a cast-iron oven as a small boy tugged at her skirts, and I ducked out of sight when she brought the pie to the window ledge to let it cool.

I rounded the corner of the house and found one of the windows on the rear wall standing open. Again, I grabbed hold of the sill and stretched onto the balls of my feet to peek into the room above me. I caught sight of a rough cot like the one I'd had in Pastor Georg's house. A male figure sat on the bed, pulling on a pair of scuffed leather riding boots. From behind, I could only see the back of his head, but the mop of blond curls identified him immediately.

I dropped back onto my heels. "Stefan?" I whispered hopefully. "Stefan!"

Gripping the sill, I pulled myself onto my toes again for another look. Suddenly an expanse of linen shirt blocked my view and hands like lion's paws hooked beneath my arms, hauling me up until my wriggling legs slid over the window ledge.

Certain that the smith himself had caught me, I kicked my feet, but they danced helplessly inches above the floor. "I—"

A mouth pressed against mine, devouring my cry. Crushed against my captor's chest, I could see—could *feel*—that it was Stefan who held me suspended above the floor. I squirmed at first, mistaking the violence of his passion for an attack.

His sure hands cupped my thighs, wrapped my legs around his waist. The sinews of his chest pushed up against the underside of my breasts, the snugness awaking nerves I had not known existed. His mouth seemed to draw the breath out of my lungs, then bellow it back in, hot with the fires of a forge. And through it all, his lips molded and melded with mine, now gentle, now fierce, as if seeking a perfect and impossible union.

This, I thought, *is a kiss, a kiss for me alone.*

I let myself drown in its deluge of sensation.

After a moment that seemed both endless and fleeting, he set me back on my feet, clasped my cheeks in his hands. "I *knew* you'd come. I knew he couldn't keep us apart."

Still breathless, I gazed up at his hero's visage, alight with the virility and invincibility of youth, like David when he slew Goliath. I already wanted him to kiss me again.

"I had to see you," I said truthfully.

"And I you. If you hadn't come, I would have come for you, Trina. But here you are, and here you shall stay." He caught me up in his arms and tumbled me onto the narrow bed.

I could not object to his audacity without admitting I knew nothing of our past intimacy, so I let him lay down beside me, his body against mine, the heady musk of his scent so close . . . I confess, I *wanted* him there.

Still, I glanced anxiously toward the door of his room. "They'll hear us."

He laughed. "I care not. Do you?"

And with that he began planting soft kisses on my ear, my chin, my bosom. At that moment, I did not care, could not think, could barely breathe. Was this love? This all-consuming, infectious mania . . . it frightened me, yet I craved it, and the fact that I would crave such a thing frightened me all the more.

I gasped to clear my head and pushed Stefan back. "I can't stay. Joseph will find out."

"Then let us ride away together. By the time he notices you're gone, we'll be a hundred miles from here." He brushed his lips along my neck, flicked his tongue out to tease the skin, came close to nudging aside the scarf that covered the scar around my throat.

I shivered and spurned him again. "I can't. Not yet. There is something I must know first."

Stefan propped his head on his hand and rolled his eyes in comic annoyance. "Yes, I really love you," he sighed, idly tracing the curve of my left breast with his fingertip.

"No, not that," I replied. "What did Joseph tell people when I . . . went away?"

"He said you were consumptive, that you'd gone to the South of France for your health." Stefan's words dripped acid. "All to avoid a scandal, of course, but I knew it was a lie."

"Yes. It was." And I tugged my scarf loose to show him the ugly white streak it concealed.

Stefan shook like a nest of angry wasps. He reached to touch the scar, but his fingers clenched into a fist before contacting my throat. "I'll kill him."

"It may not have been Joseph," I said quickly, for he was on the verge of going to murder the old man right then. "I don't remember what happened. But there is a man who knows."

I thought of Meyer the gravedigger—the gape of recognition he'd given me in the churchyard and the familiar way he'd spoken of me to Frau Hauptmann. She and Joseph knew the truth too, no doubt, but they would never tell it. But I felt sure a reprobate like Meyer would succumb to either bribery or intimidation.

"Where do we find this man?" Stefan demanded.

"I shall take you to him," I answered, "at the proper time."

The stablehand shifted restlessly, like a stallion confined to its stall. "I warn you, Trina—if I find the old man did this, nothing you say will make me spare his miserable life."

"I understand."

He tightened his arms around me. "After that, we go away together."

"Yes." I smiled. "Together."

And I lost myself in another of his kisses.

CHAPTER 11

ELOPEMENT

I spent the rest of the afternoon in Stefan's arms, luxuriating in his caresses. But when he fumbled to unlace my dress, I shrugged off his hands and jumped out of bed.

"I have to go." I pulled Bettina's cloak around me and raised the hood.

Stefan complained that he was not doing anything he hadn't done dozens of times in the past. How could I make him understand that, in the blank memory of my new mind, I was as untouched as any virgin? All I knew of lovemaking was from the sordid memory of Pastor Georg standing sweaty, nude, and red-faced in the hallway of the parsonage. I couldn't bear the thought of seeing Stefan like that.

"I'm not ready," I said.

Stefan grumbled but relented. He took me home on a tawny Hanoverian stallion he borrowed from among the horses waiting to be shod in the blacksmith's stables. "One day, I'll own a herd of these beauties," he vowed as he pulled me up onto the saddle behind him.

I had to hitch up my skirts in order to straddle the hard leather seat, and even with my knees pressed against the horse's sides, I nearly lost my balance as the animal's flanks rolled beneath me.

Stefan laughed at my clumsiness. "I see you've forgotten everything I taught you. Well, here's your first new lesson."

I didn't tell him how right he was. The ride both frightened and exhilarated me as I held my arms tight around the iron firmness of Stefan's stomach, my thighs braced against his as he spurred the horse onward. The chill of the wind only heightened the delicious warmth of my closeness to him. I imagined how thrilling it would be to ride like this, not to Joseph von Kemp's manor but to a home of our own in a distant land.

We arrived at the estate all too soon. I dismounted about half a mile from the house so no one would see me with Stefan.

"Next week, we shall go see Meyer," I told him before we parted.

He frowned. "Bring as much money as you can carry. As soon as we talk to your man, we leave."

He reared up the horse and rode off.

The sun was already setting, so I lingered at the fringe of the property until after nightfall in hopes that most of the staff would retire to their quarters for the evening. When I finally crept inside through the servants' entrance, I found the kitchen cold and deserted, its pots scoured and its counters scrubbed after the dinner hour.

My luck held as I climbed the back stairs and scurried to my bedchamber, for I met no one. Holding aloft a candle I'd lit in the kitchen, I unlocked the door and hurried into the room.

"Bettina?" I whispered as I eased the door shut behind me.

The bedchamber was dark, and the scant glow of the taper barely illuminated the hand that held it. I waved the flame toward the bed. The bedclothes lay flat and shriveled as a shed snakeskin.

"Bettina!"

I moved further into the room, gently sweeping the candle left and right so as not to extinguish the flame. I jumped when the yellow light fell upon a figure seated perfectly still in the chair by the fireplace.

"Good evening, Katarina." In the wan light, Frau Hauptmann resembled a dismal waxwork, her posture petrified, manikin hands folded in her lap, face unsmiling and unblinking. "I trust you had a pleasant afternoon."

My heart sank. How long had she been sitting there, so calm, so still, waiting for me with the patience of a stone? How vain was I to think I could deceive her!

"Where is Bettina?" I demanded.

"Why, at home, where she is every Sunday. Only this time, she shan't be back, for she is no longer in our employ."

Poor, sweet, trusting girl! Guilt throttled me so much I could barely speak.

"How could you?" I asked the housekeeper.

"How could *you*, Frau von Kemp?" She sprang to her feet, sneering my name with poisonous irony. "How could you betray the devotion of an old man whose only fault is to be foolish enough to love you?"

The accusation pierced me to the marrow. "I never asked for his love," I protested.

"No, you had it handed to you on a silver platter, like John the Baptist's head. The least you owed him was your fidelity."

I could not deny what she said, for Joseph had been good to me. Torn between what I knew to be proper—faithfulness to my husband—and what I *felt* to be right—my infatuation with Stefan—I ached as if all my scars had been ripped open. Frau Hauptmann's face rippled in my vision, and my eyes burned so much that I thought there might be something horribly wrong with them. Then an unexpected wetness trailed down my cheeks.

I had never cried before.

Unable to defend my actions, I lashed out with childish scorn. "If you think he is so easy to love, why didn't *you* marry him?"

"Because I never had the chance!" Her stone countenance cracked until she, too, trembled on the verge of weeping. "Landlords don't marry scullery maids. So I ended up with Otto Hauptmann, the valet, and had to watch Joseph squander his affections on worthless wenches like you." She sniffed, but her keen old eyes withheld any tears she might have shed. "And yet you would cast him aside for a stable boy. Well, you shall not wound him like this. Not if I have anything to say about it."

We glared at each other across the candle's flame. I had never before realized the depth of the loneliness and longing that underlay her loyalty to her master. But, obsessed with an irrational love of my own, I viewed her as merely another obstacle to my happiness with Stefan. And Frau Hauptmann had provided me with a dreadful key to achieving my desire.

"If you care for Joseph half as much as you claim, then you will say nothing of this conversation," I told her. "Because, contrary to what you might think, I *do* remember what he did to me, and I shall tell my father, the courts, and the King of Bavaria himself if you so much as mumble about me and Stefan."

The lie was a calculated gamble on my part. I knew Frau Hauptmann couldn't be certain how much I truly recalled and would not risk having me divulge whatever secret crime she and Joseph had conspired to hide.

The housekeeper wheezed in apoplectic indignation. "I brought you back because I believed it would make him happy. I see now you've only brought him more misery."

She swept past me with such ferocity that the candle blew out. I heard the bedchamber door open and slam, and I was left alone in utter darkness.

By the next morning, I could hardly believe the confrontation had ever occurred. Frau Hauptmann herself brought me my breakfast, which she served with flawless propriety. Other than an excessive formality—and too great a stress whenever she addressed me as "Frau von Kemp"—she played the perfect servant. Joseph, too, acted blissfully unaware of my meeting with Stefan. From their manner, I judged that the housekeeper had chosen to hold her tongue.

At my insistence, Bettina resumed her duties before the week was out. Not only because I wanted to make amends for getting the poor girl discharged—I would also needed her help to conceal my next planned visit to Stefan.

He and I had arranged to meet the following Sunday, when I would again pose as Bettina and have Franz drive me to Liebeheim. This time, however, I would not be coming back.

As Stefan had instructed, I brought only a small satchel. It contained all the jewelry Joseph had given me. Its treasure would fund the new life Stefan and I intended to create together.

As before, I wore Bettina's dress and hood so that none of the staff would report my departure to Joseph. Once more, Frau Hauptmann accosted me as I made my way out through the servants' door in the kitchen.

"Good-bye, Bettina," she said with disconcerting finality. Yet she made no move to stop me, although she knew perfectly well who I was and where I was going.

When I reached Liebeheim, I descended from Franz's landau and walked to the blacksmith's shop in the village. Stefan awaited me there, dressed in his riding habit, his horse already saddled. "You can't imagine how I've yearned for this day," he said softly when he saw the satchel in my hand.

"As much as I have, I hope," I said.

"We needn't go back there, you know." He regarded me somberly. "We could ride west and be in the Rhineland by tomorrow."

He peered at me with those cerulean eyes, and part of me wanted to say, *Yes, yes! Let's go far away, right now!*

"After we talk to Meyer," I insisted. "Not before."

Frowning, he helped me onto the saddle, slid my satchel into one of his saddlebags. He didn't speak again during the entire five-hour journey to Darmstadt.

Although it didn't appear to bother Stefan, I cringed every time we passed other travelers on the busy road, for I could swear that they all stared at us as if we were fugitive criminals. I kept my face hidden beneath Bettina's riding hood, but it failed to calm my conscience. Did the strangers recognize us? Would their chatter get back to Joseph?

It doesn't matter anymore, I thought.

Yet my mind continued to spin half-formed fears. When we had departed Liebeheim, a top-hatted coachman driving a landau swung in behind us, trailing our horse for miles. I stole glances at him over my shoulder but couldn't make out the driver's face. He looked like Franz . . . but hadn't I seen him leave the village after depositing me at Bettina's house? Had he remained behind to spy on me?

When he turned off onto a side road, I dismissed my fretting as silly fancy. Shortly, though, a lone rider on a gray mare appeared behind us, and my overheated imagination set to work again. While other riders sped up to overtake us, the dark-coated man on the gray lagged behind us at more or less the same distance all the way to Darmstadt. When we slowed, he reined in his horse; when we sped up, he spurred his animal to keep pace. I tried repeatedly to glimpse the rider's face, but his stooped posture and broad-brimmed black hat shaded his visage.

As we entered the city, the traffic of carts, wagons, and carriages thickened around us, and I lost sight of the rider. The mass of travelers dispersed down different avenues, and the dark figure on the gray mare apparently wandered off on business of his own.

Simply another visitor to the metropolis, with no interest in us at all, I assured myself.

In the reddening light of dusk, the long finger of the church spire touched us with its sundial shadow as we finally tethered our horse near the Stadtkirche. There seemed to be no one in sight, and I feared Meyer might have already gone home for the night.

Then my heart quickened, for I saw the groundskeeper's slovenly bulk emerge from the front doors. In my absence, Pastor Georg must have put him to work tidying the nave after Sunday services, and Meyer's laziness had made him dawdle until he was all alone in the church.

Before I had any notion of what he planned to do, Stefan stalked up the steps to stand within inches of the man. "Any chance of sanctuary for a sinner?" he asked.

Intent upon chaining and padlocking the double doors, Meyer didn't spare him a glance. "Your sins will wait, my friend. God can forgive you tomorrow."

"It's not me who needs His mercy." He shoved Meyer hard against the door, drew a hunting knife from a sheath on his belt, and held the blade against the groundskeeper's quivering double chins. Meyer blubbered but gulped down his cowardice when Stefan pressed the knife's edge close against the skin.

92

Stefan jerked his head toward the church entrance. I slid the unfastened chain off the handle of the other door and held it open as Stefan muscled Meyer inside the chapel's vestibule.

I darted a glance across the plaza at Pastor Georg's house. Its windows glowed invitingly, and a wave of homesickness washed over me.

How many sleepless nights had I caused the pastor and Birgit with my disappearance? Would they still welcome me if I went back to them now?

Yet I shrank with shame at the possibility that they might see me at this moment, sneaking into God's house to interrogate a man at knifepoint. Perhaps it was merely my guilty conscience, then, that made me think I saw a solitary spectator in the square—a dark figure on a pale horse. It withdrew into the maw of an adjacent alley and dissolved in darkness.

I hastened into the church and shut the door behind me.

Safely hidden from view inside, Stefan thrust Meyer up against the nearest wall, the point of his blade about to incise the man's jugular.

"T-t-take wh-wh-whatever you want!" Meyer babbled. "I . . . I can show you where they keep the silver."

"I want nothing from you," Stefan muttered in disgust, "but what you know of *her*."

He nodded to me, and I lowered my hood.

Even in the dimness of the benighted chapel, Meyer's eyes goggled when he saw my face. "I . . . she . . . I . . . never saw her before."

"Lying dog!" Stefan pricked the skin of the groundskeeper's gullet, and a driblet of blood trickled down the curve of the knife blade. "Did you give her that scar on her throat? Shall I give you one to match it?"

Meyer wriggled and whimpered. "No! I swear it! First time I saw her, she had but one wound on her, and *I* didn't put it there!"

My body tingled in sudden fear while my head went numb and cold, as if it were not part of my body. "What wound was that?" I asked.

"A hole in the chest, right over the heart."

The specter of a hundred nightmares rose in my mind: the decapitated cadaver on Victor Frankenstein's slab, a suppurating red gash between its stiff breasts.

93

My own voice sounded foreign to me. "When did you see this?"

Meyer gaped at me in surprise, as if I should have known the answer. "When I buried you."

CHAPTER 12

UNEARTHING THE TRUTH

"More lies!" Stefan scoffed and prepared to jab Meyer with the knife's tip again.

I held up my hand. "Wait. Let him explain."

Meyer snickered hysterically. "If anyone has lies to explain, it's *her*. She's an impostor or a witch or a devil—but she's not the girl I put in the ground. That one was stone dead!"

"Can you believe such nonsense? Let us finish him and be off." Stefan raised his blade, awaiting my cue.

"I do believe him." My speech came slowly, as if I'd just drained a cup of hemlock. "Where did you bury this other woman?"

"In the churchyard." Sensing I was on his side, Meyer addressed me, babbling quickly. "It had to be an unmarked grave—no one could know—but Herr von Kemp insisted it be in hallowed ground."

I waved Stefan back. "Let him go."

Scowling, Stefan released the groundskeeper with a shove but kept the knife poised to strike. Meyer made a show of smoothing his dirty coat as I stepped up until we stood face-to-face.

"Take us to the grave," I commanded. "And bring your spade."

The forbidden ghastliness of our errand required the three of us to tarry in the Stadtkirche until late in the evening, when no one would witness our desecration. We emerged into deserted lanes of blackened storefronts, the city as still and desolate as the cemetery we intended to defile.

The moonless night made the short walk to the churchyard seem like a descent into an underground abyss. Meyer found a lantern for us, but Stefan insisted on carrying it and kept the light hooded most of the way so as not to attract attention. He made the reluctant groundskeeper take the lead, prodding him forward with the blade of the shovel.

As we reached the graveyard's rusted gate, the slow clop of a horse's hooves echoed through the chasm of empty streets behind us.

We all froze, certain that the city's night watchmen were about to arrest us for being vile graverobbers. The peculiar amplification and distortion of sound in the vacant maze of stone walls made it impossible to tell from which direction the hoofbeats came and whether they were approaching or receding. They stopped as abruptly as they'd started, yet no horse appeared. Only the beating of our hearts thumped in our ears.

"Enough," Stefan said at last. "Let's be done with it."

The chains Meyer removed from the gate clanked like angry revenants in the night, until I thought the noise would roust the whole city from its slumber. Once inside the cemetery walls, Stefan unveiled the lantern. The gray wraiths of chiseled angels and granite crosses materialized in the gloom before us.

Meyer weaved clumsily between the listing headstones and statuary as he led the way, his bearings made fuzzy by the liquor he guzzled from a hip flask to calm his nerves.

"Here . . . this way." He paused, swaying, took another swig, then stumbled in the opposite direction. "No, wait! *There.*"

He pointed so emphatically that he nearly pitched forward and fell flat on his face.

A forlorn willow drooped its branches over a forgotten plot at the far end of the churchyard. Below the tree, a cherub perched

96

atop a marble obelisk, its baby face bowed in mourning. Unlike most of the other markers, the carving on this memorial was sharp and crisp, unmarred by the wear of wind and rain or the green cancer of moss and lichens. The polished plane that should have featured an epitaph was blank.

"Just as I told you!" Meyer trumpeted. "Herr von Kemp couldn't bury her in Liebeheim, so he paid me to plant her here, where no one would know her. There, I've done what you asked—I'm off."

Stefan blocked his exit with the shovel. "Dig."

The groundskeeper squealed like a stuck pig. Nevertheless, he grabbed the spade and jammed it into the sod at the base of the obelisk. The turf there bore shoots of fresher grass than the bedraggled overgrowth elsewhere in the churchyard.

The earth did not seem as sunken and dense as in the other plots, either. It turned easily, and, even working at his slothful pace, Meyer didn't take long to excavate a waist-deep pit. Stefan goaded him on, lantern in one hand, knife in the other.

I peered down into the growing hole, and my nose filled with the mineral-and-mildew fragrance of loam.

Meyer had dug only four feet down—rather than the usual six—when the spade struck the hollowness of wood. He'd evidently been as lazy in gravedigging as in every other chore.

No splendid casket lay in that hole, merely an oblong crate such as one might find in the cargo hold of a ship. Already damp and fragile with rot, the lid cracked when Meyer put his full weight on it. His foot broke through the wood and got snagged between two jagged planks. He dropped the spade, shouting as if the corpse had caught hold of him.

"Imbecile!" I hissed. "Get it open! I need to see."

Cursing, Stefan sheathed his knife and set aside the lantern, then jumped into the pit. He seized the shovel and staved in the makeshift coffin. As the wood splintered, Meyer yanked his foot out, tumbling back against the slope of the hole. Stefan pried open a gap in the lid above where the corpse's head should have been and lifted the lantern over it.

The box was empty.

"Ha! Just as I thought." Stefan grinned up at me. "There's no dead woman there because *you* are here—alive."

The blood drained from my face, its skin gone colder than the frigid night air. Stefan probably thought he had put to rest my worst fears when, in fact, he had confirmed them. Victor Frankenstein must have spotted the newly turned earth while foraging for cadavers to dissect and had disinterred the remains of Katarina von Kemp. That meant *I* was the headless woman on the baron's operating table . . . or, at least, part of me was. Where the rest of me had come from and how I now lived I could not even bear to imagine.

Shudders convulsed Meyer as he saw the crate's barren interior. He, of all people, knew what—or who—had been there.

"You *are* a devil." The groundskeeper scrabbled up the incline of loose dirt on the far side of the grave. Back at ground level, he ran wildly, tripping and picking himself up again and again until he vanished into the dark.

Stefan let him go. "Pay him no heed," he said, setting the lantern and spade at the grave's edge so he could climb from the pit. "Whatever nightmare he put you through is over."

He put his arms around my waist, but they failed to warm me.

My nightmare was not over. It had only begun.

Seeing me disconsolate, Stefan lifted my chin. "There is nothing to keep us apart now."

He kissed me avidly, and I clutched at his love as proof that I really was a living woman, not the thing that should have been in that grave.

The muffled clump of hooves on turf advanced on us as if from the recesses of an awful, half-remembered dream. Stefan and I started, and out of the cemetery's sepulchral night mist rode the black-coated horseman on the pallid gray mare. I believed Death himself had come to reclaim me.

With difficulty, the rider swung himself off the animal and hobbled toward us. He wore an old military sword belt, from which he drew a black walking stick that I recognized at once. Nevertheless, I was dumbstruck when the footlight eeriness of the lantern illuminated Joseph von Kemp's shriveled visage.

His complexion was ashen, and he wheezed with every step. Indomitable will alone had enabled him to survive the long journey on horseback and the damp chill of the late hour.

"Once more, you pierce my heart, Katarina," he gasped out, tears glistening on his bony cheeks. He unsheathed the sword from his cane. "Must I pierce yours again, as well?"

I dodged, slumping sideways to the ground as he thrust the blade at me. In a flash, I understood: we were doomed to reenact the original death of Katarina von Kemp, when, in a jealous rage, Joseph had skewered his unfaithful wife.

But this time, Stefan was with me. When Joseph made another feint at my prostrate form, Stefan's hunting knife deflected the killing point from my midriff.

"*You.*" Joseph narrowed his eyes in venomous hatred. "You should have been the one to die all along."

With a deft flick of his wrist, he whipped the sword's tip up to slash Stefan's forearm. Stefan cried out in pain, a line of blood oozing from his skin as his hand popped open and dropped the knife.

Disarmed, Stefan grabbed Joseph's sword hand with his good arm and attempted to wrench the weapon from him. Years of épée training, however, had made the old man swift and shrewd. With his free hand, he swung the wooden scabbard of his cane up in a vicious blow to his rival's head. Stefan sprawled beside the open grave, dazed and groaning.

Joseph towered over his fallen enemy, raised his sword for the *coup de grâce.* Scuttling on hands and knees, I snatched up Stefan's hunting knife and plunged it into the meat of Joseph's thigh. He screamed and wobbled as his weakened leg buckled, the hilt of the knife jutting from his hip like an extra limb.

The moment's interruption gave Stefan the chance to regain his senses. He grabbed the spade that lay beside him and leaped to his feet.

"*Let us be, old man!*" He swung the shovel like a halberd at Joseph's head.

A sickening *thwack* sounded as metal hit skull. Knocked sideways, Joseph collapsed into the open grave and lay unmoving on the broken box of Katarina's coffin. Spooked by the violence, Joseph's horse whinnied and ran off.

Time stopped as Stefan and I gazed down at the body in the pit, only now comprehending the enormity of what we'd done. A gash bisected the gray hair on Joseph's scalp, welling dark fluid.

"He would have killed you," Stefan whispered, as if I'd demanded a justification. "He would have killed us both."

Stefan scooped sod from the pile beside the grave and tossed it down over the still form in the pit. Dirt clung to the bloody edge of the shovel blade.

As soil salted onto Joseph's face, he moaned, eyelids fluttering, lips spitting grit. He woozily tried to push himself onto his hands and knees.

"Wait!" I said. "He's not dead . . ."

Far from stopping, Stefan shoveled faster, plowing heavy swaths of dirt in on top of Joseph. The avalanche of earth mashed the faltering old man flat. Even when sod had blanketed the entire floor of the grave, though, the soil feebly heaved, as if crawling with worms.

I gagged, remorse clotting my nostrils and windpipe like inhaled mud. I hadn't meant Joseph any harm; I only wanted to be free of him.

Even worse than witnessing my husband's premature burial was seeing the ruthlessness writ on Stefan's face as he filled the pit. How could my sweet young boy turn so brutal? And yet, had Joseph been any less savage, willing to kill me twice for the same offense? Was this what love did to men?

"Did it have to be this way?" I asked sadly as Stefan finished his hellish work.

"Yes." He stamped on the new burial mound to tamp down the loose-packed soil. "And now we have no choice but to leave this place forever. Tomorrow we start our new life, and it will be as if all this never happened."

I let him enfold me, if only to block my sight of the grave. "I pray you're right."

CHAPTER
13

ECLIPSED HONEYMOON

Stefan wiped the bloody mud off the spade and left it propped by the cemetery gates along with the extinguished lantern. He felt certain that Meyer would not tell anyone about Joseph von Kemp's murder for fear of incriminating himself, but it was only a matter of time before Frau Hauptmann sent out servants to search for her missing master. Stefan and I needed to be far away by then.

With only stars to light our path, the road out of Darmstadt was treacherous to travel. Stefan insisted that we get away from the city before sunrise, however, so he cajoled our skittish steed into picking its way forward in the dark.

After several hours of slow progress, we had secluded ourselves in the nearby forest, and Stefan at last decided we should rest until daybreak. He tethered our horse in a thicket off the side of the road, and we nestled together in the hollow of an enormous oak, wrapped together in Stefan's riding cape. Although I would have thought sleep impossible with all the terrors of the evening churning in my mind, I dropped into blessed oblivion almost at once.

I started awake sometime later, unsure how many hours had passed, afraid we'd overslept when we should have been fleeing.

101

Stefan's arm still draped across my shoulders, feeling heavier than before.

He must still be asleep, I thought.

But when I turned my head toward him, I found myself eye-to-eye with the creature from Victor Frankenstein's laboratory. It smiled in delight, gusting carrion breath over decayed teeth and graying gums as it crushed me closer for a kiss . . .

I twitched awake again, gasping as if I'd been smothered. I checked my surroundings to make sure I was not in another frightful dream. In the predawn twilight, I saw Stefan standing beside our horse, pawing through one of the saddlebags.

"Well! You're awake at last." He grinned. "It's about time! We must be on our way by sunrise. Here . . ."

He handed me a small jug of white wine from the horse's pack, then sliced some hard cheese and dry sausage for me with a jackknife. I ate ravenously but with a certain nausea, for everything reminded me of the previous night: Stefan cut the food with the jackknife because his hunting knife lay buried with Joseph von Kemp. While still in the graveyard, Stefan had used wine from the jug I now held to clean the cut Joseph had inflicted on his arm, then bandaged the wound with strips torn from his shirtsleeve. He'd since rolled both sleeves up past his elbows. Only a purple-stained rip in the cloth along his right bicep hinted at how close Stefan had come to death.

Despite this, he acted like a boy on a lark. When we finished our simple breakfast and set out on our journey again—skirting Liebeheim and the von Kemp estate by several miles—he serenaded me with Papageno's songs from *The Magic Flute*, singing in a voice more energetic than musical until I laughed with joy. The day was perfect and golden, the surrounding hills green and glorious, and we reveled in the majesty of the birds in the air and the stags in the forest. We waved in fellowship to everyone we passed, and it was easy to pretend we were newlyweds on a honeymoon rather than murderers running for our lives.

Stefan waxed romantic, rhapsodizing about our new beginning. "You shall be . . . Johanna!" he said playfully. "And I shall be

Wolfgang, since you like Mozart so much. Of course, when we are alone, you shall always be my Trina."

He reached behind him to pat my hip. I smiled and hugged him, wanting to believe the fantasy he painted. A cozy cottage of our own and a blacksmith shop that would support us and our family of adorable, tow-headed children.

Though we had not made it to the Prussian border by that afternoon, Stefan chose to stop for the night in the town of Dörnberg. We found a pawnbroker willing to purchase one of the diamond rings from my jewelry chest, and Stefan used the proceeds to buy me two beautifully embroidered peasant dresses befitting my new role as Johanna, as well as shoes and a shift and a fine new outfit for himself.

Famished from our travels, we feasted on a meal of roasted pheasant, after which Stefan secured a room at one of the finest inns in town. We ran up the stairs, giggling, giddy with euphoria.

We had barely set down our things and locked the door of the chamber when Stefan caught me up in his arms. I yelped, then laughed as he carried me to the bed.

"Tomorrow, we shall be married," he murmured with sudden solemnity, gently laying me out before him. "But I must have you tonight."

I remember almost nothing about the bed or the room, for I could look at nothing but his eyes. I felt no fear this time, but a sense of tremendous expectancy made me tremble. After tonight, I knew, neither Stefan nor I would be as we were.

His lips alighted on mine, a brief taste to tantalize me. When my mouth sought more, he nudged me away, wordless yet commanding. Then he started at my feet, as if to torment us both with prolonged desire.

After discarding my leather shoes, he pushed the skirt and petticoat of my new dress up to my knees so as to remove the garters that held my stockings in place. Peeling back the silk skin of the hose an inch at a time, he suckled upon the bare flesh beneath. The tender suction of his mouth against the inside of my thighs caused every fiber of my body to trill with sensation. In the graveyard, I'd felt that even my own limbs did not really belong to me. Now I rejoiced in being made whole again. This was *my* leg, *my* body—I was a woman, and alive!

Stefan wrapped his arms around my hips and nuzzled the haunches with swelling passion, tonguing and delicately nipping at the skin as he kissed his way up from the knees to the crux between my legs. As his questing mouth found my most secret places, I gasped to stifle a cry, for I had never known such intimacy. I hugged his sweet face with my thighs, my fingers clenching the luxuriant golden curls of his hair so that I might hold him there forever.

Too soon, Stefan ceased the deliriously ticklish kisses along the lips of my sex. I opened my eyes to see why he had stopped, and disappointment turned to delight as I watched him shed his Hessian boots and leather breeches. I barely glimpsed the fullness of Stefan's manhood before I felt it submerged in the wetness of my womb.

Now I did cry out. Nothing had prepared me for this strange invasion, the feeling that this piece of another human being was now, in some sense, a part of me. Yet this bizarre appendage filled the void within me in a way that I never thought possible, physically and emotionally bonding me to this man like an umbilicus. I wrapped my legs around him, panting as every thrust drilled deeper into the cavern of my being.

In a frenzy of lust, I tore open the front of his new white shirt to spread my hands over the broad plateau of his chest. Stefan fumbled to loosen the drawstrings of my dress, then sat me up on his lap. While still inside me, he yanked the bunched clothes off over my head, shift, stays, petticoat, and all. I threw my head back, flaunting my nakedness, shivering in anticipation of his ravishing caresses.

Nothing happened.

I looked up, wondering if Stefan were toying with me, withholding his kisses until I begged for them. He stared down at my body with such an attitude of revulsion that I crossed my arms over my bosom in sudden shame.

"What's wrong?" I glanced down self-consciously and answered my own question. In the soft light of the oil lamp the chambermaid had lit for us, the scars that fused my limbs and head to my torso stood out like ridges of livid sealing wax. In the delirium of my desire, I'd forgotten I was no ordinary woman.

But it was not my wounds that seemed to appall Stefan. Instead, he prodded a small, innocuous strawberry birthmark beneath my left breast as if it were some vile insect. He flinched from the touch in disbelief and disgust.

"Who are you?" He shoved me off him. "You are not my Trina! Who *are* you?"

I had no answer. In that instant, I realized I did not know Stefan any better than he knew me. I hadn't been in love with him—I had been in love with that look of adoration he gave me. The look that truly belonged to the dead woman, Katarina von Kemp, whose pristine, headless body did not have a strawberry birthmark.

It was a look I would never see again.

"Meyer was right. You *are* a demon." Stefan seized my throat. "*Who are you?* What have you done with my Trina?"

I shook my head. "No! You . . . don't . . . understand . . ."

He choked off my denial, pinning me against the headboard of the bed. Tears of grief flooded his eyes as he throttled me, for he must have recognized at last that he really had lost his beloved Trina forever.

I did not have time to feel sorry for him. Starved for air, my head pulsated like an apple bursting with maggots. My vision shimmering into blackness, I battered my fists against his iron chest, but he only tightened his stranglehold. I clamped my fingers around his wrists to pry his hands free, but he would not let go.

At that point, my humanity evaporated in sheer terror. As I blindly thrashed for self-preservation, a dark wellspring of strength geysered within me—a strength I hadn't wielded since the night of my birth in Castle Frankenstein. My muscles clenched and contracted with unnatural force as if galvanized by lightning.

Sharp cracks sounded as of tree boughs breaking, and Stefan's grip slipped from my neck. The screams I heard I soon realized were his.

I painfully sucked air through my lacerated windpipe. Even before my vision cleared, I could smell the blood. Gouts of it jetted from the ragged, red tears where I had snapped Stefan's wrists. His left hand flapped loosely on a tongue of skin, the ivory spar of a fractured ulna stabbing forth from the severed arm. The right dangled from the string of a single tendon, dead fingers still twitching.

His golden skin now white as alabaster, Stefan resembled a shattered Greek statue, shrieking as he stared at the ruin of his arms. With his life's blood saturating the bedsheets between us, I knew he would not live more than a few minutes in any event.

Helpless though he was, I had become a beast feral with fear. I sprang forward and locked my arms around his head. Those lips I had craved wriggled to let out another scream as my fingernails dug into that sweet face. Hugging his head against my bare breasts, I wrenched it backward on its neck. I kept twisting even after I heard the vertebrae snap apart. The tatters of his throat tore free from his shoulders, spilling crimson as his body slumped onto the mattress.

A hush descended that seemed to petrify the world. I curled, naked as a babe, with Stefan's head in my lap, his blood greasing my bosom and stomach and running down between my legs. As the red haze of my madness lifted, I did not immediately feel horror or remorse, only a wide-eyed amazement at the impossibility of the scene before me.

Who could have done such a thing? I wondered dimly, blinking at my dismembered fiancé.

It then occurred to me I had witnessed such an atrocity before, when Victor Frankenstein's creature—his *other* monster—had profaned a marriage bed with the slaughter of a newlywed.

I tilted Stefan's face up to gaze into his staring eyes, but the blue in them had already dulled to unseeing glassiness. I briefly fantasized about saving the head.

If I could attach it to another body and revivify Stefan with Promethean fire, I thought, *then maybe he would understand what it is like to be me.*

I knew such an act would be futile, however. The being I

resurrected would no more be Stefan than I was Katarina von Kemp. Besides, I had no idea how such things were done.

But I intended to find out.

I do not remember how long I sat there in a daze before I became aware of the frantic rapping on the door and the alarmed inquiries that the innkeeper and chambermaid shouted from the hallway.

"Herr Schmidt! Frau Schmidt! Are you all right?"

The names meant nothing to me at first, and I thought the inn's staff must have come to the wrong room. Then I recalled the identities Stefan had invented for us: Wolfgang and Johanna Schmidt. Of course. The innkeepers had heard his cries and come to investigate. Soon they would break down the door and accuse me of his murder, drag me away to be decapitated by the guillotine. Truly a punishment to fit the crime.

Stefan's head rolled off my lap and landed on the wooden floor with a thud as I leaped from the bed. Grabbing the wadded clothes we'd cast aside, I swabbed as much blood as possible off myself and wriggled into a fresh shift from my satchel.

Struck with inspiration, I took hold of Stefan's boots, one in each hand, and dipped the soles in the pond of blood that had formed around the bed. I stamped red footprints on the floor, alternating left and right, marking paces from the bed to the room's casement window. I unlatched the window and tossed the boots out into the street below.

Leaving the window wide open, I hastened to extinguish the oil lamp. I groped to retrieve my satchel in the darkness, then folded myself into the chamber's small wardrobe and shut myself inside.

The chamber door's latch rattled as the innkeeper tried his master key in the lock. An instant later the glow from a candle flame outlined the cracks in the wardrobe doors. The chambermaid shrieked, and I knew they had found Stefan.

"My God!" the innkeeper exclaimed. "How . . . ? Wait! Look here."

Footsteps scuttled across the room in the direction of the open window. "The fiend escaped this way. I must fetch the police at once."

I held my breath, not daring even to shiver. A swarm of other voices began to buzz. The commotion had evidently drawn the curiosity of the inn's other guests.

"Please, stand back! All of you!" the innkeeper commanded them. To the chambermaid he added, "Let no one enter this room until I return."

"You can't leave me here alone!" she protested.

"You won't be alone," he replied wearily. "Half the city is filling the stairwell as we speak."

The closing door cut off their conversation. I waited until I heard the innkeeper's key clatter in the lock again before I risked climbing out of the wardrobe. Operating as much by touch as by sight in the lightless room, I found the other new dress I'd bought that day—the one not steeped in blood—and hastily draped it over myself without bothering to put on stays or a petticoat. I then stuffed as much of Joseph von Kemp's jewelry as I could into the drawstring bag I used as a purse, which I hung around my neck.

Taking nothing else with me, I went to the open window, wincing as my bare feet stepped in still-warm, slippery liquid. I climbed onto the sill and glanced down into the street below. A small crowd had already gathered there, and among the thicket of hats I could spot the black, fan-shaped hump of a policeman's Napoleonic bicorne. Fortunately, they were all looking down to examine Stefan's bloodstained boots.

Since I had no way to get down without being seen, I determined to go up. The window was right beneath the inn's roof, but to climb onto it I would have to get out from under the roof's overhang.

I quietly reached out to pull the casement toward me. Placing both hands on top of the thick wooden square of paned glass, I lifted my right leg up to hook it over the window frame. No sooner had I done so than my left foot slipped off the windowsill.

The casement swung away from the window ledge. My left leg swayed free over the heads of the crowd three stories below as the window's hinges groaned from the strain of supporting my weight, threatening to break loose. The noise made a few of the people below squint upward in the darkness.

Now I consciously called upon the unnatural strength within

me. With the palms of both hands and the insole of my bare right foot anchored on the window frame, I managed to get my left foot planted on the casement. From this awkward crouch I balanced on the window frame and grabbed hold of the roof's edge above me, pulling myself up onto the shingled slant one leg at a time.

As confused shouts stirred the throng below, I scuttled up to the slant's peak and away along the rooftops that connected the inn with the neighboring shops and businesses along the street, just as I had seen Frankenstein's creature do in Darmstadt.

I knew I would have to find it. Him. The mate I'd scorned the night I came to life.

CHAPTER 14

THE WIDOW

"I heard the monster tore the head clean off."

My face hidden behind the curtain of my mourning veil, I managed not to react to the speaker, a languid dandy seated opposite me in the narrow coach in which we rode.

"No man could maul a body that way," said his less-flamboyant companion, a middle-aged gentleman with a staid frock coat and a neatly trimmed goatee. "More likely, the villain had a dog rip the fellow up. Perhaps even a trained wolf."

The dandy dabbed at his nose with a silk handkerchief, as if he could smell the carnage himself. "I understand he took the wife with him. I shudder to think what became of her. One can only hope they catch and send the scoundrel to the scaffold before the week is out."

Although I remained as still as I could in the lurching carriage, the more well-mannered gentleman took note of me at last. "I fear we are upsetting our gentle companion," he murmured to the dandy. "She has obviously had enough of tragedy. I do apologize, dear lady. I'm sure you have already learned more than you wanted to know about the lurid crime in Dörnberg."

"No, actually." I regarded him distantly through the mist of black lace. "I know nothing about it."

In reality, I'd heard about nothing but the savage killing of "Wolfgang Schmidt" and his wife for more than a day now. Although I had fled on foot all night to reach the neighboring town of Dörnheim, the news had traveled faster than I did, spread by itinerant merchants traveling from town to town before dawn to sell their wares. When I visited a pawnbroker to sell one of my rings, the man regaled me with the latest whisperings about the horrid double murder. When I went to buy shoes for my bruised and blistered feet, the cobbler could talk of nothing else. When I bought my widow's weeds, the seamstresses chatted incessantly between themselves while taking my measurements, ghoulishly reveling in every grisly detail of the story while pretending to abhor it. They paid no more heed to me than if I were a dressmaker's dummy.

Indeed, I needn't have worried about being implicated in Stefan's murder at all. People could not believe that a mere woman could be capable of such an act of savagery, so they assumed that I, "Johanna Schmidt," had become a victim as well, carried off to some unimaginably horrendous fate.

I wanted them to go on thinking so. Hence, my mourning attire. Not only was it appropriate given that I had lost both my husband and my lover, it permitted me to hide my face from the world. The women at the dress shop told me it would take them at least a week to sew a funeral gown for me, but I insisted that they alter one of the store's existing dresses as best they could so I could leave town by coach immediately. My journey would take me through familiar places, and I did not want anyone to recognize me as Johanna, Katarina, *or* Liesl. I vowed never again to go by a name someone else imposed upon me.

I arrived in Darmstadt that evening and signed into an inn as "Frau Neumann." All that night and the following day, I kept myself cloaked in black from head to foot. When I walked through the streets, the townsfolk made way for me as if I were the Grim Reaper himself. The clerks at the wigmaker's and the dressmaker's were somber and solicitous to me as I purchased the items I required for my new incarnation.

112

As I stepped out of the milliner's, I caught sight of Birgit emerging from the butcher shop we used to frequent. Despite my desire to remain unnoticed, I stopped and stared.

Birgit went about her business with no visible sign of distress. No doubt she'd had plenty of time to accept my disappearance. But she looked so much older and more haggard than I remembered that I wanted to tear off my veil and run to her, to hug her and say, *It's your Liesl! I'm here, I'm safe—you don't need to grieve for me anymore.*

Instead, I turned and walked in the opposite direction like the complete stranger I now was. That life was over, Liesl long dead.

I was Anna now. Anna Frankenstein, a family name I felt I owned by birthright since it had belonged to my father, my creator.

The next morning, I rose early in my room at the inn and put on one of the cheerful, fashionable frocks I'd purchased. Regarding my reflection in the chamber's mirror, I pinned up my blonde hair so that I might cover it with the wig of auburn curls I'd also obtained. I smiled at the effect. I hardly recognized myself.

When I was ready, I packed my other personal belongings in my new valise and portmanteau and hired a coach to convey me directly to Castle Frankenstein.

Memories assaulted me as we ascended the winding path up the wooded hill—the sizzle of lightning in my bones, the whistle of musket balls from the baron's guns, the whiteness of Elizabeth's rag-doll corpse flung upon her bridal bed. I regressed to the frightened newborn I'd been when I first awoke in the castle, and fought the urge to stop the carriage and flee through the forest on foot as I had before.

The panic passed as soon as the coach drew to a halt at the castle entrance. The matching towers of the old fortress, so ominous in the night, seemed stately, almost quaint in the gentling light of day. I steadied myself and followed the coachman as he carried my luggage up the steps to the front doors. I had a role to play and could not afford a moment's lapse in courage or concentration.

Fixing a bright smile on my face, I rapped the doorknocker.

As I'd hoped, Victor Frankenstein's elderly manservant opened the door, looking older and more irascible than ever.

"Hans! You dear fellow . . ." I bustled forward to clasp his hand, thereby pushing my way past the threshold. "Oh, it's even lovelier than I remember!" I gushed, making a show of marveling at the artwork in the foyer. I waved a hand back toward my luggage on the stoop. "Oh, could you have one of your men fetch my things?"

The flabbergasted butler finally found his tongue. "Forgive me, Fräulein, but . . . who *are* you?"

I feigned shock. "You don't recognize me? I mean, I know it's been a long time. I was hardly more than a child the last time I was here, but . . ." I gave him an impish smile, challenging him to identify me.

Hans studied my features, frowning with self-doubt. Perhaps he saw traces of that wild woman who'd escaped the castle tower or that "Hungarian scullery maid" who'd delivered flowers on Baron Frankenstein's wedding night.

"You *look* familiar," he admitted.

"It's *Anna*!" I laughed gaily. "Anna—Victor's cousin from Vienna. Surely he told you I was coming."

The old man wavered between irritation and embarrassment. "I'm afraid not, Fräulein. We are expecting the master's aunt Lenya and her family—all the way from Salzburg. Are you with them, perhaps?"

"No, I'm from the other side of the family." I shook my head in annoyance. "I suppose he didn't get my letter. The mail service these days! One simply can't depend on it."

"Fräulein," Hans interrupted, "the baron is not here. He has been away for more than a week."

"He's *gone*?" This time, my consternation was genuine. I had come to see Victor Frankenstein; if he had disappeared, my whole charade would be for naught. "When do you expect his return?"

"I know not," Hans replied. "I am sorry."

I twirled one end of my scarf about my finger. "Then perhaps I could meet Elizabeth? Papa was so upset that we couldn't make it to the wedding—"

"I regret to inform you that the baroness . . . passed away."

I put my hands to my mouth as if hearing the news for the first time. "How dreadful! Poor Victor must be devastated."

114

"Yes, Fräulein. It has been hard for us all."

"Alas! It seems I've come all this way in vain." I glanced significantly at the valise and trunk the coachman had abandoned on the doorstep. "Well, I don't want to intrude. I dismissed the carriage, but I'm sure I can hire another—"

The prospect of leaving a young woman without a roof over her head apparently roused the old man's spirit of hospitality.

"Oh no, Fräulein Anna, I won't hear of it!" He actually smiled and patted my hand. "I am sure the baron would not object to your stay here in his absence. I'll have the maids prepare a room at once. Allow me to have someone see to your things."

He bowed and was about to depart.

"The baron's absence . . ." I asked idly. "Does it have to do with his work?"

Hans paused, frowning again. "I beg your pardon?"

"You know. His research." I nodded toward the closed door of the tower that contained the laboratory.

A fit of palsy struck the aged servant as he contemplated the tower's entrance. "I . . . cannot say. Do forgive me." He bowed and hastily waddled off.

Hans made sure the staff treated me as an honored guest. The maids prepared my bedchamber and saw to my every need, and the cook catered to each whim of my appetite. Indeed, with the house otherwise unoccupied, they seemed relieved to have someone to serve.

Over the next few days, I took advantage of my isolation to comb through Victor Frankenstein's massive library in hopes that his books might give me the answers I could not get from him. I silently thanked Frau Hauptmann for her grueling lessons in literacy as I devoured volumes of anatomy by Vesalius and tracts on the electrical stimulation of dead muscle tissue by Luigi Galvani and Erasmus Darwin. In particular, I noted and transcribed into a journal those passages where Frankenstein had jotted comments in the margin with an inked quill.

115

Gradually, the full scope of his godlike vision—and his blasphemous audacity—became clear. As I turned the pages, my fingertips prickled as if charged with static. I was reading about my own conception.

The books, though edifying, did not tell me the two things I most wanted to learn: *how* Frankenstein had fashioned and given life to his creations and where he was now. But I had a good idea of where I might find those answers.

Late one night, long after I had supposedly retired for the evening and the entire household had gone to bed, I put on a dressing gown and crept from my room. With a single candle in my hand, I descended the main staircase to the castle's entrance hall. Dim and daunting in the candlelight, the door to the laboratory tower awaited me, pregnant with secrets. I had the uncanny sensation that I was a disembodied spectator in my own dream. At any moment, I expected to see myself burst forth from that door, half-clothed in a crude smock and trailing torn bandages, crazed with fright and gibbering like an orangutan. If that happened, I thought, I would scream in repulsion.

Nothing emerged from the door, however, and the house remained quiet. To my surprise, the latch opened when I tried it, and I ascended the flights of stone steps in the square tower with a swelling sense of *déjà vu*. A creeping, irrational fear seized me. By going back to the place where I had been made, could I somehow be *un*made, as if I were returning to the womb?

When I reached the door at the top of the stairs, I halted. Though no light peeped from the keyhole, I was paralyzed by the sudden certainty that Hans had lied—that my entire stay in the castle had been a clever trap and that Victor Frankenstein waited for me beyond that door, waited to carve up my body into its component parts and reassemble them into a better, more obedient creature.

Let him try, I thought, anger displacing fear.

I tested the latch. It was locked.

I cursed and rattled the handle, but it would not give. I could have searched for the key, but I had little chance of finding it; for all I knew, Frankenstein had taken it with him.

Then I recalled my dark reservoir of strength—the way I'd snapped Stefan's wrists like twigs.

I set my candleholder on the floor and placed my right palm flat on the door, directly above the latch. Bracing my left side against the stone wall, I inhaled, eyes shut, drew back my right hand and, with a shout, slammed the palm into the wood. The impact sent judders of pain up my arm, but I heard a metallic *clink* as the iron latch broke in two and the door finally yielded and swung inward.

The vacant laboratory had been scrubbed clean of any evidence of necromancy. Where the stench of alcohol and blood once oppressed me, there was now only a dusty, sterile odor of disuse. No vats and jars of pickled organs crowded the shelves, no shards of glass or stains of gore marked the flagstones of the floor. The marble dissection table, where the headless cadaver of Katarina von Kemp had lain, gleamed a pristine, ghostly white as I waved my candle over it. A queasy aura of unreality pervaded the barren chamber, and an entirely new fear possessed me: perhaps I was merely mad, and had imagined the whole episode of my unholy birth.

But I had not imagined the scars on my body, I sternly reminded myself, nor had I imagined the horrors I'd inflicted upon Stefan.

I moved on to the nearer end of the room, where a desk sat heaped with ledgers and parchments. One of the leather-bound books lay with its vellum leaves open. Spread-eagled on the pages was a grotesque parody of Leonardo da Vinci's *Vitruvian Man*, a detailed sketch that Victor Frankenstein had made of his proposed monster. It depicted the portions of the body he would graft together and the precise placement of the electrodes that would jolt the being to life. Frankenstein must have propped open the book to that page to castigate himself for the abomination he'd unleashed.

I pawed through the volume, panting with excitement. Here at last, I held the grimoire that would permit me to replicate the dark miracle of my creation. All I lacked now was the surgical skill for the operation.

I tucked the book under my arm and was about to leave when the light from my candle fell across the patchwork of papers scattered on the desk. They consisted mostly of pages torn from local newspapers ranging from *Le Journal de Genève* to the *Darmstädter Zeitung*. "Awful Murder" and "Child Strangled" read two of the boldface headings, accompanied by dense blocks of cramped typescript that recounted the crimes.

Along with these articles, Frankenstein had spread a map on the table. With his quill, he had drawn circles around the location of each killing and scribbled a corresponding name next to each: Wilhelm, Justine, Elizabeth, Clerval, Krempe. In addition to these circles, Frankenstein had drawn an arrow pointing to the city of Ingolstadt with the legend "Waldman?" scrawled beside it.

Next to the map rested a crumpled handbill. "Have You Seen This Man?" the leaflet asked. Its text gave an account of the suspect's alleged killings. The drawing below the print was crude and inaccurate—it softened the monster's freakish features to mere human ugliness, as though the artist did not believe the true hideousness of what the eyewitnesses must have described to him. Still, I recognized my intended mate easily enough. Except I couldn't think of him that way. We were both offspring of Frankenstein, and he felt more like a sibling to me than a paramour. My dear brother in death.

I took the handbill and map and folded them inside Victor Frankenstein's book. I knew now where I had to go.

When Hans found me waiting in the foyer at first light the next morning, my portmanteau and valise beside me, he seemed taken aback.

"You are leaving us, Fräulein Anna?" he asked, sounding rather hurt.

"Yes," I responded. "I'm afraid I must."

The servant put a hand on his chest and bowed. "I hope we have given no offense."

"Oh, no! You have been nothing but kind and generous." My gaze drifted to the valise, in which I had stashed the book and map I'd collected from Frankenstein's laboratory. "I have a . . . family obligation."

CHAPTER 15

FAMILY REUNION

At the end of two days' travel from Darmstadt, the carriage I'd hired bumped over an old stone bridge that spanned the swirling currents of the Danube. For several minutes we paralleled a high medieval wall until we came to a hexagonal, spired tower of reddish brick—the Kreuztor, or main gate to the venerable city of Ingolstadt.

After rolling through the Gothic archway into the metropolis, the coach wound between rows of buildings roofed in red clay tile. Finally, it deposited me at a local pension, where I intended to stay for the duration of my visit. My research had led me to Ingolstadt because I'd learned that Victor Frankenstein had studied under a professor named Ernst Waldman while at the university there. When I asked my driver for directions to what I supposed was a famed institution, however, I feared I'd come in vain.

"The university?" The graying coachman brushed his horses, seeming to prefer their company to that of his passengers. "Why, the school shut its doors more than ten years back. No money." He extended an arm to the south. "But you may see what's left of it if you take this street to the right."

I thanked him but secretly despaired that my efforts to find

Frankenstein had been frustrated yet again. Nevertheless, as soon as I had locked my luggage in my room at the pension, I walked down the lane the driver had indicated toward what had once been the University of Ingolstadt. Perhaps someone in the neighborhood would know where I might find Dr. Waldman.

As I proceeded along the avenue, I could not help but note the number of police patrolling the vicinity. Uniformed in black bicornes and pale blue military tailcoats with red cuffs and gold epaulettes, the officers seemed to be knocking on every door, conducting a house-by-house search. In addition to their usual heavy walking sticks, many of the policemen were also armed with muskets or swords—a rare show of force during peacetime.

The crowd of murmuring gawkers in the street became so thick that I had to plow my way through the masses to reach the university. They were clustered around what I soon learned was the school's former Anatomy Building, a two-story structure in the classical mode with symmetrical wings, a columned portico, and a semicircular cupola at its center. A hedge-lined path through formal gardens led to the entrance, but when I tried to advance toward the walkway, a stout police officer with the jowls of an old foxhound blocked my way.

"I can't let you go in there, Fräulein," he said. "It's not safe."

"Oh. Well, perhaps you could help me. I'm looking for Dr. Waldman. Do you know where I might find him?"

The policeman glowered at me. "And who would you be?"

I nearly said "Anna Frankenstein," but instinct made me withhold the name. "A friend of the family," I answered instead.

He harrumphed. "If it's Dr. Waldman the elder you seek, you're a day too late." He turned toward the Anatomy Building and aimed a sausage-thick finger up at the main window in the cupola. A hole gaped in the center of its fractured panes and fragmented glass. "Someone hurled him to his death last night," the policeman informed me.

"How horrible!" I tried to appear surprised, although I'd already guessed the worst. I pictured my brother's malformed face and imagined what those policemen with their swords and muskets would do if they found him during their manhunt through the city. "Do you know who would do such a thing?" I asked ingenuously.

"We know the very man: a former student of Dr. Waldman's named Frankenstein," the policeman asserted. "Yesterday, he was seen here, where the doctor has kept a surgery since the university closed. Frankenstein has now disappeared. But rest assured, Fräulein—we shall find him." He waggled a fat thumb over his shoulder. "Dr. Waldman the younger is there, if you want to offer your condolences."

I looked past the officer to the small fountain he indicated in the building's courtyard. A disconsolate young man sat on the fountain's rim, head in hands, as a different policeman interrogated him. The young Waldman's long, delicate fingers clenched the wavy black locks of his hair as if to pull them out by the roots. In response to some particularly probing question, he lifted his face in weary attentiveness, revealing a countenance whose cerebral brow and magnetic green eyes bore an expression of such profound sadness that it made me ache in sympathy just to look at him.

"Do you wish to speak with him?" the jowly policeman asked.

"No." I gave the grief-stricken Dr. Waldman the younger another brief glance. "Not yet."

And so it went in every town to which I tracked Victor Frankenstein. He would arrive too late to stop his creation from butchering yet another of his dearest friends or relations, and I would inevitably just miss my chance to plead with the baron before he raced off in pursuit of the murderous Cain he'd fathered.

As we moved ever northward, into the highest latitudes of Prussia and from thence into Russia, my brother began to kill complete strangers, leaving a string of mutilated bodies for his progenitor to follow. Everywhere, the pattern was the same: rumored sightings of a grotesque Goliath on the prowl; a series of hideous slayings, usually of innocent women and children; then the appearance of an ascetic, well-educated stranger who queried the inhabitants about the crimes and seemed intent upon hunting down the brutal malefactor. I knew that, unless I interceded, there could be only one outcome if Creator and Destroyer met—mutual annihilation.

When I reached the bleak, isolated port of Archangel, I thought

I had at last cornered my quarries, their flight surely cut off by the frozen swells of the icebound White Sea. I described Victor Frankenstein to the local merchants, communicating as best I could with gestures and what scraps of German, English, and French the local peasantry understood. Yes, they said, they had seen such a foreign gentleman a couple of weeks earlier. In fact, he had purchased a sledge, sled dogs, and supplies from them and set out across the desert of ice, evidently following the tracks created by the runners of another sledge that had been stolen the day before.

Indicating my desire to go after him, I asked if I could buy a similar sleigh. The Russians laughed and shook their heads.

"You would do better to buy a boat," they said, pointing out the enormous cracks that were splitting the sea's surface into a mosaic of jagged ice sheets. "The spring thaw has already begun. If your friend is still alive, he will be swimming soon."

I gazed out over the gray patchwork of breaking ice in the bay. I'd come too far to stop now. If I needed a boat to find Frankenstein and my brother, then a boat I would buy.

As Fortune would have it, when I sought a ship to hire for the search, I made the acquaintance of an adventure-seeking English mariner by the name of Robert Walton. Dauntless and ambitious, Walton had come all the way from his home in Britain to the remote Russian coast to fit out an expedition set on locating the earth's magnetic pole and seeking out a northern passage to the Western Hemisphere. He was only too happy to aid my quest in exchange for funding his enterprise with the sale of some of my remaining jewels.

"And who is this fellow you're trying to find?" the dapper young captain wanted to know.

"My . . . cousin," I replied, conducting our negotiations in Walton's native English. "He became deranged and reckless after his wife's death, and I fear for his safety."

"And I fear for yours, young lady," Walton admonished me. "The Arctic is a harsh, unforgiving place. I will do my best to rescue your cousin if I can, but I will risk neither my crew's life nor yours for his sake. Do you understand?"

I nodded gravely. "Yes."

And with that, we sealed our partnership.

Even after we had fully provisioned Walton's ship, a schooner dubbed the *Michael* in honor of the port's patron archangel, it languished in the icebound harbor. I agonized in suspense for weeks as we waited until the water had cleared enough for us to set sail. Every day that passed increased the chance that Frankenstein and his creature would kill each other—or that the fathomless Arctic sea would swallow them both.

When at last we embarked, the days had already become unnaturally long, with only a few scant hours of night to divide dusk from dawn. We sailed out into an ocean still treacherous with massive bergs of floating ice whose hidden crags could stave in our hull. Walton posted a round-the-clock watch in the crow's nest, and several times the crew scrambled to bring the ship about when the cry of *"Iceberg!"* rang out.

With the ice sheet fragmenting around them, Frankenstein and my brother could have headed in only one direction: north, toward the pole. And so we followed the quivering needle of the ship's compass out of the White Sea, through the Barents Sea, and into the Arctic Ocean.

As we neared the pole and the summer solstice, night disappeared altogether and time seemed to stop, suspending us in a dismal limbo of overcast gray. The flat plane of the still water reflected the serrated landscape of glaciers on the horizon and the bleak slate of sky above, creating the illusion that the entire world had been inverted. Becalmed for days due to lack of wind, we would drift like a derelict between breathtaking palaces of ice. Their pinnacles reached twice as high as the ship's masts, and melting runoff had hollowed vast nautilus chambers in the hearts of the bergs.

As such times, I would stand on the prow for hours, inhaling salt and cold, keeping vigil until my face went numb from the frigid air. Every time we passed one of the floating glacial islands, I would scan its white banks for stranded castaways. My pulse quickened once as I spotted—*There!*—a misshapen, hulking creature lying beached on a berg's shore. But, no—the fat form rolled over, and a tusked-and-mustached walrus lazily flopped into the water.

After more than a month at sea, my hope dimmed. Then a Norwegian trawler sailed into view, the first sign of humanity we'd encountered since leaving port.

"Ahoy!" Captain Walton shouted as our ships passed each other. "Have you seen any dogsleds on the ice around here?"

When it appeared that no one on the other vessel understood English, he found a Russian crewman on the *Michael* who spoke rudimentary Norwegian to translate the question. Yes, the Scandinavians replied, they had seen two sledges, one of which seemed to be driven by a thick-limbed ape of a man. The news cheered me, and I redoubled my vigil at the ship's prow, sleeping only a couple of hours each night.

Just then, when prospects for our search had seemed to improve, a thick fog moved in, reducing visibility so much that it became too hazardous to move. We dropped anchor and waited. Still, I scrutinized the roiling mists for any shadow of movement.

And then I heard it: a gunshot, ripping through the deadening tufts of fog.

I knew the sound as intimately as my own heartbeat. It was the crack of the same dueling pistol Frankenstein had fired at me the night I was born. I was sure of it.

I leaned over the ship's rail, wishing I could part the silver mist through sheer force of will. Instead, I had to wait another half a day for the fog to lift.

When it did, we found ourselves within a league of the vast polar ice cap. We cruised alongside the frozen shelf, seeking the source of the gunshot we'd heard. It wasn't long before a sailor on the ship's port side called out, "I think I see something!"

I rushed to look where he pointed. At first, my heart shriveled with disappointment. The irregular brownish lump on the white landscape that the seaman had sighted was clearly just another walrus.

As we drew nigh to it, however, we saw that the great fanged mammal lay dead, its belly *slit open* to disgorge entrails and blood. Beside the carcass rested a weather-blasted sled piled with sealskin packs. Two wolf-size Siberian huskies were tethered to the sledge, and they tore at a hunk of raw meat that had evidently been sliced for them from the slaughtered walrus.

But where was the sled's driver?

Captain Walton sent a contingent of the ship's crew to investigate. The men rowed a lifeboat over to the ice sheet. I watched, unblinking, as the sailors poked around the apparently abandoned campsite. One of them happened to be the ship's cook, a grizzled Siberian ever on the lookout for a cheap meal to serve the crew. He bent down to scrutinize the flayed walrus to see what meat he could salvage, then let out a cry of surprise and revulsion.

The cook motioned for his comrades to help him, and together they reached inside the slain animal and pulled out a babbling, barely living man. Smeared as he was with drying blood, the man was unrecognizable, yet I sensed at once he was none other than Victor Frankenstein. He had obviously sought shelter from the deadly Arctic chill in the insulating blubber and still-warm body cavity of the dead walrus.

While the search party busied themselves with Frankenstein, I scoured the surrounding icescape with a spyglass, looking for other signs of life. If the baron had fired his pistol to kill the walrus, then maybe my brother was still . . .

A black spot flicked across the shaky white circle of the telescope's eyepiece. When I swung the lens back to where the spot had been, the dark shape slipped out of sight behind a ridge of ice overlooking Victor Frankenstein's encampment. Another walrus? I could not tell.

Despite his desperate condition, Frankenstein resisted the efforts of Walton's men to rescue him. They had to restrain him in the rowboat as they ferried him back to the *Michael*.

Although I was standing at the bulwark railing as the sailors dragged the baron aboard ship, the stricken nobleman did not even look my way. Perhaps it was because I had the hood of my fur coat pulled up so he could not see my face. Or maybe he failed to recognize me out of context; I'm sure I was the last person he expected to encounter on a ship in the middle of the Arctic. But I think the real reason he did not know me by sight was that I was no longer the same woman he'd fabricated in his laboratory.

Still stained with blood, Frankenstein was so weak that he would have crumpled into a heap on the deck if a young boatswain hadn't propped him up. Yet a manic energy animated him, and he seized the lapels of Walton's coat, shouting German in the captain's face.

Walton patted the baron's arm to soothe him. "Easy, friend! You must rest . . ."

Frankenstein switched to English, desperate to make himself clear to the British captain. "No! You can't take me. Don't you understand? The demon is still out there! *It's still alive!*"

A shiver rippled through me that had nothing to do with the polar cold. Was it fear? Or exhilaration? Possibly both. Frankenstein hadn't succeeded in killing my brother. There was still a chance I might see him again.

The crazed nobleman raved about "the monster" and "the devil" as the boatswain half carried him to one of the ship's cabins and laid him on its berth. The ship's "doctor"—a carpenter by trade who practiced little medicine other than amputating gangrenous limbs with his saw—stripped off Frankenstein's soiled clothes, washed the dried walrus blood from the patient's body with warm water, and then wrapped him in heavy blankets. The baron slipped into a mumbling semiconsciousness. "Must find . . . can't let it live . . . "

For more than two days, he remained in a feverish delirium, and I fretted he would die without ever regaining his wits. With the temperature outside well below zero, he twitched in a private inferno, teeth chattering, face burning red, sweat bleeding from every pore.

At last, in the middle of another night that was not night, Walton came to my cabin to announce that the baron's fever had broken. "He's awake now," the captain said. "Do you want to speak with him?"

I found myself unable to answer. Here it was, the moment for which I'd waited my whole brief life, and now that it had arrived I felt myself completely unprepared. I'd had so many questions to ask, so many emotions to express to this confounding man who'd given me life, yet I was tongue-tied, my mind a blank.

126

"I'll come," I told Walton, "but don't tell him who I am. The shock . . . might be too much for him."

With the captain's permission, I accompanied him when he next went to check on Frankenstein. Wearing a plain dress and my auburn wig, I brought with me a cup of bouillon and a ship's biscuit. While Walton stood off in a corner near the door, I seated myself on a three-legged stool at the side of the sick baron's bunk, broke off a piece of the salt-crusted hardtack, and dipped it into the broth to soften it.

Frankenstein rested in the bunk, propped up by a pillow and folded bolts of rough canvas. Peaked and skeletal, he nevertheless turned his mouth away when I tried to feed him.

"No! There's no time for that. The demon will escape."

"Then you will need your strength to hunt it," I countered.

The baron ceased his feeble resistance and permitted me to place the sodden biscuit in his mouth. He peered at me with heightened interest.

"You are German?" he asked, noting my accent.

I smiled, remembering all I had learned about Victor Frankenstein while pursuing him. "My father was Genevese," I said.

The apparent coincidence brightened his spirits. "I'm from Geneva as well! At least, I was until I assumed my family's ancestral title and estate." He sighed, regarding me with a look both fond and wistful. "A ministering angel from home!"

I did not realize until that instant how much I had secretly craved his approval and affection. We hardly knew each other—he had been little more than a frightful ogre from my past—but it didn't matter. The uncharacteristic warmth in his gaze filled my heart with a homesickness for a family I'd never had. I wanted him to accept me as his own, always.

Would he be as warm to me if he knew who I really was? I doubted it. Yet I didn't want the illusion to end.

"That mouth should be eating instead of talking," I chided playfully, and fed him another bite.

He coughed out a chuckle and permitted me to nurse him without further complaint. Let him think I was just an ordinary girl, if it endeared me to him like that.

The broth and biscuit restored the baron enough that Walton stepped forward to engage him in conversation. I surrendered the stool to the captain and retreated to the cabin's corner, where I could listen unobtrusively.

Walton turned out to be the ideal confidant to elicit the baron's story—a father confessor to whom Victor Frankenstein could unburden his accumulated sins against man and Nature. Over the next several days, I gave Frankenstein his meals, then eavesdropped as he related the entire sequence of events that had led him to his present misery: how he had extrapolated the heretical theories of his mentor, Ernst Waldman the elder, to conceive the first artificial being; how the being's hideousness had caused it to be shunned by even the humblest humans; and how the creature's anguish of loneliness had devolved into rage against humanity in general and his creator in particular.

Then Frankenstein came to the part where the monster had demanded a female companion to ease his isolation. I fought the urge to weep as I heard the revulsion with which the scientist described the "filthy process," as he called it, and the "abomination" he had fashioned as a mate. Frankenstein was either so ashamed of his actions or so convinced I was dead that he lied to Walton and claimed he'd dismantled the female before ever granting it life.

That was the unkindest cut of all—complete omission from my own life story. I felt as unwanted and orphaned as my brother must have.

With Baron Frankenstein safely aboard ship, Captain Walton wanted to set sail for the pole again, but I begged him to hold off. "My cousin Victor's health is too precarious," I told the Captain. "We must give him a few more days to convalesce."

In reality, I was thinking of the black shape I'd spotted with the spyglass. If that *had* been my brother, my best hope was to lure him to me with Victor Frankenstein as bait.

I stalled Walton for several days more, but my brother did not appear.

Then the baron's health took a turn for the worse. His fever rose, and he bobbed in and out of consciousness. When I came to feed him, he jerked awake and grabbed my skirts.

"Elizabeth," he breathed. "Please stay with me—I've missed you so."

128

I wanted then to tell the truth, to reveal myself and reconcile with him while there was still time, but he sagged back onto the pillow and his eyes rolled shut again.

"We've got to get him back to civilization," insisted Walton, who stood behind me. "He'll die out here otherwise."

I sighed, gazing out the cabin window at the desolate and barren ice shelf. "You're right, of course. Let us head for port at once."

We agreed to depart as soon as the crew had slept for the night, although in the weird perpetual twilight in which we floated, "night" was an arbitrary designation. Since Frankenstein occupied the ship's only cabin, I went down to the berth below decks that Walton had prepared for me. A considerate gentleman, the captain had nailed sheets of canvas around the bunk to sequester me from the male crew. Attached to the curved wall of the hull, the narrow wooden niche bounded me on all sides but one as I crawled into it.

The smell of oak and tar became stifling in the claustrophobic box that night, the bunk's roof barely a foot above my face. The dankness of the ship's hold seemed to blacken further, and I was seized by the impression that I lay not in a berth but rather in Katarina von Kemp's coffin. Gasping and shrieking, I clawed at the closed lid until splinters needled up under my bloody fingernails . . .

I banged my head on my ceiling as I jerked up in the berth. Despite my restlessness, I must have slipped into sleep and nightmare. The throbbing thump on my forehead brought me fully awake, and I rolled out of the bunk with a groan. Giving up on the prospect of rest, I crept out from my canvas stall. Around me, sailors still snored in berths like mine, the atmosphere in the hold rancid with the pent-up stink of their sweat. I tiptoed up the wooden steps and onto the main deck, preferring fresh air—no matter how frigid.

I could not tell what time it was as I paced the ship from prow to stern. The clouds overhead remained ashen, illuminated from behind by a sun that never set, yet which we could not see. With the crew absent, the *Michael* seemed as desolate as a ghost ship. I guessed it to be about three in the morning, and looked up at the crow's nest to see if the night watch was still alert.

The lookout wasn't there.

I glanced around to locate the seaman who'd abandoned his post. Although the ship was at anchor, any number of perils could still threaten her, and someone needed to be vigilant and rouse the crew in case of danger.

Turning to the aft of the vessel, I spotted a dark figure that appeared to be standing in front of the winch used to haul in the anchor. I believed it to be the missing lookout, for he wore the same sort of thick, fur-lined coat and cap the other sailors did. He did not move as I approached, nor did he acknowledge me as I hailed him, even though he seemed to stare straight at me. His face bore a ghastly gray-blue cast in the bleak day-that-was-night, and I soon saw why.

The anchor chain had been wrapped around his neck, the thick iron links digging into his throat until they cut off the flow of blood to his head. The dead sailor only stood upright because the chain lashed him to the giant horizontal spindle of the anchor winch. His sightless eyes goggled from their sockets in a stare of permanent terror.

I clapped a hand over my mouth to suppress a cry.

I should have rung the ship's bell right then to raise an alarm and wake the crew.

Instead, I went and looked over the stern railing. The anchor chain ran from the spool of the winch down to an irregular polygon of ice that floated on the water a few yards astern. Because we were sailing in oceanic depths, the crew had replaced the shore anchor with a sea anchor, a construction of wooden beams and canvas cut from torn sails. The canvas sheets would increase the anchor's drag in the water to slow the ship's drift.

But someone had pulled up the anchor and wedged it into the raft of ice to tether it to the ship. A large ax and a makeshift paddle fashioned from the wooden planks of a sled also lay on the ice, indicating how the raft had been crafted and propelled.

He must have climbed the anchor chain, I thought as I raced toward the cabin where Frankenstein lay dying. *If only the crew will stay asleep . . .*

The cabin door stood open, yet an opaque blackness blocked my view of the bed. The choking sobs I heard revealed what was in my way. Even on his knees, my brother's massive frame virtually filled the low doorway.

"I knew you'd come," I said.

He started, more frightened by the fact that I knew who he was than by any harm I could do him. "Who are you?"

I pulled off my auburn wig and unwound the scarf from my scarred throat. "One like you."

"You." He regarded me as if I were an apparition. Then his amazement curdled into contempt. "You are nothing like me."

"But I am." I put my hands out to him, yet he cowered from my touch. "I've felt what it's like to have no home, no family, no self."

"Oh? Have you felt what it's like to have people chase you from their doors at the very sight of your face?" Tears glistened like fresh gouges in his grotesquely veined visage. "No. You are beautiful, so they take you in, shower you with comfort and affection, fight with one another over who will have you. You are *nothing* like me."

I realized then that he was grieving not for Frankenstein, but for himself.

"I know how much you've suffered," I began, "but—"

He reared up, his height making the ship's cabin resemble a room in a doll's house. "Know? How could you possibly know? You *left*."

The accusation stung like a whip's lash. "I didn't understand then. I do now."

I went to the bunk where Victor Frankenstein lay, his face as gray and cold and still as the nightless day outside. I touched his throat, the stiff skin resisting my fingertips. There was no pulse.

"We have only each other now," I told my brother.

"No," he replied. "You have the whole world. I have nothing and no one. Listen. Here comes your proof now."

The cabin floor shuddered from the percussion of the waking crew moving about belowdecks. Soon they would come up top and see the murdered lookout. Then they would see my brother.

"There's still time," I said. "We can leave now. Together."

He took a step toward me, the thick floorboards moaning under his weight, and his expression softened with a sweet wistfulness. "You would do that? You would forfeit all human company to spend a life alone and outcast with me?"

The description struck me like a death sentence, but a sense of duty and familial loyalty forced me to accept it. "Yes."

"And would you . . . *LOVE ME?*" He thrust his face at mine, more ferocious and bestial than ever.

I flinched and could not answer. I felt a kinship with him due to the bond of our common creator and unholy conception. I'd come to understand and even pity him for his lonely, wretched existence. But love? No. How could I explain that I could not feel that way about him, and that it had nothing to do with his appearance?

A hatred far more revolting than disfigurement contorted his features. "I thought as much."

He moved to leave, crouching to duck beneath the doorframe. I rushed to stop him, to beg for another chance to show I had not rejected him like the rest of the world had. As I caught hold of his elbow, though, I heard Walton outside, yelling, "Search the ship!"

"You've got to get away from here," I whispered.

He shook off my grasp. "It doesn't matter."

It mattered to me, though. As long as my brother lived, I might someday reconcile with him.

The moment we emerged from the cabin, four angry sailors surrounded us, some of them only half-dressed. They brandished boathooks and skinning knives—whatever weapons they could lay hands on.

I stepped in front of my brother, attempting to shield him, like an ant trying to defend an elephant. "Leave him be!"

An unshaven man to our right swore in Russian and stabbed a harpoon at the monster beside me. With the barbed point an inch from piercing his heart, my brother grabbed hold of the harpoon's shaft. He wrenched it from the sailor's grasp and clubbed the attacker in the stomach, batting the man into his comrades, who fell together like tumbling ninepins.

The commotion brought other crewmen running. With his way clear for only a moment, my brother thundered aft-ward, where he'd anchored his ice raft. He spared me only one backward glance—part sorrow, part scorn—before vaulting over the railing.

I dashed forward to see whether he'd landed safely, but Captain Walton got to the rail before I did. He lifted a musket to his shoulder and sighted along the barrel at a downward angle.

I didn't need to see his target. Lunging forward, I shoved the gun's stock just as the flintlock's hammer fell.

The musket ball flew wide of its mark, and Walton cursed. In a lather, he took the horn of black powder from his side and began the laborious process of loading and tamping the muzzle for another shot. He soon gave up, for when he glanced out over the water, he saw that my brother had already freed the ice raft from the sea anchor and had pushed adrift from the ship with his makeshift oar.

"Are you mad?" the captain shouted at me. "Don't you know what that beast is? Don't you know what it's done?"

"Yes. I know." I watched the black blot on the ice raft paddle away until it dwindled to a tiny speck on the pristine whiteness of the Arctic wastes.

I never saw my brother again.

CHAPTER 16

THE PROFESSOR'S SON

I waited more than a month after the *Michael* made port before I returned to the abandoned university in Ingolstadt. A month I spent poring over Victor Frankenstein's research papers as a profane vision took shape in my mind.

To realize my awful fantasy, however, I would need skilled assistance. And that is when I recalled the forlorn figure of Ernst Waldman the younger, crumpled in grief where his father had been thrown to his death.

Autumn had brought early darkness and drenching rains to Ingolstadt by the time I arrived at the university's former Anatomy Building. Drops spattered the fabric of my sodden umbrella and sluiced off around me in thick rivulets. I gazed up at the lightning fracturing the sky overhead, its thunder reverberating in my bones, and I inhaled the charged air as if I could taste its divine power.

Soon, I thought.

I had no reason to expect that anyone would be at the Anatomy Building on that night, at that hour. Yet I was not surprised to see that the shattered window of the hexagonal cupola had been restored and that a solitary lamp glowed within.

I knew why Ernst Waldman still haunted the place. Like me, he had lost a father and now sought in vain for answers to unasked questions. I intended to offer him those answers in trade for his help, and so I carried Victor Frankenstein's notebook beneath my cloak.

Folding my rather useless umbrella, I approached the structure's main entrance and knocked on the door, though I thought there was little chance Waldman would hear me over the thunderclaps. I rapped, waited, then pounded and waited again.

Soaked to the marrow and shivering, I tested the door's latch. Locked, of course. I glanced at the deserted avenue behind me. All the townspeople had sought shelter for the night. Surely no one would see if I broke the door open.

I drew my hand back, ready to ram it against the lock with all my unnatural strength. But just then the door pulled away from my palm, and I had to catch myself to keep from stumbling over the threshold.

"What do you want?" Ernst Waldman glared at me through the narrow opening. The lamp he held gave his handsome face a sallow complexion, and he looked as if he hadn't slept or eaten for days. Perhaps it was only the coarse shading of stubble on his cheeks that made them appear sunken and malnourished.

"I must speak with you," I said.

"I can't be bothered. Good-bye."

He thrust forward, intending to slam the door. I braced it open with one arm, unnerving him.

"Who *are* you?" he demanded.

"Someone who shares your sense of loss. You may have heard about the recent death of my cousin Victor."

His green eyes, quivering from fatigue and distraction, suddenly fixed on me with dagger-keen intensity. "I have nothing to say to a Frankenstein. And the only regret I have to offer you is that I was not there to watch him die."

"My cousin did not kill your father," I vowed. "But I know who did. And I can prove it if you'll let me."

I took Victor Frankenstein's notebook from beneath my cloak.

Waldman frowned with mistrust but opened the door and brusquely motioned for me to enter. "If you know who committed this slaughter, why haven't you gone to the police?" he asked as he led me up a wooden staircase. "Unless you're protecting the villain . . ."

"I haven't gone to the police because they would never believe me, for the murderer is no ordinary cutthroat. Only a man of science will comprehend the truth. Victor tried to tell your father. Now I hope you will listen to me."

Waldman paused at an upstairs door, held the oil lamp close to my face as if to read in my expression whether I was lying. I gazed steadily at him.

He opened the door and we passed through into a large chamber with six angled windows overlooking the courtyard. It appeared to be a dissection room for educating medical students. The tables topped with white marble, each carved with gutters to channel drained blood, chilled me as if I could feel the cold, polished stone pressing against my bare back.

How many corpses, I wondered, *have been carved up to create me?*

Waldman set the lamp on a desk cluttered with papers that were crammed with arcane diagrams and notations. This was obviously the place where he kept his lonely vigil—the very spot where my brother must have slain his father.

"You've been studying his work," I observed.

"Only to find out why anyone would brutalize a harmless old man. It's all a load of nonsense anyway."

I idly skimmed the sheets of foolscap. "Victor didn't think it was nonsense. Your father was his mentor."

"Frankenstein was mad. He probably flew into a murderous rage when my father told him his insane designs were impossible."

"They weren't impossible." I threw Frankenstein's notebook on the desk, flattened the pages open at the drawing of the creature that had become my brother.

Fascination flickered in Waldman's expression as he compared how Frankenstein had refined and extrapolated his father's concepts. Then he shook his head as if to dislodge such ideas from his brain. "Revivifying dead tissue? Doomed to failure!"

"Victor succeeded. Twice."

I loosened my scarf, let Waldman see the unbroken chain of scar tissue that encircled my throat. He trembled, eyes wide, and I couldn't tell whether he was thrilled or repulsed. As a physician, he knew no human could have survived such a cut.

I leaned forward, flaunting the gash. "Look at it! I am a living vindication of all your father's theories. Don't you want to see his reputation redeemed?"

Waldman recoiled. "It . . . it's madness. More mad if true than if not."

"You think your father mad?" I gestured to the drowsing city outside the window. "Is that how you want the world to remember him? Or do you want history to recognize him for what he really was—the man who discovered the key to life itself?"

Waldman's expression wavered, twisted by some internal debate. "You said you could identify my father's killer. Who was it?"

I put a hand on the drawing in Frankenstein's book. "This creature that Victor created—his first—became crazed by its own hideousness. For the misery of its existence, it sought revenge on everyone Frankenstein held dear."

Waldman nodded with grim satisfaction. "As I thought. Only evil can come of this blasphemy."

"*I* have not become a raging beast." Guilty thoughts of Stefan billowed in my mind, but I stuffed them back into the dank hole whence they came. "The process of creation itself does not make the creature mad. It is how it's treated after it's born."

Waldman spat breath dismissively. "What is the point of making such a monster? Aren't the masses already rutting and reproducing enough to breed more wretches than the world can abide?"

"But *we*—you and I—could make a being who would never be poisoned by the wickedness of this world, who would remain untainted by sorrow, bitterness, or fear," I countered. "A being fashioned from such beauty, raised with such purity and nobility, fostered with such *love*, that it would embody all the good of humanity and none of the bad. A being that could shine as a paragon of the godly perfection to which every mortal aspires. Wasn't that your father's dream?"

138

Waldman rubbed his haggard face in an agony of indecision. His gaze fell upon the illustration in Frankenstein's journal. Unlike my brother, the creature in the sketch exemplified a celestial grace unknown to mortal flesh. A seraph incarnate.

His choice made, the physician hung his head. "God forgive me," he whispered.

CHAPTER 17

ASSEMBLING AN ANGEL

Even after I convinced him to help me build my demigod, Waldman and I argued over how best to procure the raw materials for our creation.

To my surprise, he had no moral objection to graverobbing. "The practice of medicine would not exist without ghouls," he said dryly, referring to the acquisition of the cadavers from which doctors learned their art. For the sake of expediency, though, he thought we should simply raid the churchyard there in Ingolstadt, as he and his fellow medical students had done for decades.

I objected. Like Darmstadt, Ingolstadt was a small, sleepy, peaceful town. The infrequent deaths there tended to be of the old and decrepit, the fat and the frail. I needed the flesh of the young and virile, limbs and organs in superlative physical condition.

Waldman threw up his hands in exasperation. "So you want to wait until a dozen young people in perfect health suddenly drop dead? That could take years!"

"Not if we get them from *here*." I unfolded a map on which I'd circled the town of Dutweiler in the Saar region of western Prussia.

The surrounding land was one of the principal coal-mining areas of the country. Strenuous and dangerous work, coal mining built men into muscular drudge animals, then slaughtered them at their prime in vast numbers. Tunnel collapses, poison gas leaks, black lung disease, spontaneous explosions—barely half the miners survived to the age of forty, yet dire poverty ensured there were always enough desperate souls to take the places of the deceased.

Waldman shook his head again. "Why go to so much trouble just for a pretty face? Isn't it enough that the beast look human?"

"No," I said. "People only embrace beauty. He must be beautiful."

The young physician gave me a penetrating look. "So the creature must be a male, eh?"

For the first time, I couldn't meet his gaze. "We already have a female specimen," I reminded him, laying a hand on my bosom. "Another female would be . . . redundant."

Waldman grinned with maddening cheekiness. "I see. When you put it like that, your plan makes perfect sense."

I think I blushed.

We both had numerous preparations to make for our charnel theft, so we parted company and agreed to rendezvous in Dutweiler in five weeks. I used the time to set aside as much fresh blood as I could donate. Every three or four days, I drew another pint from my veins with a catheter, collecting the plasma in empty wine bottles I stoppered with a cork. On the days in between, I gorged myself on calf's liver and red meat, washing them down with pitchers of water and heavy French clarets to replenish my body. My creation would be bonded to me from birth, for his blood would be my own.

To preserve the vital fluid, I loaded the bottles of blood into a butcher's wagon filled with ice—huge, sweating chunks of glacier I paid to have imported all the way from the Alps. Adopting the guise of a butcher's wife, I kept slabs of beef and pork in the wagon's rear compartment to allay the suspicions of anyone who might look inside. But I intended to load the wagon with meat of a far more precious sort.

142

With morbid eagerness, I sought out reports of untimely deaths in Dutweiler and felt a shameful aggravation when weeks passed with no fatalities. Fretting my plan was a failure, I set out for the Saarland in my butcher's wagon anyway. I was half a day's travel away from Dutweiler when I received news of a terrible cave-in at one of the local mines, with many lives feared lost. Sickened by the excitement with which I welcomed such a tragedy, I drove the wagon's horses hard to get to the town before the bodies had been recovered from the rubble.

Once I secured lodging at the best inn the village had to offer, I intended to send a letter to Waldman, asking him to come to Dutweiler immediately. I soon found the correspondence unnecessary, however.

"Herr Dr. Waldman has been expecting you," the concierge informed me upon my arrival. When she told me he was not in his room that afternoon, I dashed off a brief note that I sealed in an envelope and left for him at reception. "Meet me at the Burning Mountain tomorrow at dusk, and wear black," it read. "Until then, I think it's best if we are not seen together."

I ordered some cold meats and cheeses to sup on in my room but could hardly eat. Although I went to bed early, I lay wide-eyed in the dark for hours, thinking, scheming, imagining. At some point I must have dozed off, for I had a dream. At first, I feared it would be the nightmare I'd had all too many times in the past: I was nude, and a great looming creature reached toward me out of the darkness with consuming lust.

As it emerged into the light, however, I saw that it was not the same as my brother at all. The figure was that of a man, but a man unlike any I'd seen before. He, too, was naked, and had fine seams of scar tissue where his head and limbs had been sewn to his body. Other than these superficial flaws, the figure possessed sculpted sinew of such perfect heft and proportion as to be almost divine. Stefan would have seemed a boy in knee breeches beside such a Samson.

When his massive arms enfolded me, I shuddered not with fright but with desire. I lapped hungrily at the salty sheen of the polished breastplate that was his bare chest. His face drew close to mine, shedding its husk of shadow. His face . . . his glorious face . . .

I awoke with a scream of climactic ecstasy that degraded into a growl of frustration when I found myself alone in my bed at the inn. I lay there all morning in a lassitude of dejection, vainly trying to recapture the fantasy the dull daylight denied me.

By that afternoon, when I went to meet Waldman, my inflamed passion had calmed to cold resolve. I would make that unfulfilled dream a reality.

The bank of sulfurous rock known as Brennender Berg, or the Burning Mountain, resides at the bottom of a deep gorge outside Dutweiler, not far from the city's cemetery. As I brought the butcher's wagon to a halt beside a nearby oak and descended to put feedbags on the horses, I could feel the heat emanating from the gravelly earth. It warmed my feet even through the thick leather of my boots. Eddies of rising heat made the barren branches of the surrounding trees appear to ripple and waver.

I approached a large block of stone wedged into the hillside, its face the colors of fire: yellow and orange and infernal red. A cleft in the wall exhaled a hot gust of brimstone that smelled like the forge in Stefan's blacksmith shop. Feathers of black smoke occasionally wafted from the crack, and deep within the fissure an orange glow pulsed like a demonic heart.

A vein of coal beneath this ground had caught fire more than a century before and had resisted all attempts to extinguish it. For all anyone knew, it might smolder forever. Goethe had once visited the place, and it was easy to imagine that the spot had inspired his visions of Hell in *Faust*.

I was grateful for the warmth, however, for the dolor of late autumn frosted the air. Having spent the entire summer in the Arctic, I could hardly remember the last time I hadn't been cold. The repeated bloodlettings had also left me vulnerable to chill. I leaned back against the flat plane of rock and shut my eyes, basking like a lizard in the sun.

"I take it you are here for the funeral, Fräulein." The male voice jarred me alert. "My condolences on your loss."

I glanced at my widow's gown, the one I'd purchased to disguise myself after killing Stefan. I'd worn it to blend in as a mourner and decided I'd better play the part. "Thank you, Herr . . ."

"Doktor," the man corrected as I turned to him. "Doktor Waldman."

Little wonder I hadn't recognized him at first! He hardly resembled the gaunt and haggard physician I'd seen in Ingolstadt. His strong jaw was clean-shaven, the muttonchops neatly trimmed, his thick, dark hair combed and coiffed. His face had filled in and regained its color, as if he'd resumed eating properly, and his eyes glittered with the animation of an incisive-yet-playful intellect. He was more handsome than I remembered.

"Oh. I see you got my note." I indicated his immaculate black suit and tall, brimmed hat, which lent him the appearance of a well-heeled mortician.

He tipped his hat. "I always believe in dressing for the occasion. And in being prepared."

Waldman took his left hand from behind his back long enough to show that it held a shovel.

"How many are we disinterring today?" he asked. "Six, was it?"

"Seven."

"Well! How . . . *fortunate* for you."

"For *us*," I said, mimicking his arch tone. "The procession will pass along there." I pointed up the rise toward the end of the ravine where the road led to the graveyard. "We'll wait here until after dark, when all the mourners have left, but no longer. I want the specimens as fresh as we can get them."

Waldman gave a mordant nod. "You show tremendous promise as a ghoul, Fräulein Frankenstein."

His sarcasm nettled me, and I didn't reply.

Before long, we saw a parade of solemn figures marching across the horizon in the direction of the cemetery. I realized then that Waldman and I were overdressed. These poor laborers and their families could not afford to buy special black mourning attire, so they had come to bury their dead in the same dingy linen clothing they wore to mine their coal or clean their houses. The men carried the rough, unvarnished, oblong boxes of the coffins on their shoulders, their faces still grimed with coal dust and sweat from digging their friends' bodies out of the rubble of a collapsed tunnel. The women carried their fatherless children, and even at a distance I could hear the wails of widows and babies.

Waldman eyed me severely several times as the procession went by, perhaps to see if I suffered any pangs of conscience about what we intended to do. I didn't. Those men were dead regardless of our actions, and they would no longer miss the bits of flesh and bone we would take from them.

The mourners filed on up the road and out of view. We waited. After about two hours they returned, headed back toward town, their formal ranks scattered into small groups of family members that clung together in grief. Still, we made no move to leave.

The sun went down. As darkness deepened around us, the crack in Brennender Berg glowed with unquenchable fire. Perhaps sensing I was not going to break the ponderous silence, Waldman finally spoke up.

"Did you ever consider getting a man in a more conventional fashion?" he asked in a tone of idle curiosity.

I growled and turned my back on him, hoping he couldn't see my face flush with embarrassment.

He shrugged with insufferable nonchalance. "I only ask because, if you doubt your ability to attract a suitable match, you needn't worry. I can think of at least a dozen of my former classmates from the university who'd fall to their knees with marriage proposals the moment they laid eyes on you."

"You wouldn't understand." I sighed, picturing Stefan's head on my lap, his blood running down between my bare thighs. "I'm not fit for ordinary men. I need one of my own kind."

I almost laughed then. My brother must have said exactly the same thing when he demanded that Frankenstein create *me*.

"Well, I admit you'll probably find a better husband in a graveyard than you will in the taverns of Munich." Waldman shouldered his shovel. "Shall we get on with it?"

We rode together in the butcher's wagon to the cemetery. Watching for any laggards who might have remained behind, we discreetly ventured forth onto the grounds, Waldman with his spade, I with my hooded lantern.

It wasn't hard to find the graves we sought—heaps of freshly turned earth marked with humble crosses of wood, the perishable monuments of those who could not afford chiseled granite cherubs. Waldman shed his coat and rolled up his sleeves for the work ahead.

"Can't say I've really missed this part of the job," he commented as he stabbed the shovel's blade into the first mound.

"So why *are* you here?" I asked when he'd dug himself waist-deep in the pit.

He cast a look of mild annoyance up at me. "You said it yourself. I want to know whether or not my father was a lunatic. This will prove it, one way or the other."

"Is that the only reason?"

He turned more clods of soil up onto the grass beside the hole and smirked. "Oh, I don't know. If it works for you, maybe I'll make myself a woman. Haven't had much luck getting one the old-fashioned way."

I let out a dry laugh. "I was sewn together from corpses less than a year ago. What's your excuse?"

He paused to consider. "I think I've been spending too much time with cadavers rather than people. Present company excepted, of course."

He tipped his hat, then jabbed the shovel back into the floor of the grave. It made a hollow thump.

I crouched on the edge of the pit and raised the lantern. Waldman scraped the rest of the dirt from the coffin and jammed the shovel's blade under the lid to pry it open. The coffin nails tore free with a groan, and Waldman bent the board up to allow the lantern light to fall into the box.

"Ugh!" The jaded surgeon recoiled against the wall of the pit, hand over his mouth, face rumpled with revulsion.

The body in the coffin would have been beyond the cosmetic

repair of even the most talented mortician. The head and the left half of the torso were simply *gone*, most likely crushed beneath rock and timbers in the mine's collapse. Only a sickening red cavity remained in the cage of ribs that had once housed the man's heart and lungs.

Yet the man's right side remained eerily intact, the beefy pectoral still smooth and unscathed where exposed by his ripped and bloodied shirt. And that arm—its bulging musculature tapered down to fingers of surprising delicacy. Was it only fancy that made me certain I'd seen that hand before, had *felt* those fingers stroke my skin and hair?

Waldman shook his head. "I don't think this one will be of any use . . ."

I grabbed the cloth sheaf of surgical implements he'd brought with him and tossed it into the grave. "Get that arm," I said. "I need it."

CHAPTER 18

THE CREATION

With seven graves to plunder that night, we were able to cull many of the parts we needed to piece together our Osiris. I immediately packed the prospective limbs and organs in a wooden tub filled with ice chunks I'd chipped off the blocks in the back of the butcher's wagon. I covered the tub with a tarp and heaped sides of beef and ham hocks on top to hide our ghastly cache.

Several of the wounded survivors of the mine disaster passed away within days, and a few more nocturnal visits to the graveyard gave us the rest of the body I'd envisioned. But the proper head eluded me. All the dead miners were either baby-faced boys, like Stefan, or careworn family men, old before their time.

That face—the captivating face I'd glimpsed in my dream. I could almost see it whenever I closed my eyes. I had to find it.

My pickiness vexed Waldman. "Isn't it enough for your lover to look like a man?" he griped as we stood beside yet another grave I'd had him open only to reject its contents. He lifted his spade toward the wagon loaded with human flesh. The ice in the compartment was already melting into puddles. "Every hour we spend searching for a pretty face," Waldman said, "the rest of your demigod begins to *rot*."

He was right, of course. Too much delay could spoil all the body parts we'd gathered so far. But without a suitable face, the rest would be worthless anyway. How could I make Waldman understand? He'd never known my brother.

"It's not enough for him to be normal," I insisted. "He must be *beautiful*. He must have every advantage that Victor's creature never had. Please . . . let us search just a little more."

"Very well." Waldman threw the shovel at my feet. "But *you* do the digging."

So I did.

The next grave yielded nothing; neither did the one after that. I was on the verge of giving up and taking whatever homely head I could lay my hands on. There was but one new grave left to raid, and I exhumed the coffin with the lethargy of hopelessness.

When I opened the casket, it seemed all my effort *had* been a waste. The dead man inside had been mashed to such a pulp that the undertakers had merely scraped what remnants of bone and bits of meat they could recover into the box without even attempting to reconstruct the whole. Nothing but an unidentifiable red mass lay at the coffin's head.

I was about to slap the lid shut when I happened to glance toward the other end of the casket, about where the deceased's knees should have been. There, as if carelessly tossed in at the last moment, lay the head, miraculously intact and unscathed. A mane of thick, sandy-brown hair surrounded the most beguiling countenance I had ever seen, frozen in age at masculinity's peak of ripeness, just when the vigor of youth acquires the character of maturity. This was the face of a *man*, not a boy—a man who had enough worldly experience to know about life and love but not so much that he had become embittered by them. The features firm with strength and ardor, yet gentled by a soulful, empathetic nature. Half artist, half angel, just as I had dreamed.

The eyes were open, and revealed clouded gray irises. Nevertheless, the head appeared to gaze up at me expectantly, its lips parted in soundless invitation. I cupped it in both hands and lifted it from the swamp of entrails in the coffin.

"Here you are at last," I whispered, finally speaking the name I had secretly chosen for him. "My Raphael."

With our wagon of blood and body parts brimful and the ice inside dissolving by the hour, Waldman and I sped back to Ingolstadt. We drove the horses for as long as they would go, even traveling at night whenever there was enough moonlight to illuminate the road.

Waldman's father had bequeathed him an extensive estate outside the town proper, and we chose to perform our necromancy there rather than at the university so we might be secluded from the local citizenry. A narrow dirt road took us through verdant pastures in which a few cows grazed and past a copse of walnut trees before we came to the manor house. Not quite grand enough to be called a *schloss*, it featured the plain yet elegant architecture common in Ingolstadt, with a stark white facade, smallish windows, and red shingles and trim. With its steep, peaked roof, the house was three stories high—and as long as a city block. It seemed too large a home for one man.

"Where is the rest of your family?" I inquired as we climbed out of the wagon and walked to the front door.

"I have none," Waldman said with stoic bluntness. "My mother died giving birth to my sister, who was stillborn. I was only two at the time, so I don't even remember them. After that, reviving the dead became my father's obsession."

"Would you have wanted him to bring them back if he could?" I asked. "Your mother and sister, I mean."

Waldman rapped the brass knocker of the home's front door. "As a physician, I've devoted my life to the living. I wish my father had done the same."

His tone bespoke the resentment of a son neglected in favor of his dead relations. If the emotion pained him, he brushed it aside, for he greeted the matron who answered the door with a winning smile. "Ah, Wilhelmina! May I present our guest, Fräulein Anna Frankenstein."

Distracted and out of breath, the woman gave a hasty curtsy. "It's an honor, Fräulein."

151

"Thank you, Wilhelmina—"

"Minna, if you please, Fräulein." She must have been only about forty, but perpetual worry had creased her brow and mouth prematurely. She shifted her feet and wrung her hands as if late for an appointment. "I do apologize, sir. I was so busy readying your rooms that cook and I have only just started dinner—"

"That's quite all right, Minna," Waldman soothed. "I need some time to show Fräulein Frankenstein around the house, so we'll dine late. And tell Oskar and Gert not to unload the wagon—we'll take care of that ourselves this evening."

He issued the order in such an offhand way that Minna didn't think it unusual. Only I understood why he did not want his servants to see the cargo we'd brought.

A gracious host, Waldman collected my satchel and valise and showed me to the bedchamber where I was to stay. We then toured the house—all but the attic—and chatted idly until dinner. Even as we ate, our conversation lolled over bland trivialities, neither of us daring to speak of the dreadful project that preoccupied our thoughts. The hours lagged until I wanted to scream with impatience.

Finally, the household staff went to bed, leaving Waldman and me alone. He led me upstairs to the attic and opened its door with a flourish.

"Here it is, as you requested. I only hope it's fit for a Frankenstein."

I smiled at the laboratory he'd cobbled together. In addition to the requisite chemical vats and dissection slab, Waldman had obtained fresh ice. The frigid blocks lay stacked around us like bricks in the walls of some frost giant's prison.

"Splendid!" I declared. "Let's get the pieces of our angel."

Waldman looked as if he'd swallowed something he'd rather spit out, but he said nothing. We returned many times to the butcher's wagon, retrieving the body parts one at a time and carrying them upstairs to the attic. In case any of the servants happened to see us, we wrapped each piece in loose linen to hide the horror of our endeavor.

"Enough for one night!" Waldman grunted as we swung the hammocked torso onto the dissection slab. "I'm so tired, I'll sleep as soundly as this poor fellow."

"No. We must start now."

He massaged his brow in exasperation. "Are you mad? This will take days. Weeks, even."

"And the longer we wait, the more we risk failure. Do you want that, after all we've gone through?"

Waldman shook his head and grabbed one of the cloth-wrapped legs from the floor. "Christ!"

Together, we laid out the scraps of men we'd collected on the marble slab and set to work.

At first there was little I could do but watch as Waldman, the trained surgeon, painstakingly hemmed up every tiny blood vessel and muscle fiber that strung together our marionette of flesh and bone. He toiled in the attic's freezing confines in order to prevent the body's decomposition. Waldman wore fingerless gloves to keep his hands nimble for sewing, but had to stop repeatedly to warm his numb digits on the glass flute of an oil lamp.

For three nights he labored that way, operating only in the wee hours so that we would have complete privacy. The slow progress made me frantic. Even amid the clean coolness of the ice, I fancied I could detect the first fetid whiff of putrescence—the stink of failure. Finally, I could take it no longer.

"Birgit taught me to stitch as well as anyone," I said. "Skin can't be that much harder to mend than cloth. If you show me what to do, I'm sure I can help."

Waldman was engrossed in wrapping muscle about the ball-and-socket joint of bone on the body's right shoulder, but he abruptly threw down his needle and thread with a sigh. He'd slept at most an hour or two during the days, and the fatigue had aged him so much he resembled the portrait of his father that hung in the second-floor library. He evaluated me for a moment, then nodded. "Very well. You can't make any more of a mess of it than I have."

He beckoned me to where he stood beside the operating table and demonstrated how he was stitching a deltoid muscle on the torso's back to the nub end of a severed tendon on the arm. "Like this. See?"

He offered me the needle. As he had done, I pinched together the muscle fibers to be joined and looped the needle in and out of the meat to bind it with thread. I flinched a bit at the stickiness and gooey pliability of the tissue but ultimately found it no worse than trussing up a goose.

I could feel Waldman staring at me as I toiled, and his scrutiny made me wonder if I was doing everything wrong. But his gaze was on my face, not my hands.

I finished repairing the tendon and anxiously presented it for his approval. "Well?"

At last, he smiled. "You would have made an excellent surgeon, Anna. Provided, of course, that the university had ever accepted women, which it didn't."

He clapped me on the back like one of his fraternal classmates.

I gaped at him. "*What* did you call me?"

This time, his cheeks reddened. "Forgive me, Fräulein Frankenstein."

I smiled coyly. "There is nothing to forgive . . . *Ernst*. Now tell me what to do so you can get some rest."

After that, the work went much faster. It was not only that I could assist Ernst and relieve him when necessary. We had suddenly turned from strangers into colleagues, with a new rapport and mutual respect. Ernst continued my education in medicine as we labored for as long as fourteen hours at a stretch, pausing only to drink the hot coffee the servants left at the door of our icebound laboratory.

When we finally needed to rest, he had a private meal served to us in the parlor, after which he charmed me by playing whimsical tunes on his pianoforte or reading to me from the poetry of Schiller and Byron. Lulled by his mellifluous voice, I leaned back in my chair and shut my eyes, resisting the urge to nap. I only wished that I had something—some skill or pleasure of my own—to give him in exchange for all he gave me.

Yet as we neared completion of the body and my excitement began to grow, Ernst became distracted and withdrawn again.

Attaching the head made him especially agitated. He sat on a stool and brooded as I closed the seam around the creation's neck. It took a long time, for I used the tiniest stitches I could to minimize the scarring. I was determined to spare Raphael the humiliation my brother and I had endured.

"What if he won't have you?" Ernst asked. The man seemed to have the most vexing ability to read my mind.

"I beg your pardon?" I glanced up, pretending I hadn't heard what he'd said.

"You've told me how *you* spurned Frankenstein's beast," he said. "Suppose your homemade groom rejects you in the same way?"

I didn't have a ready riposte. I won't say the possibility he raised hadn't occurred to me, but I'd refused to entertain the idea.

"Victor's creature frightened me because of my own ignorance," I protested. "I couldn't understand his desire for me. I'll surround Raphael in my love at once, and he will have no reason to fear me."

"So it's 'Raphael,' is it?"

My face warmed under Ernst's glare, and I bent my head over my work so I wouldn't have to look at him. "Everyone needs a name."

I yanked the final stitch tight with such force that I accidentally stabbed my thumb with the needle. A pearl of blood dripped from the puncture and landed on Raphael's gray mouth. The fluid colored the ridges of his cold lips until they appeared to bloom with red life.

Ernst grunted, as if he had expected just such a mishap. "I sincerely hope that is the only pain your Raphael causes you."

He stalked out of the laboratory without admiring the completion of our handiwork. Irked at him for spoiling what ought to have been a moment of triumph, I stanched my bleeding thumb with a bit of gauze, then snipped the excess thread from Raphael's neck. I started to wipe the blood from his mouth with the gauze, but my hand slowed as I dabbed at the unfolded petals of those lips. He lay there before me, naked, complete, and perfect but for the pallor of his marble skin. A hero petrified, as if Perseus had dared to stare at the Medusa. I leaned down to whisper in his ear of stone.

"Soon, my Raphael."

And I kissed his frigid lips.

With the body whole and the veins sealed, we pumped fresh blood into the vessels in preparation for when that succulent plum of a heart began to beat. All we needed was the sacred fire of electricity to surge life into the shell we'd made for it.

Perversely, though it was the middle of November, when rain and thunder ordinarily bombarded the Bavarian countryside, the skies remained obstinately blue and cloudless, the days maddeningly sunny. Incensed to the point of distraction, I began to wonder if God was deliberately withholding His thunderbolts to prevent our blasphemy.

To keep from going mad with aggravation, I concentrated on preserving Raphael as best I could. With the aid of a pump, I circulated the blood several times a day to keep it from coagulating, and Ernst and I would rotate the body as if basting a boar on a spit so that the fluids would not settle in the flesh. Nevertheless, I despaired whenever I noticed even the faintest purpling of his pure skin. To have him before me, waiting to be born, only to watch him decay to corruption . . . it would be more than I could bear.

I packed ice close around the body when I wasn't attending to it, and I rearranged the laboratory in anticipation of the electrical storm I had faith would come at any moment. Yet each day broke with a sunrise of infuriating radiance, and Raphael's body turned as blue as the damnably clear sky above.

I roamed the house in impotent frustration, peering out of one window after another—east, west, north, and south—scanning the horizons for any sign of coalescing thunderheads. Ernst paced the floor as well, but with the wary slowness of a zookeeper afraid of rousing a sleeping tiger.

For a week we hardly spoke to each other. Then, as I lifted the curtains aside for the hundredth time to gaze out at the appallingly pleasant weather outside, Ernst softly cleared his throat behind me. "Perhaps it's for the best—"

"No! *No!* I refuse to accept that." I wheeled on him. At last, my wrath had a target. "And you shouldn't look so pleased, for Raphael *shall* have life."

If any apologies or arguments came out of Ernst's stammering mouth, I couldn't hear them over the pounding of the blood in my head. I stomped upstairs, into the laboratory, and slammed the door. The heat of my fury burned so intensely I felt as if I would melt the remaining ice in the room. I looked at Raphael's ghastly lividity and saw not an angel, but a corpse.

I sank down on a stool beside the slab and spread my hands over my crumpling face. Almost immediately, though, I balled my hands into fists and gulped deep breaths to stop my tears. Anger was better than sorrow.

I remained at Raphael's side the rest of that afternoon and into the night, rocking back and forth on the stool and muttering unholy prayers.

As if in sympathy, the weather darkened with my mood. By noon the following day, nimbus clouds had turned the heavens to soot, claws of lightning raked the sky.

In manic ecstasy, I flitted about the laboratory yanking the remaining ice away from the body and snapping the manacles about Raphael's wrists and ankles. Iron chains led from the cuffs toward a hole in the ceiling. There, the strands linked to one master chain that rose upward to connect with a row of half a dozen lightning rods on the roof of the house.

The windows and walls of the laboratory shimmered with the ghost-light of another lightning flash as I fastened the iron bands over Raphael's forehead and across his heart. I realized then that, if I had contact with the metal, the very bolt that I hoped would give Raphael life might strike me dead. What a grand joke that would be: the Lord taking away what He had never given.

Someone rapped on the door, and I nearly screamed at the interruption. I yanked open the portal to find Minna shivering in the hall, a silver tray with hot soup and cold meats in her hands. "Yes? What is it?"

She jumped as thunder rattled the rafters and torrents of rain lashed the roof. "Forgive me, Fräulein, but are you sure it's quite safe here . . . ?"

"No. It's extremely dangerous." I grabbed the tray from her. "Now send Herr Dr. Waldman up at once."

I slammed the door. Although I hadn't eaten in over a day, I shoved the food aside. There was no time for that. Instead, I drank in the electricity that even now prickled along my skin and floated the fine strands of my hair.

I pumped the blood to circulate it through the body again. Peals of thunder began coming closer together, almost on top of one another—so loud that I didn't hear Ernst enter the room.

"Where have you been?" I demanded the moment I saw him standing next to me. "I had to do everything myself, and we've nearly missed the storm!"

His face tightened with sour reluctance. "I *thought* you'd given up."

"Thought, or *hoped*?" I threw down the pump, shouting to be heard over the thunderclaps, and the more I shouted, the angrier I became. "Do you care nothing about all our work? About your father's reputation? About your own?"

"And what about *you*?" he yelled back. "Seems to me your only concern is your new plaything and his . . . *equipment*."

"Indeed! Well, if all I wanted were the perfect man, I would have sewn his mouth shut. Then I wouldn't have to—"

A bone-shattering boom severed the thought. The chains that dangled from the ceiling rattled and swayed, the ropes of iron limned in a bluish phosphorescence like St. Elmo's Fire. The glowing fog of charged air enveloped the cadaver on the slab, and the corpse convulsed so violently I thought the seizing muscles would rip loose the stitched limbs.

Ernst and I could do nothing but stare at the body as it thrashed and contorted, banging against the bonds of its metal straps until it began to tear free the bolts that fastened the hinges to the wood. Certain that Raphael must be writhing in pain, I started forward to free him. Ernst blocked my way, for the irons crackled and spit sparks that would surely have killed me.

Then the light dimmed and the body slumped flat again. I fancied I could see the massive chest heaving in the sudden darkness, but I could hear nothing over the ringing in my ears. Again, I moved to release Raphael, yet Ernst tightened his arms around me.

"What are you doing?" I tried to shrug him off. "Let me go!"

"No, Anna!" He still shouted, like a deaf man who can't hear the volume of his own voice. "Don't you understand? *The storm is right overhead.*"

As if to drive the point home, another lightning stroke caused the room to flare with phantasmal luminescence. Another jolt racked Raphael, whose quivering skin began to sizzle and smoke.

"It's killing him! *Let me go!*" I flung Ernst off me with the full force of my freakish strength, crashing him into a shelf of glass beakers and alembics. I didn't even look to see whether I'd hurt him. Raphael needed me.

The popping sparks spooked me. I waited until they stopped for an instant, then lunged to unfasten the iron straps from his chest and forehead. Without the lifeblood of electricity coursing through him, Raphael flopped, moribund, onto the slab, still as a stone once more. The stench of singed hair and smoldering flesh wafted off his slack face.

I scrabbled to release the shackles from his wrists, but my agitation made it impossible for me to hold the turnscrew steady. The tool slipped off the bolt head, and Raphael's arm slithered from my grasp like a lifeless eel. I shrieked in anguish.

"He's dead! He's dead! I've failed, and he's dead!"

I slumped over the hard mountain of his chest, hardly caring that another thunderbolt could sear us both at any moment.

Then the mountain heaved beneath me.

As I fell back in surprise, hands groped at my head, thick fingers knotting themselves in my long hair to pull me back. I yelped and tugged myself free, my scalp stinging as if the strands had been yanked out by the roots.

With a *crack* of splintering wood, the demigod on the slab wrenched loose the iron straps across his brow and chest, which clattered onto the stone floor. Remembering the terror of confinement I'd felt at my own birth, I'd chosen not to bind him with leather straps; I had not counted on his Herculean strength.

All that secured him now were the chains that connected him to the lightning rods above. The links rattled and snapped taut as he reared upright on the slab. Held fast by the manacles, his hands lunged at me like leashed mastiffs. I pressed myself to the floor, the grasping fingers inches from my face.

Raphael sprang forward with such force that he slipped off the edge of the slab. Supported only by the shackles on his wrists and ankles, he swung in the air above me, whipsawing the chains around him in a frenzy, like a puppet frantic to shake loose from its strings. He let out a simian roar, and my heart ached.

Is this my artist-angel? Have I succeeded only in producing a mindless brute?

I had no chance to consider the consequences. Spectral white light flickered over Raphael's suspended form as another thunderclap boomed above our heads. At any second another lethal bolt could strike the rods atop the house.

Yet there was an even more dire threat. For in the momentary glimmer, I saw Ernst creeping close, a long dissection knife in his fist.

"No!" I yelled as Ernst plunged the blade toward Raphael's back. I jumped up and caught Ernst's wrist so hard he cried out. The knife fell from Ernst's hand just as its tip grazed Raphael's skin. Raphael snarled and shook his chains like a captive gorilla.

"He's nothing more than a beast!" Ernst snapped, echoing my own fears. "Worse than your brother."

"No. No, he's not. I'll prove it to you." I wasn't sure whether I could prove anything. Nevertheless, I stooped to collect the turnscrew and inched closer to Raphael, cooing as if to calm a stray dog. "It's all right, Raphael. I won't hurt you."

Thunder pealed again, and Raphael howled and writhed in his fetters so violently I was afraid the lightning had pierced him after all.

Despite the danger, I reached to stroke his cheek. "*Shh, shh,* Raphael. Anna is here to help you."

The giant ceased struggling, and the pendulous swinging of his body slowed. Trembling, he peeked down at me, eyes wide and white through the tangles of his tousled hair.

"Na-na?"

I nodded and beamed at his halting syllables. "Yes! *Yes!* Anna." I touched my breast.

"Na-na!" He pawed the air, and I took his hand and pressed it to my face.

"Yes! Yes!" I smiled at Ernst over my shoulder. "You see? He understands."

Ernst did not return my smile. Indeed, he frowned more than ever as he rubbed his injured wrist.

I looked back at Raphael, lifted the turnscrew. "Just hold still. I'm going to release you."

A tremor shuddered through him, but he did not resist when I bent to unbolt the shackles on his ankles. Breathing evenly to steady my hand, I unscrewed the manacles on Raphael's legs. His feet swung free, his toes sweeping back and forth a mere inch from the floor.

As I started to unfasten the cuff of his right wrist, another thunderclap pounded, louder than all the rest, and my hands shook as if I could already feel electricity coursing through them. I managed to hold onto the tool, however, and when I'd freed Raphael's right arm, the balls of his feet touched the stone beneath them.

With a few final twists, the remaining screw in the left manacle popped out. As Raphael's arm dropped loose, he fell forward onto me, his weight toppling us onto the floor in an accidental embrace. Another crash of thunder rocked the room, and blinding claws of electricity sparked between the swinging chains where Raphael had hung an instant before.

He curled closer to me, his muscled immensity shivering against my breast like a frightened kitten. "Nana! Nana!"

I clasped him, my fingers spread over the rippled smoothness of his bare back. "*Shh, shh*, Raphael. Everything will be all right now."

I glanced up in time to see Ernst stomping out of the laboratory.

161

CHAPTER 19

THE NEWBORN

I had hoped for Ernst's help in handling our newborn, but I was soon disappointed. He did not return to the laboratory within the first few minutes, and I didn't have the patience to remain sprawled on the floor with Raphael until my colleague recovered from his fit of pique.

I rose and grasped Raphael's hands, urging him to stand as I did. He squatted before me with the gape of a perplexed baboon, and again I fretted that I'd brought a body to life with no mind inside it.

"Like this, Raphael." I bent my knees and mimed standing several times, tugging on his arms and smiling encouragement.

He timidly aped my movement, as if unsure whether he could remain upright. When he straightened at last, I let out a small gasp, for he towered before me like a Nordic deity, massive and male and nude. While he lay lifeless on the slab, I had been able to maintain a certain academic detachment from that mass of tissue and bone. Now his flesh was warm, the complexion flush with flowing blood, the skin supple and exuding a masculine musk I could not ignore. It seemed that my own pulse throbbed in time with the beating of the heart in that leonine chest.

163

"*Good*, Raphael." With his hands still in mine, I tugged him forward as I stepped back, as if conducting a dance lesson.

He took a lumbering first step, heavy and graceless, then a smoother second one. I smiled and nodded, and he did the same, pleased with himself for having pleased me.

Then another thunderclap cracked sparks between the chains behind him, and he stumbled forward to cling to me, shuddering. For the first time, the flickering light illumined the deep wells of shadow beneath his brow, and I saw I had not entirely succeeded in making Raphael appear a normal human. Perhaps too much blood had drained from his eyes, or perhaps some chemical degradation had blanched them, but the irises were the color of lightning—stark, almost luminous, white rings around the ebony pellets of his pupils. They were eyes that should have been blind, should have been *dead*, yet they stared at me with an uncanny intensity.

I resisted the impulse to recoil from him in fright and instead moved to comfort him. His girth was such that I could barely reach my arms around his shoulders. "It's all right, Raphael. You're safe now."

I herded him toward the laboratory door, my arm still around him, both of us hobbling together like one hybrid creature. Just when I thought Raphael had calmed enough to walk on his own, we exited into the hall beyond and nearly collided with Minna. The matron gasped and came close to dropping the tray of stew and bread she carried.

"F-forgive me, Fräulein! I thought you might need some supper." She blushed and averted her gaze from Raphael's exposed manhood. "I did not know you were . . . busy."

Now I flushed with embarrassment. To add to my discomfort, Raphael grabbed me about the waist, cowering behind me as if for protection from the older woman. His loins pushed against the seat of my dress.

"This is Raphael, a patient of mine." I strived to make the introduction sound detached, professional. "He has suffered a severe brain injury, and Dr. Waldman and I shall be treating him for the next several weeks. I ask that you attend to him with all the deference and patience you can. Now be so good as to prepare a guest bedroom for him."

"Of course, Fräulein." She curtsied without looking at Raphael and hurried off.

Her eagerness to avoid our unclothed guest made her even more efficient than usual. By the time I coaxed Raphael to the third-floor room I'd requested, Minna had already turned down the bed and brought a washbasin, chamber pot, and towels.

In the wan light of the single candle the maid had left burning, Raphael blinked at every item in the chamber with a mixture of apprehension and bafflement. While his back was turned, I locked the door and hung the key around my neck. I knew that, with his tremendous strength, the door would not stop him if he wanted to burst through it. I only hoped locking it would discourage him from leaving the room until I was ready to let him out.

Raphael happened to be standing near the chamber's dressing table when another thunderbolt flickered outside the window. A black slate in darkness, the table's mirror abruptly shimmered with Raphael's silvered image, menacing him with his own reflection. Startled, he crossed his forearms in front of his face, as if to shield himself from the phantom figure's expected blows. When he saw the reflection move as well, he swung one mallet fist toward the attacking mirage in front of him.

I caught hold of his arm before it could strike the glass. Strong though I was, Raphael nearly hurtled me through the mirror with the force of his punch.

I caressed his clenched hand to soothe him. "No, no! You shouldn't be afraid. See?"

I snatched the candle from the sconce by the door and held it in front of the two of us, so that the flame gilded the perfect proportions of Raphael's face and frame in his mirrored reflection. I vowed that he would never detest his own image the way my brother had.

"See, Raphael—see how beautiful you are!" I stroked his cheek so he could see that *he* was the Adonis in the glass. "My beautiful, beautiful Raphael."

At first he peered at himself with the same mixture of curiosity and trepidation with which he regarded everything in the unfamiliar world around him. Then he touched his face, stroking his cheek the way I had, and watched his twin do the same. For the first time, he mimicked the smile of delight I wore.

I'd naively hoped that I could take Raphael to his room and put him to bed for the night so that I could sleep as well. I suppose I should not have been surprised that, having been roused from the slumber of death, Raphael refused to consider even a nap. He meandered about the room, peering and prodding at every object in a state of wonderment.

I stifled a yawn and shambled along behind him. The euphoria of the birthing process had dissipated, leaving me in cathartic exhaustion. But since it seemed Raphael would give me no rest, I decided I might as well begin his education at once.

"Stool," I said as he stooped to run his palm over the dressing table's polished wooden seat. "Raphael . . . stool."

I pointed to him, then to the furnishing, as if introducing the two of them.

His eyes lost some of their idiot-dog stupor, acquired new depth. "Sssooool."

I smiled and nodded, repeated the pronunciation with exaggerated movement of my teeth and tongue. "St-st-stool."

"Sssst-sssst-stooooool." His expression brightened with comprehension, and he gestured to the dressing table excitedly.

"Table," I said to keep the word simple. "Ta-ble."

"Taaaaa . . .llllll."

"Ta-*ble*."

His mouth struggled to shape the syllables. "Taaaaa . . .buh-buh-*bllllle*."

"Yes! Good. Now say it again. Ta-ble."

Too eager for repetition, Raphael yanked me by the hand to the next item and the next, his pointing finger demanding to know the name of each. Mantel, wall, wardrobe, door, bed, bowl, candle, curtain—we played the game for hours, until we'd named everything in the room. Now I knew how Birgit must have felt when teaching me, and I prayed that I might have her patience.

More than once during the night, I lay on the bed for a brief respite, but Raphael would shake me awake, bleating my name.

"Nana! Nana!"

"Anna," I corrected him. "*An*-na."

"Na-na!" he repeated, more emphatically this time.

I let it go. There would be plenty of time to teach him later. With a groan, I sat up in bed and pointed to the stool. "What is that, Raphael? What is that?"

Hours passed, and the storm abated. Raphael's nakedness—the press of its solidity against me—I could think of nothing else when he was so close. The soft hair of his arm would tickle the bare skin of mine, and my gaze and mind would wander to the curly thatch between his legs, wondering what *that* hair would feel like against the delicate skin of my midriff and thighs. At such times, I had to shut my eyes and count to ten to regain my concentration.

As the windows grayed with the light of a gloomy dawn, I again lay back on the pillow, eyes aching for sleep. But before the lids drooped shut, I caught sight of Raphael at the chamber door, frowning as he rattled the handle.

I vaulted off the bed and pulled his hand from the locked door.

"Let's continue our game, shall we?" I smiled weakly.

For an instant, Raphael lost interest in the door, but Minna chose that same moment to knock. "Fräulein? Are you still . . . occupied?"

Stark naked as ever, Raphael grabbed the latch and shook it, snarling and pounding the wood when it refused to open. I heard Minna yelp.

I clamped both of Raphael's hands in mine with a stern look. "Give us a few minutes," I told Minna.

As the maid's footsteps scurried off down the hall, I tugged Raphael toward the center of the room, away from the door. "I have a new game to play," I announced.

I shook out the folded nightshirt Minna had left on the dressing table and moved to drape it around Raphael's shoulders. He backed away with a scowl of distaste.

"No, it's all right." I pulled at the fabric of my chemise. "See? Like this."

I unfurled the nightshirt again, but Raphael yanked it from my hand and flung it aside. Then he grasped at my dress and ripped at the bodice, intent that I should be as naked as he was.

"No!" I batted his hands away and retreated toward the door, one hand on my bosom to hold closed the frayed rip. "Very well. We shall have to work on that later."

I fumbled to take the key from around my neck and unlock the latch. "Stay here," I commanded Raphael, as though he would actually understand and obey me.

I exited into the hallway and locked the door behind me, hoping that it would hold Raphael inside until I came back. Hurrying downstairs, I found Minna waiting anxiously in the kitchen.

She noted the tear in my clothing with alarm. "Oh, Fräulein! Are you hurt?"

"It is nothing." I scanned the room, saw the iron pot hanging in the fireplace. "I need two bowls of stew. Immediately!"

"Yes, Fräulein."

The maid ladled the food into two wooden bowls and placed them on a tray. "Would you like me to . . . ?"

"No. I'll take it."

I carried the tray from the kitchen, but before I returned to the bedroom upstairs, I went to the laboratory and searched the shelves of Ernst's medicines and tinctures until I found a brown bottle of sleeping draught. With no idea how much I would need to sedate Raphael, I poured more than twice the dose for a normal man into one of the bowls of stew.

"Here, Raphael," I said as I soon handed him this same bowl. "Let me show you how we eat."

I lifted the other bowl—the one without the narcotic—to my lips and drank the broth. A lesson in utensils would have to wait until I was better rested.

Seated across from me on the floor, Raphael sniffed at the thick soup and seemed surprised by its savory, beefy aroma. Imitating me, he sipped from his wooden bowl. The flavor must have appealed to him, for he ravenously gulped the rest, nearly choking on the chunks of meat until he learned to chew before swallowing. Gravy dribbled down his chin and onto his chest, and he swabbed the bottom of the empty bowl with his hand, licking the residue from his fingers. He thrust the bowl toward me, demanding more.

"Here." I exchanged his bowl for mine with a sigh.

Did I not use enough of the sleeping potion?

His energy undimmed, Raphael gorged himself on the rest of my stew and badgered me for more.

"Later." I wiped his face and chest with a towel from the washbasin, then took his hand and led him to the bed. "Let me teach you another word."

I reclined on the eiderdown-stuffed mattress and pulled Raphael to me. Leaning against the carved mahogany headboard, I coaxed him to lay beside me. He looked at me with expectant curiosity, those extraordinary eyes alight with celestial innocence. The eyes of an angel.

"And *this* is 'love,'" I whispered, and caressed his sculptured chest.

Despite the frigid night, his skin smoldered feverishly beneath my fingertips. I traced every rise and ridge of rib and sinew from his breastbone to his stomach to the thicket of dark hair between his naked thighs. The lolling serpent of his manhood shivered and awoke, thickening and lengthening as I touched its pulsing veins.

Raphael gasped, startled that he had lost control of part of himself. Before he could cry out, I put my mouth to his—a kiss I had rehearsed on his cold corpse. This time, his lips were supple and warm, and I dug both my hands into his mane of wild hair to hold him there. In that moment, I lived that awful, wonderful, maddening dream that had plagued me for months.

Then Raphael's mouth went slack, and he began to nod. He blinked and shook his head but could not shake off the drunken drowse into which he sank. The sleeping draught had finally taken effect.

I pressed his drooping head to my breast, and he did not resist. Before long, he slipped into the placid doze of an infant. I fought the overwhelming temptation to keep kissing his sleeping form, to have my way with his helpless body.

For the better part of an hour, I didn't dare to move although his sprawled bulk weighed heavily on me. The nearness of his flesh, his heat . . . my heart thumped so hard that I feared its beat alone would wake him. When he did not stir, I gingerly edged out from under him, cradling his head in my hands until I could rest it upon a pillow. I eased out of bed and crept from the room, glancing back to make sure he hadn't moved before locking him alone in the bedchamber.

Lust had drained the last of my vigor, and once I'd left Raphael's presence, exhaustion collapsed upon me like a demolished tower. I wanted only to go to my own bed and sleep the day away. It was midafternoon by then, and I could hear Minna and the cook already puttering with dinner down below. I also heard other activity that I could not identify: a rapid thudding of wood against wood on the stairs.

I peeped over the top landing's banister and saw Ernst dragging a large cedar chest up the stairwell, banging it over each step as he went. His rumpled shirt and shadowed, sunken eyes told me that he, too, had spent the night sleepless, which made his current exertion all the more perplexing.

I pattered down to the second-floor landing and followed him as he carried the chest into the hallway. "Are you leaving?" I asked.

"No. You are." Ernst hefted the chest through the doorway into my bedchamber, dropped it on the floor, and threw the lid open. He grabbed the gowns from my armoire in a great, sloppy bundle and stuffed them in the wooden box.

"Stop it!" I scrabbled to keep him from plucking fistfuls of underthings from the drawers of my dresser. "What are you *doing*?"

"You've got your handmade lover. It's time you were off on your honeymoon." He jammed petticoats and chemises in with the dresses.

"You can't send us away now. Raphael . . . he isn't ready. He doesn't know how to behave, can hardly speak."

"That is none of my concern. As I recall, I never invited you to spend the rest of your life in my house, and I certainly didn't invite *him*."

170

"But your father's work—"

Ernst seared me with his expression of disdain. "Ha! Your only interest in my father's work was using it to populate your bed."

I stayed his hands as he moved to seize my slippers. "Please, Ernst. You're my friend—the only one I have. As a friend, I am begging you for a little more time. Enough to prepare Raphael for the outside world. Then we'll leave, if that's what you want, and you'll never have to see us again."

Ernst turned his head away as if determined not to look at me. When he finally did, the taut anger on his face fell into sad weariness.

"Very well," he said. "You have a month."

CHAPTER
20

THE EDUCATION
OF RAPHAEL

Ernst's ultimatum hung over me like the waiting blade of a guillotine. How on earth could I possibly civilize Raphael in only a month? I might as easily have schooled the horses in the stable to speak Latin in that time.

Although I was so tired I could have slept for days, I planned to nap for only four hours before dealing with Raphael again. The instant Ernst left my room, I crawled into bed without even shedding my clothes. But it seemed I had barely shut my eyes before I heard an explosive *crack* of splintering wood accompanied by the shrieks of a woman.

Not enough sleeping draught, I thought, even before I heard the petulant shouts of *"NANA! NANA!"* I ran upstairs to find Raphael cornered in the hallway, the white starbursts of his irises flickering wildly as he glanced around like a feral hyena. Behind him, the broken bedroom door canted on one bent hinge.

"Those eyes!" Minna whimpered. "He's possessed by a devil, surely!" She cowered before him, covering her face either to keep him from striking her or to keep herself from staring at his nakedness.

Ernst stood beside her, a pistol aimed at Raphael's heart. *"Back,* you beast," he commanded, the way we talk to dogs we know cannot understand us.

I gasped, remembering how I had first learned the power of a gun. Raphael had no concept of how much danger he was in.

He caught sight of me as I came up behind Ernst. "Nana!"

He started forward. Ernst cocked the pistol, but I rushed in front of it. "It's all right," I told them both. "I'll handle this."

Ernst lowered the gun, his hand shaking. "See that you do. Otherwise, I might reconsider my decision. Come, Minna—he won't harm you now." Ernst put an arm around the sobbing maid's shoulders and gently led her away.

As soon as they were gone, Raphael clutched me with a greediness that reminded me of my brother's first embrace. *"Nana."*

Again, I wrapped myself in his unquestioning adoration as if it were a fur coat. But such pleasures would have to wait—there was too much to do.

While I coaxed Raphael back into the bedchamber, I glanced at the wreckage of the ruined door. Obviously, I'd have to find some other place to house my impetuous angel until he could be tamed.

Before I did that, however, I had to find some way to clothe Raphael so he wouldn't scandalize the servants. The problem was that Raphael couldn't fathom the use of clothing. Despite the drafty house, he padded around the bedchamber like an unadorned Adam, chest, haunches, and buttocks covered only in downy, dark hair. When I tried to throw a red satin brocade robe around his shoulders, he swatted it away and scowled at me as if I'd tried to snare him in a net.

"No, Raphael, you don't understand." Struck by inspiration, I pulled him toward the mirror where he'd first admired himself. "See how beautiful it makes you?"

I draped the robe about him like a royal cloak. "You remember what 'beautiful' means, don't you? See how beautiful you are now!"

It was true. He looked like the pasha of some exotic princedom. He stroked the unfamiliar fabric as he peered at his reflection in the glass, seeming to enjoy the feel of its smooth gloss against his skin.

"Here—let's put it on you."

Raphael let me slide first one arm, then the other into the robe's sleeves. The garment was almost too small for his colossal musculature, but he smiled and preened, a peacock pleased with his new plumage.

I showed him how to tie the sash that held the robe closed in front. At least now he wouldn't embarrass the staff. But that still didn't solve the problem of how to keep him from breaking out of his quarters to roam the house or even, God forbid, the outside world. Short of chaining him to a wall, I could see only one way to make sure he remained in seclusion.

I would have to stay with him. At all times.

"Let's show the others how handsome you are." I led him out of the bedchamber and down the stairs. The staff would have to become accustomed to Raphael as soon as possible . . . and so would Ernst.

We found them huddled together in the kitchen. Ernst hunched in a chair at the small wooden breakfast table, arms folded, his expression as bitter as the black coffee in the half-empty cup in front of him. Next to him sat Minna, shivering and hyperventilating. Nadja, the cook, who stood only as high as Minna was seated, urged her to swig a dram of sherry to calm her nerves. The moment Raphael lumbered into the room, Minna yelped and leaped from her seat.

"Don't be afraid." I gestured to Raphael. "You see, he means you no harm."

Still panting, she blinked up at him fearfully. He simply stared at her with those luminescent white eyes, as sharp and impenetrable as an owl's.

"I need your help," I told Minna. "I need you to make up a room in the wine cellar. Have the stable hands put two beds down there—cots will do—and—"

Now Ernst jumped to his feet, bumping the table so that it rattled the china. "Have you lost your mind?"

When Raphael cocked his head in sudden interest, Ernst eyed him with heightened alarm. It had evidently not occurred to him that Raphael might understand what he said.

Ernst moved closer to me, lowered his voice to a whisper. "Do you actually intend to share a room with him?"

"He needs supervision," I murmured. "*Constant* supervision. Surely even you would agree with that."

Ernst grimaced. "One month," he reminded me, as if I had forgotten. "In the meantime, I'll see that your bridal suite is prepared."

I looked at the floor as he pushed past me and went to fetch his men.

Ernst and I didn't speak for days after that, but I was too consumed by my work with Raphael to regret the fact. Ernst's sarcasm had stung, however, so I insisted that the makeshift bedchamber in the cellar be furnished with two narrow cots rather than one large bed.

My attempt at propriety did little good. Every evening Raphael crawled in beside me, nuzzling his naked heat up against me like a languorous cat. His broad frame took up so much of the mattress that I was forced to sleep on my side, my head pillowed on the hard hill of his pectoral muscle. All night, I felt those moon-white eyes peering at me through the basement's darkness. I slept little, and woke exhausted from the effort of frustrating my own lust.

Not yet, I kept telling myself. *Only when he's ready.*

I felt certain that wouldn't be long. Every day he grew more independent and more restless. I let him roam the house in hopes that this small measure of freedom might pacify him for confinement in the cellar at night. Minna fled every room he entered, of course, while I had to hitch up my skirt and scamper at his side to keep watch on him.

I tried to occupy his attention to keep him out of trouble, and so took him into Ernst's library one afternoon to show him an enameled globe of the world and the collection of pickled frogs and reptiles displayed in jars on the bookshelves. But Raphael gravitated instead toward the nearest window.

"Out," he breathed, gazing hungrily at the green pastures that surrounded the Waldman estate and at the clustered buildings of Ingolstadt in the distance. *"Out!"*

It was a word I could not remember teaching him. He understood it all too well, though, for he pounded on the glass. The leaded panes fractured into starbursts of cracks beneath his fists.

"No, Raphael!" I grabbed his arms, but all my superhuman strength was nothing compared to his. So, rather than restrain his hands, I kissed them instead. "Please . . . *stay*. Stay with me."

The coiled tension in his muscles eased, but he did not lower his hands. When I bowed my head to kiss them again, he grabbed my hair and pulled my face up, forcing my lips to mold to his in ferocious passion. The kiss was so brutal my mouth felt bruised, yet I didn't stop him. Didn't *want* to stop him.

When he had satisfied himself, he released me and smiled. Those lunar eyes of his shone with new luster, for he had learned the power he had over me.

That night, I had Minna lock Raphael and I together in the cellar. It would do little good, I knew, if he wanted to get out, but it calmed me enough so that I could sleep a few hours.

Raphael made such rapid progress that it amazed and unnerved me. He learned to speak more quickly than I had, as if he merely had to pull stored-up words from the brain of the dead miner whose head he wore. His observation was so keen that he could use almost any device, tool, or utensil after seeing it demonstrated only once. I made sure to have Ernst and the servants hide the keys to the house, as well as any obvious weapons or implements Raphael might employ to escape. A futile gesture, perhaps, given his strength and cunning, but I hoped such measures would prevent him from leaving before I'd prepared him for the world of humanity.

As fast as he matured in some ways, Raphael remained stubbornly infantile in others. Matters of personal grooming were the worst. He couldn't seem to see the point in such activities as shaving or bathing, so he refused to do them. Yet he also mistrusted me to do them for him. It took an hour of cooing and cajoling to get near him with a straight razor the first time I tried to shave him, but the instant I grazed the tender skin of his Adam's apple with the blade, he shoved me away. The razor left a shallow, oozing red nick just above the faint ring of scar tissue around Raphael's neck. The bleeding stopped within minutes, but Raphael wouldn't let me near him with a blade in my hand for days afterward. He soon grew a thicket of stubble, which gave a manly, untamed cast to his lean face.

Perhaps this change in his appearance led me to think him more mature than he was, or perhaps my own impatience was to blame for what happened next.

Raphael's aversion to bathing had become intolerable, so I instructed Minna to heat a cauldron of water in the kitchen. Oskar and Gert, the grooms from the stable, carried the steaming water down to the cellar in oaken buckets, complaining all the way.

"No one ever took so much trouble to give *me* a hot bath!" Oskar grumbled, sloshing water on the stairs.

"Wish they would," Gert muttered, wrinkling his bulbous nose as he trudged downwind of his partner.

They emptied the buckets into the large, round wooden tub I'd had the servants bring from the upstairs laboratory. It was the same tub in which I'd preserved the body parts I'd used to make Raphael.

He watched the workmen pour the steaming liquid into the vat with the skittish curiosity of a cat. I deliberately requested that the water be nearly scalding so it would stay hot during the hour or more it took to prepare the bath. I then needed to add several buckets of cold water brought directly from the nearby cistern to lower the temperature to a comfortable level. Oskar moaned that he'd never be able to stand up straight again after toting those heavy pails, so I gave him and Gert each a handful of pfennigs and sent them on their way.

With the workmen gone, I beckoned Raphael to the bath. "Come. It won't hurt you."

I laved my hands in the tub's warm water to prove the point.

He shied back and shook his head.

I sighed. As with everything else, I would have to show him by example.

178

I pushed the sleeves of my dress off my shoulders and let it slip to the floor. Then I pulled my shift off over my head, shivering in the dank cellar as I stood naked before him.

"Like this." I stepped over the rim of the tub and lowered myself into the bath, both to ward off the chill and to hide my body from the twin moons of those staring eyes.

Raphael padded forward and bent to study the bathwater. He dabbed the fingertips of one hand below the surface and held them there, apparently waiting to see if the water did anything to him. When it didn't, he stepped in and lowered himself beside me, gazing at me expectantly.

I picked up a cake of lye soap I'd balanced on the tub's rim and lathered it against my palm in the water. Raphael shrank from my hand as I reached to rub the soap's sheen on him.

I laughed. "It's all right. It feels good. See?"

I spread the foam over my left shoulder, smiling, then refreshed the lather on my hand. This time, Raphael let me glide the soap over the swell of his chest. Taut over the bunched muscle and slick to the touch, his skin had the delicious smoothness of polished marble.

My breaths grew heavier as I washed the rest of his chest and arms. Though I avoided looking at his face, I could feel that silver-white gaze boring into me. I didn't know how I was going to wash the lower half of his body without touching him . . . down there.

"There! You see how easy it is. Try it." I held the cake of soap out to him, hoping he would finish the task.

Raphael took the soap and rubbed it in his hands as he'd seen me do. Instead of washing himself, though, he reached toward me.

Startled, I splashed backward to the far rim of the tub. He moved forward, pinning me against the wood. Before I could wriggle away, he stroked soap over my left breast. I gasped as his hand glided over my skin, then cupped and gently kneaded the flesh. My nipple stiffened in the gap between his fingers, and he lightly pinched the aureole to pucker it even more, studying the effect his caress had on me.

"Love," he said.

Despite the water's warmth, I shivered. He had never spoken that word before. Yet he clearly remembered how I had taught it to him the day he was born—how I had touched him just as he touched me now. Total and unquestioning adoration illuminated his features, and I believed that here at last was the hidden face from my dreams, the visage I'd craved to see.

Pent-up hope and longing spilled from my heart. I pressed his hand into the cleft between my breasts so he could feel the pounding in my chest. *"Yes,"* I breathed. "Love!"

He pulled me against him . . . or I wrapped myself around him . . . I didn't know which, and didn't care. The space between us closed, and we were like twins in the womb, our bodies folded against each other while the water swaddled us in warmth. His hands glided over the contours of my body with almost frictionless ease, tracing the curve of my spine to the small of my back, then grasping the fullness of my hips to widen the spread of my thighs. He instinctively rubbed my sex against his firming manhood but did not know what to do next. Hungrily, I reached down and fed him into the opening chasm within me, kissing him deeply as I did so. I entered him with my tongue, he entered me with his shaft, and in that moment we felt inseparable.

Straddling his lap, I lifted and lowered myself upon him, gently at first, then faster and more forcefully, swallowing him further and further. My inner walls pulsed with his arousal, as though his heart itself had been stuffed inside me. Pressure swelled up through my stomach, my chest, my throat, my brain, until it wanted to burst from my mouth in a scream. I clamped my jaw to keep it in, digging my hands into Raphael's mane of hair to hold back the eruption—a vain, greedy attempt to hoard his passion in my body forever.

"Love!" Raphael's husky voice cracked, quavered on the verge of sobbing. *"Love!"*

I threw my head back, shrieked in triumph. "Yes, my angel! Yes!"

Prickling fire exploded from my loins to every part of my body, until my toes and nipples and scalp tingled with fever-heat. No, no, I could not hold it back a second longer. I groaned in almost painful ecstasy and sagged against Raphael in a narcotic delirium.

But Raphael still bucked beneath me, the two of us bobbing so violently that the bathwater washed over onto the basement floor. "Love!" he cried, shuddering in climax. "Nana! *Nana!*"

I ground my teeth. That name—a baby's babble.

Why can't he say it right?

I suddenly felt sick. It all seemed wrong now. To have him sagging inside me, like an indigestible meal . . .

"No! Not 'Nana'!" I stood, water drooling off my body. "My name is An-na. *Anna!*"

I bumbled out of the tub and wrapped myself, still damp, in a dressing gown. Raphael just sat there in pitiful confusion. My nausea increased. I had done a terrible thing, and knew terrible consequences were sure to come.

I bolted and barred the cellar door as I left. Behind me, I could hear Raphael bleating "Nana! Nana! Nana!"

I ran upstairs, dripping bathwater on the polished teak floor all the way. So distracted was I that I bumped into Ernst when he stepped from his study into the hallway.

"Anna?" He stood back and looked at me. "What is it? Are you all right?"

The gentility and concern he displayed made me feel worse yet. *What would he think if he knew what I've done?*

I rushed off without answering him. I dashed into the bed-chamber that used to be mine and slammed the door. Alone, I sank to the floor and covered my face, as though the whole world stared at me.

CHAPTER
21

BROKEN COMMANDMENTS

After that, I resumed drugging Raphael's food every evening. Guilt stabbed me each time we took dinner together, as he waggled his head, woozy and perplexed, before slumping into a bovine doze. But I knew that it was less of a sin than if I permitted myself to go on making love with him. So, once he was deep in slumber, I locked him in the cellar and went up to sleep alone in my bedchamber.

I'd put my selfish lust ahead of Raphael's well-being. I would not do so again. As his creator, I had an obligation to be his mentor and protector, to prepare him to thrive in the life I'd given him. To make good my pledge, I resolved to school him in the morals of the human race he would one day join.

With the month Ernst had allotted me for Raphael's preparation slipping away, I drilled my pupil around the clock. He slouched at the desk in the library and fidgeted while I taught him his letters. At first, I would stand beside his chair and indicate the text I'd given him to read, but he inevitably tried to plant kisses on my cheek and neck every time I bent near him. To keep us both from temptation, I took to standing on the opposite side of the desk and tapping on the open book with a wooden pointer that I borrowed from Ernst's classroom at the university.

Despite being an unruly, inattentive student, Raphael quickly became fluent in both spoken and written German. As soon as he was able to read, I gave him passages from the Bible to recite aloud, as both Birgit and Frau Hauptmann had done with me. I particularly stressed the Ten Commandments. With me, Frau Hauptmann had harped on "Thou shalt not commit adultery"; with Raphael, I insisted that he repeat "Thou shalt not kill" over and over in hopes that he might escape my brother's fate.

One day near the end of our month of instruction, after hours of such tedious lessons, Raphael lost patience.

"Who is this God?" He brushed a hand at the page of Scripture in derision. "Why should I follow his rules?"

I gave the answer I had been taught. "He is our Creator. He rules the universe, and we must obey Him."

"Then who are this father and mother I am supposed to honor?"

I was not prepared for Raphael to ask about his parentage. Should I invent some comforting lie? Tell him that he was an orphan, that he lost his memory in some terrible accident? But those were the same sort of lies that Frau Hauptmann had told me. I could not deceive him that way, for I knew how devastating it would be when he ultimately learned the truth.

"You are . . . *different* from other people," I said. "Someday, you will understand—"

"Then I see no need to bother with this." He flung the Bible off the desk. It landed on the floor facedown, like a dead bird, the wings of its brown covers splayed over a heap of onionskin feathers.

I inhaled deeply. "Very well. You deserve the truth."

I crossed the library and took Victor Frankenstein's notebook down from the shelf. I drew another chair up close to Raphael and sat with the leather-bound volume propped upright on my lap, facing him.

"You have seen this, haven't you?" I pulled off my scarf and touched the scar around my neck. "And there is one like it here . . ." I turned back one lapel of his loose-fitting, ruffled shirt and grazed the faint line across his throat with my fingernail. The stubble on his throat pricked up at my touch. His angel-white eyes lost their defiance, quivered between fear and fascination.

"You and I—we were not *born*. We were *made*." I opened Frankenstein's journal to his schematic drawing of my brother. "The man who wrote this book put me together from pieces of other people. I made you the same way."

"You . . . *made* me," Raphael repeated, as if to make sure he'd understood me correctly. "Why?"

The question struck me mute. Should I confess how I had manufactured him simply to be my lover, so I would not be alone in the world? I recognized now how little thought I'd given to Raphael's own happiness as a free and independent being.

When I failed to answer, he batted Frankenstein's book out of my hands and yanked me from the chair, gripping my head in his huge hands to force my lips to his. I wriggled in his grasp even as I reveled in the savagery of his kiss.

I pushed to break loose from him, but his constricting embrace only tightened. A growing fright welled within me as I pushed harder and harder, a scream corked in my mouth by his relentless, questing tongue.

Finally, I rammed his chest with all the strength I'd used to knock doors off their hinges. The blow would have sent an ordinary man careening into the wall, but it barely tipped Raphael off balance.

He let go of me and staggered backward a step. Then he wiped his mouth on his sleeve. "That's enough for today's lesson."

He swaggered over to the nearest window and gazed out over the countryside with the air of a prince surveying his future kingdom. I was already losing control of him, and I didn't know what to do.

That night, I put twice the usual dose of sleeping draught in his food—I knew I was dangerously close to poisoning him. But I needed at least a few hours to myself so I could think.

Raphael's breath was shallow, almost imperceptible, when I locked him in the cellar and trudged upstairs to the library to sulk by the fire. I'd hoped for nothing more than solitude and a glass of cognac to tranquilize my panic. Instead, I had barely slumped in the chair by the hearth when Ernst entered, nonchalant and relaxed in his satin evening robe.

"Allow me." He took the decanter of brandy from my hand and poured some into the snifter I held, then helped himself to a glass. "So . . . only a few days left in the month. I trust you shall have Raphael quite ready to make his way in the world?"

He made a mock toast and took a languorous sip of the liquor.

I gulped mine in one burning swallow and cupped the glass in my palms. "If you came here to gloat, you needn't bother. I'm miserable enough."

He sank into the chair opposite mine, and his expression softened. "I know how hard you've been working . . ."

"And for what?" I stood and flailed a hand toward the basement where I'd imprisoned Raphael. "I tried to teach him to be a decent human, and all I've done is make him a brute."

Ernst contemplated the liquor in his glass. "Perhaps that's all he can be."

"*No.*" I shook my head. "I created him. The responsibility is mine. And I failed. I'm no better than Frankenstein."

"Raphael is a thinking being," Ernst said, his tone stern but not unkind. "He makes his own choices, just as you did. And *you* didn't become a monster, did you?"

"I don't know." The eyes I'd inherited from Katarina von Kemp quivered with tears as I remembered the slickness of Stefan's blood on my breasts, the weight of his severed head in my hands.

Ernst rose and quietly refilled my cognac. Then, to my astonishment, he undid the sash of his heavy robe, shrugged it off his shoulders, and spread it on the floor in front of the hearth. "Here, sit close to the fire."

I couldn't guess what he had in mind—possibly some special humiliation—but at that moment, I felt like I deserved whatever he had in store for me. As instructed, I sat on the padded satin spread of his robe and gazed into the coal-fed flames. I hadn't realized how cold I was until the fire's warmth salved my skin.

186

Now clad only in a nightshirt, Ernst crossed to one of the bookshelves and selected a small, thin volume with a shiny new leather cover. "I know your fondness for the recent English poets. I think you'll like this fellow Shelley. A friend of Byron's, I believe."

He plumped down beside me, paged through the book.

I sniffed and sipped brandy. "Fiddling while Rome burns."

"Shush! Now listen."

Propping himself on one arm, he leaned close to recite the verse in my ear, as soft and gentle as a sigh.

"And said I that all hope was fled,
That sorrow and despair were mine,
That each enthusiast wish was dead,
Had sank beneath pale Misery's shrine.—"

His voice lulled me again, the way it had after those long nights we'd spent stitching together Raphael's body. I was tired, so very tired, and I reclined against his firm shoulder and closed my eyes, shutting out everything in the world but that soothing voice.

"Seest thou the sunbeam's yellow glow,
That robes with liquid streams of light;
Yon distant Mountain's craggy brow.
And shows the rocks so fair,—so bright—
'Tis thus sweet expectation's ray,
In softer view shows distant hours,
And portrays each succeeding day,
As dressed in fairer, brighter flowers,—
The vermeil tinted flowers that blossom;
Are frozen but to bud anew,
Then sweet deceiver calm my bosom,
Although thy visions be not true,—
Yet true they are,—and I'll believe,
Thy whisperings soft of love and peace,
God never made thee to deceive,
'Tis sin that bade thy empire cease.
Yet though despair my life should gloom,
Though horror should around me close,
With those I love, beyond the tomb,

Hope shows a balm for all my woes."

A reverent silence followed, and in the stillness, my borrowed eyes wept tears that were truly mine. For one who had been born in horror, whose cradle was a tomb, and who had no God to call her Maker, the verse came as absolution—as a promise that even such a misbegotten creature as I might have hope for salvation.

And Ernst had believed it all along.

I sat up and looked at him. In the firelight, he resembled Lord Byron, the book held casually in his right hand, his loose-fitting nightshirt open at the neck to reveal the shadowed grace of his clavicle.

I sniffled and laughed. "A poet. And an angel." I touched his dark, curly hair, his strong jaw, and high, noble brow. "What a fool I was to think I could build a man better than you."

"Anna." Ernst put aside the book and took my hand in his, pressed my palm against his cheek. It fluttered as if with the quickening of his heart, and he seemed in sudden agony. "Oh, how many times have I wished I could make myself into the man you wanted."

"Ernst, you *are*. You always were. I see that now. But I was afraid I could never be with you." An image of my blood-sodden wedding bed flashed through my mind, except it was Ernst's headless corpse I saw there instead of Stefan's. "I'm still afraid."

"I'm not." Ernst bent forward to brush his lips to mine in a kiss of sweet, delicate tenderness. As I responded, his ardor increased, and he grasped my face at the temples to prolong the contact, as if afraid I might vanish if he released me.

I pulled back, weeping. "You don't know what I am. What I've done—"

He put his forefinger to my mouth. "I know all I need to know."

He kissed me again, and this time I held onto him, wouldn't let him stop. I continued to cry, and he kissed away each tear. When he lifted his hand to stroke my hair, I touched my lips to his palm and pressed it against my cheek. Its strength comforted me, its touch so tender that I had no fear of it. This was a hand that would never do me harm.

I took his hand from my face and placed it on my left breast, right above my heart.

The gentlest of gentlemen, Ernst flinched as I guided his fingers underneath the open collar of my chemise and held them against my bare skin. He no doubt feared he was taking advantage of me. I kept his hand in place with my left and slid my right hand under the lapel of his nightshirt. I brushed my fingertips along the thatch of hair that fringed his chest, then flattened my palm over his heart, kept it there until I could feel the soft percussion of our pulses beat in unison.

As one, we leaned closer, touched lips. A kiss as light as the brush of a feather . . . then another that lingered longer, pressed harder. Our mouths tugged at each other in delicate, delicious suction, and Ernst slowly traced the oval of my lips with his tongue. I knotted the fingers of my left hand into the thick black curls of his hair to hold him there, as my right hand slid around the swell of his chest to claw at the rippling expanse of his back.

The hand that Ernst held on my heart moved to caress my left breast. My breath quickened as he fingered the aureola, rubbing and lightly pinching the nipple until I shivered with delight. I wanted to cry out, but that would have meant taking my lips from his, and I could not do that for even an instant. Instead, I let him fill my mouth with his tongue, lapping and sucking at it with my own.

Ernst's hand glided lower beneath my shift, down the smooth curve of my stomach, tickling the hair between my thighs as it sought the delicate button of flesh that nested there. He rubbed its tiny circumference in circles—slowly at first, then faster and faster—as if running his finger along the rim of a crystal goblet to make it ring. My body vibrated until I thought I would shatter.

Snarling now in animal desire, I ached to give him the same ecstasy. I reached down inside his nightshirt until I grasped his manhood. It was already firm and full, pulsing with life that I wanted to pull from it. I pulled and I pulled, and Ernst moaned more loudly each time.

The heat from the fire seemed to intensify until the thin nightclothes we wore felt stifling, intolerable. We scrambled to undress each other with clumsy impatience. I tried to pull his nightshirt up over his head at the same time he yanked my unbuttoned shift off my shoulders to drop at my waist, and we became a tangle of arms and cloth.

When at last we freed ourselves, Ernst seized me in a tempestuous embrace, kissing the arc of my neck from jaw to shoulder, massaging the muscle with his mouth. His hand again moved to my nether region, and I gasped as his finger curled down to probe and penetrate the salivating walls of my sex.

It wasn't enough. I pushed Ernst back flat on the robe that overspread the floor and lowered myself onto his jutting spire. It sealed the void within me, became part of me, kissed the roof of my soul with each thrust. I collapsed on top of him, sucking his tongue into my mouth, wanting him in every part of me at once.

Ernst obliged better than I could have wished. He caressed my hindquarters as we made love, pushing himself more deeply inside me. Then, at the height of our passion, he gently inserted a finger between my buttocks to tap softly at the valley's tender hole. Though the touch was slight, it rippled in rhythm with the surging waves of sensation from his shaft, cresting and crashing in my head.

"Anna," Ernst panted, spilling his seed inside me. We wailed together at the consummation, kissing frantically to draw out the climax even as it settled into a blissful afterglow.

Afterward we lay on the rumpled robe in a happy lassitude, our nightclothes draped over us like bed sheets. The comfort of the fire, the feel of Ernst's arm across my breasts, the light susurration of his breath on my neck—they lulled me into the best sleep I'd ever known in my short life, and I dreamed of no lover but him.

A creeping clamminess jarred me awake. The fire had burned to embers, and the library was now dark and cold. I shivered and sat up, apprehensive.

How much time has passed? It's still night—surely the drug has kept Raphael asleep this long. But how much longer?

Ernst rolled onto his side, still asleep. I wanted nothing more than to nestle beside him again. Instead I stood and put on my shift, taking care not to wake him, and made haste to return to Raphael.

Before I went down to the cellar, however, I paused in my

bedchamber upstairs and filled a washbasin with water from a pitcher that the servants had left there. I inhaled the delicious aroma of our lovemaking on my body, the mingled musk of our sexes. Then I scrubbed Ernst's scent from my skin, sponged his seed from between my thighs so Raphael would not detect my infidelity.

I carried a single candle as I crept into the basement, shading the light with my hand so it would not shine on Raphael. The room was absolutely silent, and I stepped as lightly on the stone floor as if there were creaking boards beneath my feet.

Raphael lay on his cot with his massive back to me, without the slightest motion or sound. A nauseating dread filled me.

Is he dead? Did I feed him too much of the drug?

I couldn't bar the cellar door from the inside, so I merely eased it shut. I inched forward but still could not see or hear Raphael breathe. The candlelight settled on the hill of his cheek and the valley beneath his jaw. Finally, I saw it: the worm of a vein pulsing beneath the tender skin of his throat. He was alive.

Although I should have been relieved, a new anxiety gripped me. I suddenly had the terrible certainty that he was lying there, wide awake, waiting for me.

From the angle where I stood, the hollows of his eyes remained black with shadow, and I could not tell if they were open or closed. If I took even one step closer, or held the candle out at arm's length, I might see those luminous orbs staring into the cellar's darkness, fixing their white gaze on me with all-consuming wrath . . .

I blew out the candle immediately and buried myself in my own cot, pulling the blanket over my head as if those baleful eyes might stare at me even in the basement's coal-black night.

CHAPTER 22

ANGEL'S FALL

The image of those white eyes peering at me through the darkness possessed me so thoroughly that I could not tell whether I was seeing or dreaming them the rest of that night. I thought I might still be dreaming when I woke and relit the candle in the morning, for Raphael had rolled over in his bed to stare at me in my sleep.

I gasped, startled. "Are you all right?"

"Of course." His luminous irises gleamed like polished coins. "Why shouldn't I be?"

"Did you . . . sleep well?"

"Very." He sat up in bed, stretched and yawned, languid as a caged lion. "I can hardly wait to start today's lessons."

True to his word, he proved an exemplary student that day, the complete opposite of his behavior the previous afternoon. Calm and attentive, he answered every question with a quickness and precision that revealed his uncanny intelligence. Yet the change in him disturbed rather than encouraged me. Although he obeyed my every direction without complaint, he regarded me with a brooding coolness, his white eyes half-lidded but unblinking.

Had he guessed what Ernst and I had done the previous night? If so, he said nothing of it.

Nevertheless, I slightly increased the dose of narcotic in Raphael's dinner that evening. And when I was certain he was asleep, I went to spend the night with Ernst.

In this fashion, Ernst and I stole many wonderful hours together in the week that followed. Each time, I had to leave the sweet sanctuary of his embrace to return to the cellar before Raphael's medication wore off.

Raphael said nothing. But he stayed at my side constantly throughout the day, watching so intently that I could feel his glare if I so much as passed Ernst in the hall. I took to looking at the floor whenever Ernst was around so I wouldn't let Raphael see us exchange a glance.

"I don't know how long I can go on like this," I confessed, pillowed on Ernst's bare chest in one of our midnight trysts. "How can we be together if he won't ever leave us alone?"

Ernst teasingly stroked my arm with his fingertips. "You could turn him loose. Let him make his own way in the world. At least he can speak now."

I groaned. "He's not ready for the world. And the world is not ready for him. I'm not sure it ever will be."

Ernst toyed with my hair for a few moments before speaking again. "There are other ways to be rid of him."

Gooseflesh stippled my skin, and it was not from the pleasure of his touch. "You don't mean that."

"You gave life," he replied. "You can take it away."

The crack of musket fire reverberated in my memory, and I was once more running through the woods, rain pelting my face, branches tearing at the unraveling bandages I wore.

"No. That's something Frankenstein would do." I climbed out of Ernst's bed, put on my shift, and used a spill to light a candle from the embers in the fireplace. "I owe Raphael more than that."

"Anna, wait. I didn't mean to—"

I swept out of the room without listening to his excuses. He'd shocked me with his cold-bloodedness. If I'd been the unwanted monster, would he have killed me, too? That was not the kind, tender, patient Ernst I knew . . . the one I loved.

He doesn't understand, I told myself as I whisked down the stairs. *He doesn't believe I can civilize Raphael. I'll simply have to work harder. When I succeed, I'll fulfill my obligation to Raphael and* earn *my right to be with Ernst.*

I reached the bottom of the stairwell and froze. The cellar door, which I had secured from the outside, had been thrown wide open. The thick iron bolt had wrenched its metal plate out of the wood, and the heavy oak bar I'd placed across the door had snapped in two. Beyond the doorway lay dead silence and darkness.

Wheezing with panic, I plunged into the cellar and held my candle aloft. I already knew Raphael was gone. But I needed to find out *how.*

My nose told me the answer even before my eyes could see it—an acid stench of bile so strong I had to cover my mouth to keep from gagging. Raphael had vomited his drugged dinner into his chamber pot.

Rushing back upstairs, I started my search for Raphael where I most feared I'd find him: in Ernst's bedchamber, where I'd been not half an hour before.

Raphael was not there, and neither was Ernst.

The vacant room only sharpened my fright. What if Raphael had already found Ernst and taken him somewhere . . . done something to him? Or maybe Ernst had ambushed Raphael first, had "taken away" the life he'd helped create. With two jealous lovers bent on killing each other, any meeting between them could only end in disaster.

I darted from room to room in the house, hoping to find Raphael and Ernst unharmed. But I couldn't risk calling out to either of them lest the other one hear.

Then I noticed a faint yellow light seeping into the hall from the library. The door stood ajar, as if in invitation.

I entered and found Raphael alone, sitting in the chair he occupied each day for our lessons. He wore only a loose dressing gown tied with a sash. An oil lamp rested on the small writing desk in front of him, and he pored over a large tome, so engrossed in his reading that he did not seem to notice me.

A cold apprehension made me stop halfway across the room. "Raphael?"

He did not look up.

"Couldn't you sleep?"

"I wasn't tired." He turned a page.

"But your dinner—"

"Didn't agree with me."

My throat tightened. If he had figured out I was drugging his food, I would have no way to subdue him. I fought to keep my tone light, cheery. "What are you doing?"

"Learning. You know, this book is far more educational than all the others put together."

He lifted the volume from his lap, and I recognized it as Victor Frankenstein's notebook.

My skin prickled as if he'd walked over my grave. "That's good, Raphael. I want you to know how you were created."

He stood and sauntered toward me. "Ah! But that's not what *I* wanted to know. I wanted to know *why.*"

As he left the halo of lamplight, only his incandescent white eyes shone through the shadow. He tapped the notebook's cover. "You made me for yourself, Nana."

I backed away from him. "I told you not to call me that. My name's Anna."

Raphael didn't seem to hear. "You made me for yourself, and now you would throw me away for that twig of a man?" He flung aside the book. "I'll snap him in two!"

I resisted the impulse to retreat any further. "If you dare—"

But I was secretly relieved. His threat meant he hadn't harmed Ernst. Yet.

"If I dare *what*? This?" Raphael surged forward to try and snatch me around the waist. I dodged him, but he barricaded the door, then swung around to pin me against the wall with the iron girders of his arms.

"Am I not what you wanted, Nana? Is this not all you dreamed it would be?" He pulled open the front of his dressing gown, unveiling the beautiful body I'd tailored for him, his manhood hard and eager. Yet there was something inexpressibly sad in those silver-white eyes—the plaintive longing of a neglected child.

I shook my head. "Raphael, we mustn't—"

"We *must*." He tore at my shift, rending the fabric down to my crotch. The frayed linen slid off my left shoulder, and Raphael peppered my breast with seething kisses.

I wanted to cry out but was afraid of what might happen to Ernst if he came to my rescue.

Raphael pressed me against the wall, forcing me to feel the hardness of his erection. "You know this is right. It's what you wanted from the very beginning."

He ground his mouth against mine. When I clamped my jaw shut, he clenched my throat until I gagged, then wormed his tongue between my parted lips. His breath still tasted sour from vomit. Though I thrashed with all my might, Raphael's hands pinioned me as firmly as Frankenstein's manacles.

My body slackened in resignation. Perhaps it was better this way. Raphael and I deserved each other; our life together would be a fitting punishment for our mutual vanity and selfishness. And Ernst would be free of both of us.

I ceased struggling and pretended to return Raphael's kisses. At last, he let me pull my mouth away to speak.

"Yes! Yes, my dearest!" I gulped in fresh air, stroking Raphael's tangled hair in mock affection. "Let's go far away from here. Now! This instant!"

Eyes still watery with emotion, he smiled and stroked my cheek. "We shall, sweet Nana. As soon as I have you."

Then he seized me under each thigh, spreading my legs wide and leaning back as he jammed his engorged shaft inside me. I couldn't help but shriek at the pain of violation as he lifted me from the floor, ramming himself deeper with each thrust. *Please let Ernst be free*, I prayed as a raw ache filled me.

"*Love*," he grunted, as if he'd just learned the word again. His shouts rose to a shriek. "Love, love, *love, LOVE!*"

Raphael reared back, let out a wail so loud I thought he had climaxed, and let go of me.

I fell off him, legs flailing as I thumped to the floor, and scampered away on hands and knees. When I glanced back, I saw that Raphael was groping behind his back, trying to grasp a metal rod Ernst had stabbed deep into the soft tissue below his ribcage. It was the catheter I'd used when creating Raphael, the pointed tube with which I'd injected blood into his empty veins.

The pump Ernst held did not circulate blood. Instead, he'd inserted its siphon into a corked flask whose shape and label I recognized from the laboratory. It was the sleeping draught I'd been putting in Raphael's food. While Raphael struggled to wrench the catheter loose, Ernst pumped in enough of the colored fluid to kill a dozen ordinary men.

The metal rod still in his back, Raphael wheeled around, jerking the pump from Ernst's hands. The half-empty flask of poison flew aside to smash and splatter the wall. Already lurching from the drug's effect, Raphael lunged toward Ernst, hands outstretched. Ernst stumbled backward, but Raphael caught him by the throat, raising Ernst from the floor until his feet fluttered helplessly in a hanged man's dance.

With only an instant to act before Raphael snapped Ernst's neck, I scanned the room for a weapon. I ran to snatch the first thing that caught my eye: the oil lamp on Raphael's reading table. The glass chimney tumbled off as I swung the lamp down onto Raphael's head.

The oil reservoir shattered, dowsing his hair in oil and slicking his face and shoulders with a greasy sheen. The guttering wick struck his scalp immediately after, and Raphael screamed as his dark mane ignited into a halo of fire. Hurling Ernst away from him, he slapped at the flame to put it out, but it engulfed his entire head. His eyes and mouth became black blurs beneath a mask of fire as he flailed blindly about the room, the iron spike of the catheter still protruding from his lower back. I could hear his skin fizz and pop like the crackling of a roasted pig, and the air filled with the stink of burning hair.

With one hand clutching his neck, Ernst got to his feet, dodging as Raphael nearly careened into him. "Come on!" he rasped, nodding toward the door.

I gaped, aghast at what I had done. "But we can't leave him—"

Raphael blundered against one of the library's windows. Pawing at the heavy drapes, he tried to wrap himself in them to smother the blaze but succeeded only in setting the lace curtains afire.

"There's no hope for him." Ernst yanked my arm. "We've got to get out of here!"

As I let him tug me from the room, flames lapped at the ceiling and fanned out toward the crisp kindling of the books that lined the library's shelves. Raphael pirouetted drunkenly amid the inferno, yowling piteously, a mad dervish whirling in Hell.

Tendrils of smoke followed us into the hall. Ernst dragged me back to his bedchamber, where he hauled a small valise out from under the bed and threw it on the mattress. "Dress quickly," he commanded. "And take only what you can put in here. Pack valuables we can sell."

I didn't argue. Trying not to think about Raphael, I took the valise into my bedchamber and stripped off my shredded shift. I wriggled into the first outfit I could lay hands on, though I was shaking so badly I could barely lace my ribbons or button my shoes. Without a pause, I thrust what remained of Katarina von Kemp's jewels into the case, then tossed in some clean undergarments and other small articles of clothing. There wasn't room for another dress, so I'd make do with the one I wore. All my worldly possessions now fit in a box no bigger than a sewing basket. Despite the warmth of the spreading fire, I put on the heavy, hooded coat I'd worn in the Arctic. The night outside was cold, and I had no idea when we might find shelter again.

When I returned, I saw Ernst unlock a metal chest he kept in his wardrobe. He withdrew several leather pouches. These he stuffed into a large drawstring knapsack, then crammed a few crumpled shirts in on top of them. He cinched the sack shut and slung it over his shoulder.

A searing torrent of heat hit us as we hurried out into the hall, toward the stairs. Our travel preparations had been the work of but a few minutes, yet in that time a black cloud had billowed out from the library to fill the corridor. We covered our mouths, choking on soot, and stamped down the stairs. I couldn't stop myself from casting a glance back at the library doorway.

Raphael's cries had stopped.

Minna and Nadja bustled up to us as we reached the base of the stairs. Each held a lit taper, and both were still barefoot from bed, wearing only nightgowns and kerchiefs.

"Herr Doktor!" Minna cried. "What is happening? We heard screams, smelled smoke—"

"The house is on fire," Ernst said. "We must leave at once. Go wake Oskar and Gert and have them hitch horses to two wagons—one to take both of you into town, and one for me and Fräulein Frankenstein."

Minna shook her head. "The house . . . ?"

"The house is lost."

I could not believe it any more than Minna did. Ernst's beautiful manor. But he was right: by the time the men could fetch buckets of water, it would be impossible to quench the flames.

"But what's to become of us?" Nadja pleaded.

"Don't worry, I'll provide for you. Now please hurry."

"And what about . . . the other gentleman? Your patient." Minna glanced downward, obviously thinking Raphael was still confined in the cellar.

I looked at Ernst, but his expression remained impassive, resolute.

"He perished," Ernst told her.

I had to accept that as fact, too.

A loud popping and cracking reverberated through the ceiling, punctuated by the thud of some heavy chunk of wood on the floor upstairs. The servants scampered to scavenge what belongings they could bundle into their bedsheets before Ernst shepherded them to safety outside. There was no need to wake the stable hands by then, for the men were already stumbling from their quarters half-dressed, Oskar hopping on one foot as he tried to pull his boot on while running. It was the fastest I'd ever seen him move to complete any task.

As the men readied the wagons, I had little to do but gaze at the flames gutting the house from within. Every window in the face of the house was still dark, except for the second floor, where the library casements shone a brilliant, flickering orange. The heat had already shattered the glass from the panes, and fire lapped around the windows' blackening frames. Soon it would spread to the adjacent rooms, consuming the upper story until it collapsed into the ground floor below. Then every window in the stone shell of the manse would be bright with gaily dancing firelight.

Ernst busied himself with bridling the horses, never looking back toward the ruin of his ancestral home. I took hold of his hands, made him put aside the reins.

"I'm so sorry," I said.

He regarded me somberly, and I feared he was angry. Then he chuckled. "Someday, we shall think back on this night and celebrate it as the beginning of our new lives."

He hugged me, his eyes shining brighter than the fire, and I laughed until I cried.

CHAPTER 23

VIENNA

It was impossible to obtain a room at an inn at that hour of the night, so Ernst and I were forced to seek shelter with Minna. Her uncle and his wife lived above their small bakery in Ingolstadt, and Minna convinced them to host us until we could lodge elsewhere. Ernst handsomely rewarded both Minna and the uncle for their kindness, giving them each the equivalent of a year's salary from the cache of coins he'd brought with him.

Minna's poor relatives had little space and no accommodations to offer us, so we slept fully clothed on the floor of the bakery, wrapped in a rough woolen horse blanket, our coats folded beneath our heads as makeshift pillows. Despite the night's disaster, the loss of everything I'd worked for, and the uncomfortably hard boards on which we bedded, I slept well, safe in Ernst's embrace.

Around five in the morning, after only a few hours, Minna's uncle woke us, for he had to begin the day's baking. He apologized profusely for having to disturb us and offered us the use of his own bed if we wished to go back to sleep, but Ernst refused.

"There is too much to do," he said, and asked if we could have a bit of bread and cheese to eat.

Before we even finished our breakfast, Ernst drafted glowing letters of recommendation for Minna and Nadja and made a list of his personal acquaintances with whom they might find employment. He then wrote a missive to a wealthy cousin of his in Vienna, informing her of the calamitous fire that had consumed the family manse and humbly beseeching her to provide a temporary home for him and his "wife."

I read the word over his shoulder as he wrote, and Ernst smirked when he saw the uneasy look on my face.

"A tiny lie for the sake of social propriety." He took hold of my hands, his smile softening as he looked into my eyes. "I shall make it true as soon as I can."

He dipped his fingers in the breast pocket of his waistcoat and took out two rings—one an engagement ring with a brilliant-cut diamond, the other a simple gold wedding band. Following German tradition, he slid them gently onto the third finger of my right hand. "I'm told that these were my mother's. If you don't like them, I can get others later—"

"No, no! They're perfect."

I returned his smile weakly. Ernst had assumed I wanted reassurance that his intentions were honorable. He did not know about the last time that I'd pretended to be someone's wife and what had become of my prospective bridegroom.

I sloughed off the memory of Stefan's severed head as if it were a husk of dead skin. Ernst was right: the purifying fire had burned away our past sins, and we had commenced a new life. Our life together.

It took us nearly a week's journey to travel to Vienna, and with each passing day and mile that separated us from Ingolstadt, my heart grew lighter. We stayed at inns and boarding houses as husband and wife, and everyone treated us as if we were any ordinary married couple. We made glorious, intoxicating love in our rooms at night, and nothing bad happened. It began to feel less like an escape and more like a genuine honeymoon.

When we arrived in Vienna, it seemed we'd entered a whole other world. Compared to the sleepy hamlets of Darmstadt and

Ingolstadt, the Austrian capital was a monumental metropolis. Stone facades five stories high flanked the broad avenues and narrow side streets, their neat rows of windows framed with carved pediments of a grandeur and elegance that I had seen only in engravings of the architecture of Paris and Versailles. Palatial public buildings, columned and corniced and domed, ornamented the city like Roman temples. The market squares thronged with more people than I had seen in my entire life, and several times our carriage had to stop to avoid plowing into groups of well-dressed pedestrians and shouting street vendors.

As we wended our way to his cousin's house, Ernst pointed out the home where Haydn had died and another where Beethoven still lived. The city breathed life and beauty, and I exulted in it as if seeing the glory of the sun for the first time. At times, I nearly deluded myself into thinking I was just an ordinary woman, young and in love, with the simple joys of a home and family to look forward to.

But I was not an ordinary woman, and I made sure that my scarf was wound tightly over the scar around my neck before Ernst introduced me to his cousin.

Her name was Klara, a slender, handsome woman of late middle age whose wig of dark brown ringlets looked a trifle too young to match her shriveling face. Yet her gay manner made her seem younger than her years, and she greeted us at the door of her elegant townhouse with the fawning fussiness of a mother hen.

"Oh, you poor dears!" She hugged Ernst, kissing him on both cheeks. "First your dear father's murder, then the house set fire! At least you're both safe."

"Yes," Ernst said. "Anna and I can hardly repay your kindness—"

"Oh, nonsense! Think nothing of it." She took hold of my hands. "And isn't she lovely? Ernst, you were really quite wicked for keeping her a secret from us."

He smiled. "Well, I'm delighted to share her with you at last."

"Dear cousin!" She kissed my cheeks as well, then ushered me into a charming antechamber adorned in the latest fashion, accented with golden wallpapers and satin draperies that made the room glow like spring sunshine on a field of daffodils. "I hope you will be comfortable here."

"It's only until I can set up my practice and obtain a place of our own," Ernst said as the serving girl who'd let us in shut the door behind him.

"Nonsense! Stay as long as you wish. Now that the children are grown, Friedrich and I hardly have company." Klara laughed as she led us up a narrow stairwell to the second-floor bedchambers. "Do forgive us for cloistering you in our daughters' old room."

The apartment she presented to us was much smaller than the parlor downstairs but equally quaint. Burgundy diamonds patterned the carpeting while stenciled green vines snaked up the wallpapers. Rows of porcelain figurines lined the shelves of a small china cabinet like tiers of spectators in an amphitheater. All the furniture in the room—the chairs, the writing desk, the dressing table, the wardrobe—appeared to be a size too small, as if fitted for a doll's house. Two identical beds sat parallel to each other at the far end of the room.

"We shall have a proper bed for the two of you put in as soon as we can," Klara promised.

"It's perfect," I murmured. "Thank you again . . . cousin."

She smiled graciously. "I'll let you two refresh yourselves before dinner. There's a bell rope by the bed if you need to ring for the maid."

She withdrew and shut the door. Ernst waited until her footsteps receded down the hall, then pushed the two small beds together to mimic a larger one. He caught me around the waist and pulled me onto the paired mattresses with him. I let out a small squeal of surprise and had to stifle a giggle as the wooden bed frames creaked so loudly under our weight that I was sure the whole house would hear us. The beds were so short, Ernst's feet stuck out over the floor.

"Will it do for now, Frau Waldman?" he purred.

I ruffled his hair. "Splendidly, Herr Dr. Waldman." I sighed. "It's all so like a dream, I'm afraid of waking up."

"So let us sleep forever." Ernst rolled onto his side, massaging my mouth with his in an ever-deepening kiss, and we lost the afternoon in lovemaking.

For the first two weeks we were there, the dream lingered. Ernst and I dined at lavish parties hosted by Klara and Friedrich, strolled in the shade of the horse chestnut trees in the Prater, attended the latest opera at the Leopoldstadter. Ernst even tried to teach me to waltz, although I danced so badly I joked that Frankenstein must have given me two left legs.

We might have gone on this way, joyously oblivious, for the rest of our lives if Ernst hadn't insisted on reading the newspaper during one of our afternoon visits to his favorite local coffeehouse.

The establishment was among the oldest and most venerable in the city, its interior still boasting the traditional Turkish style, with a high, arched ceiling and floor of brown brick. A large and loyal clientele clustered around its small wooden tables: frock-coated dandies wooing their women, old men frowning over games of chess, self-styled intellectuals debating art and philosophy for the pleasure of hearing themselves talk. We inevitably had to wait to seat ourselves, and it was during such an idle moment that Ernst purchased a copy of the *Wiener Zeitung* from the proprietor—a portly, mustachioed man robed in purple Ottoman attire.

A few minutes later, when we at last found a vacant table, this same gentleman poured us each a demitasse of thick, steaming brown coffee from a long-necked brass pot. Ernst settled back in his chair and shook out the newspaper broadsheet, skimming the dense paragraphs on the front page while I stirred sugar into my coffee. He folded back the first sheet to peruse the second page and lifted his own cup, but he set it down before it reached his lips. Some article had captured his attention, and he paled as he read it.

"What is it?" I asked, wondering what could have upset him so.

He glanced up, startled, and forced a laugh. "Politics!" he said, shaking his head. He folded the paper and shoved it between his thigh and the arm of the chair in which he sat. "Now, let's talk about this wedding we've been putting off . . ."

With strained gaiety, he peppered me with questions about where we should hold the ceremony, what sort of dress I wanted to wear, and whether to invite any guests given that we were pretending to be married already. I mumbled answers that I hardly thought about, and found it difficult to keep my gaze from flicking to that newspaper. I wanted to jump up and snatch it from him.

Finally, I cut off his trivial chitchat and rose from my chair. "I'm sorry. Would you excuse me?"

Ernst stood and bowed like the gentleman he was. "Of course, my dear."

I moved off in the direction of the side exit to the coffeehouse, which led to the detached privy outside. Before I reached the door, however, I looked back through the crowd to see Ernst retake his seat. As soon as I left him, his false cheer dropped away, and he rubbed his chin pensively, staring at whatever unseen object occupied his mind.

When I was sure he wasn't watching, I took a couple of coins from the pouch on my dress, went to the front counter of the coffeehouse, and bought another copy of the *Wiener Zeitung*. I hurried out the side exit and opened the newspaper to the second page, skimming the blocks of type.

Each paragraph had a heading of one or two words, and at first they all seemed the usual assortment of international affairs and local events. Then I came to an item titled "Awful Murders." I braced myself against the outside wall of the coffeehouse to keep from collapsing in despair as I read: "The unidentified madman known as the Fiend of Bavaria has perpetrated another ghastly slaying, this time in the town of Babenhausen . . ."

I might have dismissed the story if it hadn't gone on to say that the string of five killings had begun in the city of Ingolstadt just three weeks earlier. My heart sickened as the writer speculated that the murders might be the work of the same lunatic who was responsible for the brutal decapitation of a young man in Dörnberg in the spring of the previous year.

The present victims, however, all happened to be beautiful young women. The authorities felt certain that the slayings were committed by the same individual, for in each case the malefactor had severed and stolen a different portion of the body, abandoning the rest of the corpse. From one girl, he took the left leg. From another, the right arm. Then a right leg and a left arm. And in the most recent atrocity, he'd absconded with the woman's torso, leaving her head and dismembered limbs in a jumbled heap like discarded doll parts.

Although the Fiend had commenced his parade of horrors in Bavaria, he had moved steadily north and west into Hesse with his subsequent crimes. Ingolstadt, Nuremberg, Schlüsselfeld, Hösbach, Babenhausen . . . the authorities could only guess where the killer might strike next.

But I could tell exactly where the path led, as if a trail of breadcrumbs had been laid out for me. Raphael could have killed only one woman to obtain the body he desired, and Ernst and I might never have learned of his butchery. Instead, he picked the pieces one-by-one, town-by-town, so that we would recognize the signature of his crimes and his ultimate destination.

He wanted us to follow him.

I strode back into the coffeehouse and stood before Ernst's chair, confronting him with the article. "Why didn't you tell me?"

He sighed but did not seem surprised that I had discovered the story. "It's nothing. Just some lunatic. Nothing to do with us."

I glared at him. "You know very well who it is."

"That's impossible!" Ernst checked the roomful of chattering patrons to see who might be listening and hushed his voice to a whisper. "I gave him enough poison to kill ten men."

I laughed hollowly. "Too bad for you he's the equal of twenty."

Ernst raised a hand to silence me. "He died in the fire."

"Did you see him die? Did you find a body in the ashes?"

"There was no need."

"Then you can't be certain." I bent closer to him. "You know where he's going. And you know what he'll do when he gets there. Don't deny it—I see it in your eyes."

"Enough!" Ernst turned his back to me. "No more of this insanity!"

I moved around to kneel before him, took his hands in mine. "Please. If I'm wrong, then there's no harm if we find nothing. But until I'm sure, I'll never have a moment's peace."

Ernst considered me with a sullen look. "Suppose you are right. What will you do if you find him?"

I squeezed Ernst's hand. "He was dead when I brought him into this world. He shall leave it the same way."

Ernst sighed. "Very well. Then I shall go with you."

CHAPTER
24

HOMECOMING

Ernst and I barely spoke during the weeklong trip by coach out of Austria and back through Bavaria. Although we maintained the pretense of being married, our fellow passengers must have taken us for strangers, for we sat opposite each other, staring out the window—he gazing back toward Vienna, I looking ahead to Darmstadt.

Every day, I checked the newspapers for word of another murder. When no further killings occurred, it only intensified my anxiety. Raphael wasn't done with his work. What was he waiting for?

You, his voice replied inside my head.

The weather turned as dismal as our mood. The sky pressed down in gray blankness, misting the air with a cold drizzle that saturated us in clammy misery every time we descended from the carriage to find an inn for the night. On the day we crossed the border into Hesse, the clouds clotted into a great gout of inky darkness. Deep within the thunderhead, the first shimmers of lightning pulsed—the palpitations of a black heart stuttering to life.

Perhaps we were already too late.

A thunderclap boomed louder than cannon fire, and the drizzle became a deluge. Water sheeted down around us until we could hardly see through the streaked curtains of rain. The coach rocked and splashed as the downpour flooded the road, turning the ruts and potholes into craters of mud. The conditions grew so treacherous that on the outskirts of Darmstadt, the carriage lurched so violently to the left that it nearly tipped over. The team of horses whinnied in terror, and I was thrown into the lap of the flustered clergyman seated beside me. A young novice of the Catholic church, he struggled to help me up without actually touching me.

As Ernst and I and our fellow passengers all righted ourselves, we found that the coach itself still canted to the left. The driver's whip cracked, the horses stamped and strained, but the shuddering carriage failed to roll forward. I heard the coachman curse.

"Anna!" Ernst groaned as I leaned out the crooked coach door into the tempest.

The stout coachman squatted beside the left front wheel, spitting oaths. His feet had sunk past the ankles in the same muck in which the wheel was lodged.

"How long before we can move again?" I shouted to be heard over the storm.

He looked up at me in exasperation, rain pelting his face so hard he could barely keep his eyes open. "We're not going anywhere, pretty one."

I jumped down into the river of silt, soaking my skirts. "What if we push?"

"Useless! The axle is cracked."

Already, I was as wet as if I'd been fished out of the ocean, and I clawed aside the sodden hair that ran into my eyes. "But we *must* get to Darmstadt tonight!"

"Impossible."

Ernst leaped down beside me. "Then how much for one of your horses?"

The coachman wrinkled his face in disbelief. "Are you mad?"

"That one there." Ernst pointed to a lean, muscular, brown gelding at the head of the team. "Name your price."

The coachman looked up at the worsening storm, down at the

broken wheel. "Well, then, let's see just how mad you are," he said to Ernst, and demanded five times what the horse was worth.

Ernst paid him at once from the purse in his coat pocket, on the condition that we could keep the bridle and cut the reins that joined the gelding to the rest of the team. "And since we can't take them with us, you can sell our things as well," he added.

We jumped back up into the carriage compartment briefly, and Ernst wrested two items from our luggage: a cutlass in its scabbard that he'd wrapped in black felt and a small wooden box. Ernst strapped the cutlass to his side with his leather belt, and from the box drew a pair of flintlock pistols. I'd seen him load the guns as we'd prepared for our journey and knew what he planned to do with them. These he also stuck under his belt, then tried as best he could to cover them with the tails of his coat to keep the flints and powder dry.

The clergyman still huddled inside the coach, shivering as a fusillade of raindrops bombarded the roof. "Y-you're quite sure you want to go out in this frightful flood?" he worried aloud.

"*Want* has nothing to do with it," Ernst muttered. "We *must*."

"Then God be with you." The young priest made the sign of the Cross.

"I'm afraid God has nothing to do with it, either," I said.

Ernst and I abandoned the shelter of the disabled coach and went to claim our new horse. The carriage driver shook his head and climbed inside to sit with the priest, where it remained relatively dry. The road was now a river, and I had to lift my skirts to wade forward to the brown gelding. Torrents of rain soaked our clothes until they weighed on our shoulders like chain mail.

Ernst grabbed the makeshift reins he'd cut from the team's leather tack and pulled himself up onto the horse, settling himself so far forward that his legs were nearly astride the beast's front shoulders. "No saddle, so we'll have to ride bareback," he shouted. "Hold on tight!"

He held out his arm to help me climb on behind him. The horse was so slippery that I nearly slid off as I hitched up my dress and swung my leg over to straddle the beast.

Before I'd had a chance to get my balance, the horse lurched ahead. Again, I nearly fell off, and I caught hold of Ernst around the waist with such force that he cried out in pain.

"*Ugh!* Not *that* tight."

Thunder cracked like a riding crop, and the skittish horse trudged forward, plucking its hooves from the mud with every step. I clamped my legs on its flanks and clung to Ernst, glancing over his shoulder at the terrain ahead. Hair kept running in my eyes, but I didn't dare let go of Ernst for a second to brush it aside.

The trees at either side of the road were little more than dark blurs seen through the rippling curtains of water, and at times we seemed to be swimming in place. With every clap of thunder, the gelding balked and attempted to bolt in the opposite direction, but Ernst reined in the horse and prodded it onward.

Night fell, the starless dark so deep that we were grateful for every bolt of lightning that fitfully brightened our path. A crooked trident of quicksilver split the heavens, and we saw that the forest had given way to rolling hills of fields and vineyards. And there in the distance cowered a tiny cluster of buildings with the modest spire of the Stadtkirche at its center: Darmstadt.

"Thank heaven!" Ernst said. "At least now we have someplace to stay the night—"

"No," I insisted. "No, we have to go on. That way." I pointed to the left.

He frowned but snapped the horse's reins, veering it in the direction I indicated.

Before long, the terrain sloped upward at a steeper angle, and the cleared croplands disappeared from view as we plunged into another dense thicket of forest. Clammy from the constant wet, I tingled with recognition at my surroundings.

With a boom that sounded like mountains colliding, a bolt struck an elm barely a hundred yards ahead of us. The tree flared with blinding blue fire, its trunk splintering shards of bark. An enormous bough creaked, broke off, and crashed to the ground. Terrified, our horse reared and stamped, throwing both Ernst and me into the mud.

Our clothing splattered and our faces smeared, we scrabbled up onto our feet, but the horse had already clopped off into the darkness, its loose reins whipping in the wind.

"That does it!" Ernst despaired. "We'll never get there now!"

He yelled, but I could barely hear him over the ringing in my ears. "No!" I cried. "It's not that far. We can make it on foot."

"How do you know?"

"I've done it before."

I grabbed his hand and yanked him with me as I darted through the forest, leaping over tree roots and stomping through puddles. It ought to have been impossible to find my way under those conditions, but the memory of my first night was fixed so clearly in my mind that I felt I could have retraced my steps blindfolded.

Up and up we went, until we at last broke free from the forest into a wide clearing.

"Look!" I indicated a tiny yellow light that appeared to hover in midair far above us. Only when the next stroke of lighting flashed could we see the stone facade of Castle Frankenstein before us. The solitary light shone from one of the rectangular windows near the top of the tower. Every other window in the structure was utterly black.

With the shimmer of another thunderbolt, the heavy double doors of the entrance flickered into visibility. We approached, and I was about to pull the bell chain when Ernst grabbed my hand and put a finger to his lips. He gestured to the right-hand door, and I saw that it stood slightly ajar, as if someone anticipated our arrival.

I eased the door open and crossed the threshold. Rain gusted through the archway behind me, the wind and spatter echoing in the marbled cavity of the foyer. It was dark as a crypt and we had no means of lighting a candle, so I inched forward with my arms extended, fingering the air like a blind woman.

Ernst edged in beside me. As we advanced, our drenched clothes dripped trails of water on the floor. At least we had a roof over our heads.

As I pawed my way toward the right, seeking the stairway to

the tower, my foot struck a soft-yet-cumbersome object on the polished stone. It slid away as I inadvertently kicked it. Afraid of tripping over the thing, I moved to nudge it aside, but my toe hit a larger, heavier bulk that resisted my efforts to push it with my foot. I almost slipped, for the floor was slick with what I assumed was the rainwater I'd tracked inside. I would have stooped to feel what the obstruction was, but lightning flashed outside the open castle door, throwing cold light onto a face mere inches from my own.

It was the old servant, Hans. He glared at me in wide-eyed affront, his shriveled mouth agape.

I staggered back against Ernst, certain that Hans was about to raise the alarm and rouse the whole house against us.

Lightning flashed again, showing me that I had nothing to fear from the servant. The truth was far, far worse. The old man's severed head had been impaled on a pike held by the suit of armor that stood to one side of the castle's entry.

A scream caught in my throat like a bone, and I choked to release it. Ernst slapped a hand over my mouth to hold it in.

The flicker of illumination playing over the floor revealed that the object I had kicked was Hans's arm, twisted and ripped from the body as if it were the leg of a roast goose. Black blood coated the floor, smeared by shoeprints where I'd stepped in it.

Beside the arm lay the corpse's headless trunk, and beyond that other pieces of dismembered anatomy. Too many to belong to one old man. *We're expecting the master's aunt Lenya and her family,* Hans had said the last time I had come to the castle. My heart sank to think that what I saw before me might be them.

A mosaic of human limbs extended into the darkness, laid out with horrid humor. The head of a little girl—a cherub-faced waif with blue ribbons still entwined in her auburn curls—had been stitched onto the neck of a fat, middle-aged man in a great coat and riding boots. The bodies of a blue-veined crone and a peach-skinned maiden had been stripped naked, cut in quarters, and reassembled as mismatched patchworks, mirror images, each with one full, supple bosom and one sagging, wrinkled breast.

Was Raphael simply mocking the atrocities that Frankenstein and I had perpetrated? Or was he . . . *practicing* them?

I tore Ernst's hand from my mouth and stalked in the direction of the stairs. He rushed to take the lead, shushing me when I tried to protest. Without thunderbolts to light the cavernous stairwell, we had to feel our way upward a step at a time. Ernst drew his sword and sliced it through the darkness ahead of him in case anyone silently waited in the thick shadows to prey upon us.

As we scuffled up the last flight of steps to the top floor of the tower, a wan yellow glow greeted us. The light offered no relief. No doubt it emanated from the single lamp we'd seen in the tower window. I'd expected that the door to Frankenstein's laboratory would be shut and bolted against intruders, but instead it had been left wide open for us.

Still brandishing the sword with his right hand, Ernst fumbled one of the two flintlock pistols out from under his coat before approaching the door. I took advantage of his momentary distraction to enter the room first. Ernst glowered and shoved in beside me, weapons raised.

The air inside the laboratory was frigid, and my wet cheeks and hair stiffened as if rimed with frost. Chuffing out white vapor, I soon saw the cause of the cold: half-melted blocks of ice surrounded the wooden slab where I had been born. And on that plank lay a nude female form, its delicate arms and graceful legs sewn to a voluptuous torso with such fine stitches, that, once the wounds closed and the black thread had been removed, the scars would hardly be visible at all.

Raphael had obviously honed his skill as a surgeon.

He had not completed his creation, however. The neck remained a ragged red bundle of loose tendons, disconnected veins, severed windpipe, and spinal column. Yet the body lay ready to receive the final spark: manacles dangled from chains beside the delicate ankles and wrists, and another chain ran to a circlet of electrodes that rested in the vacant place where the head would be, awaiting the brow it would crown. Once the iron bonds had been fastened to the finished woman, the next thunderbolt that struck the tower's lightning rod would surge down the chains and into the dormant beauty, rousing her in violent resurrection.

Beyond the slab, at the far end of the room, burned the lamp in the window we'd seen from below. Its sickly halo outlined the silhouette of a hulking figure hunched on a wooden stool. The reflected light from the bald dome of its head gleamed slick and red, as if the skin had been peeled from the scalp.

"I knew you'd come, Nana," it said.

The voice was Raphael's, but the words had an odd, slobbering lisp to them. Ernst needed no further proof of the speaker's identity, however. He aimed the flintlock at the figure's heart and pulled the trigger. The hammer snapped, but the pistol didn't fire. The rain must have saturated the gun's black powder too much for it to ignite.

Raphael gave a gurgling chuckle as he rose from his seat. "And you've brought Herr Dr. Waldman. How fortunate! It saves me the trouble of finding him."

Ernst threw down the useless gun and switched the sword to his right hand, point extended. Raphael ignored the threat.

"Your murders brought us here," I said coldly. "What do you want?"

"Why, to show you everything I've learned." He lurched toward the slab with a limp that favored the left leg, his arms and hands held in an almost arthritic cramp. He passed a window just as lightning glimmered outside, frenetically illuminating his shadowed form.

I gasped. *My beautiful Raphael . . .*

I saw now why he gurgled and hissed—his right cheek had nearly burned away. A grotesque halfgrin permanently exposed his teeth and tongue, so that he had to slurp up spittle to keep from drooling. He rolled his eyes up until the irises nearly disappeared, and I realized that his eyelids had shriveled like parched rose petals, leaving him unable to blink. Not a hair remained on his entire body, and scabs and scars encrusted every inch of skin. He moved with pained, mincing deliberation, as if any reckless gesture might cause his wounds to crack and bleed anew.

"You see? I saved it." Raphael held aloft a large, leather-bound book, the edges of its vellum pages singed to feathery ash. Though its cover was blackened beyond recognition, I knew it was Frankenstein's notebook. "The rest I learned from you."

His horrible grin widened with pride as he lifted a hand to indicate the unfinished body on the slab.

"You came all this way just to make a woman for yourself?" I muttered. With Ernst's house burned to the ground, Raphael needed the only other laboratory in existence that would suit his purpose: Victor Frankenstein's.

He shook his head. "You should know by now that no other woman will do for me, Nana. And I mean to have you—one way or another."

He smiled at the headless cadaver on the slab. I put my hands to my throat, trembling. Now I understood why the body was not complete. Raphael wanted to top his creation with my head, to fashion his own "Nana" that he could teach and tame and possess, just as I had wanted to possess him. It hardly mattered whether he could succeed in revivifying Katarina von Kemp's borrowed visage a second time; I would be dead regardless.

"Pathetic creature," Ernst said. "If you have a soul, may God have mercy on it."

With the stance of a seasoned fencer, he circled toward Raphael, lunging and feinting with the sword, inviting his rival to enter the swath of his blade.

Raphael advanced on him, beckoning. "Yesss . . . come, little stick-man. Let me break you."

The gap between them closed. Ernst swished the blade, but Raphael dodged, remaining just outside the sword's radius, his arms raised as if they, too, were weapons. The rivals danced around each other in a seeming standoff, then Ernst thrust the sword in a lethal jab toward Raphael's heart.

Raphael had no fear of pain. He grasped the blade with both hands before the point touched his chest and did not even flinch when the keen edge razored his palms. The gashes leaked blood as Raphael twisted the sword out of Ernst's grasp and broke it in two with a snap of ringing steel. He cast aside the pieces and slouched toward Ernst with an unhurried air, grinning at the easy kill to come. Ernst backed against the wall and pulled the other dueling pistol out from his belt. The flintlock's hammer clacked impotently as Raphael seized Ernst by the throat.

Unable to find a weapon of my own, I dove toward the slab with its headless maiden. I dragged the naked cadaver off the wooden plank and held it up in front of me as if modeling a wedding gown. "Is *this* what you want?" I sneered to Raphael.

Raphael froze, Ernst gagging and gasping in his grasp. One small squeeze of his mighty hands and Ernst's neck would crumple like a paper lantern.

With my left arm around the body's waist to support its weight, I ran my right hand over the cold, porcelain flesh, cupping my fingers under one turgid breast and massaging it seductively. Syrupy blood dribbled from the open neck to stain my chin.

Raphael licked his raw lips as he watched me. "You leave her alone," he rasped.

I flicked my gaze toward Ernst. "Whatever you do to him, I do to her."

Raphael growled, shaking with frustrated rage. Then he threw Ernst against the wall and stepped away.

"Good," I said. "Then take your plaything."

With all my unnatural strength, I hurled the slack-limbed corpse at Raphael. The nude body slapped into him like a sack of flour, loose arms flopping over his shoulders. Despite his massive size, the blow nearly knocked Raphael over. He grabbed the headless woman around the waist, and they did a macabre, teetering waltz as Raphael tried to regain his balance.

Before he could steady himself I charged, hands poised like the horns of a stampeding bull. I barreled into Raphael and his unfinished bride, and the three of us tumbled to the floor together in a hideous *ménage à trois*.

I pushed myself off him, but before I could get to my feet Raphael shoved aside the corpse and grabbed my head with both hands, as if he meant to wrench it off my neck right then.

Instead, he pulled my mouth to what remained of his burned and blistered lips for a loathsome, slavering kiss. My own lips touched the slimed ivory of bare teeth where the flesh had burned away. Even his tongue had stiffened and deformed with scar tissue. I slammed his chest with all my force, clawed the cooked meat of his face until it squished under my fingernails, but he did not loosen his grip.

Then there was a sound like ripping curtains. Raphael howled and let go of me. As I rolled away, panting for breath, I saw that Ernst had taken off his coat and wrapped it around the broken end of the sword blade, which he'd driven deep into Raphael's abdomen.

Before Ernst could release the blade, Raphael snarled and caught hold of Ernst's forearm. With a single turn of his enormous fist, Raphael snapped the bones as easily as dry branches. Ernst screamed as his right hand flapped from a sagging sleeve of skin and muscle, the pinkish splinter of the fractured ulna needling out through torn flesh.

I did the same to Raphael's leg.

Gripping him just above the left ankle with one hand, I rammed the palm of my other hand against his shin until I heard it crack. Raphael shrieked, releasing Ernst so he could reach for me.

I yanked on the broken leg. Raphael wailed and kicked wildly as I dragged him back toward the slab and the chains that dangled beside it.

"*Ernst!*" I yelled, struggling to lift Raphael's leg toward the closest of the iron manacles. "The key!" I jerked my head toward the metal ring that hung from the wooden peg on the wall behind me.

Tears of agony streaking his face, Ernst propped his useless right arm against his chest and ran to snatch the ring from the peg with his left hand. I had to hold on to Raphael's ankle with both hands to keep him from wriggling free. He tried repeatedly to get upright, but each time he sat forward it nudged the sword blade further up into his chest cavity, inching it toward his heart.

Holding the key ring in his teeth, Ernst opened the cuff of the manacle with his left hand. He pulled the chain toward Raphael's foot, but it didn't quite reach.

My grip on Raphael's ankle slipped, and he thrashed even harder to shake me off. Hugging his leg to my chest and leveraging all my weight against it, I gave a final tug. Ernst snapped the shackle shut around the ankle. He did his best to hold the manacle closed while I took the key from his mouth and screwed it in to secure the lock.

The chain rattled and stretched taut, jerking the ring from my hand before I could remove the key from the shackle. Raphael crabbed forward on his hands and his one free foot and groped for the key. Still unable to sit upright, he extended his fingers toward the clattering ring that swung from the lock but couldn't reach his elevated foot.

Roaring in frustration, he pounced at me, scrabbling along on his three good limbs until he'd pulled the chain as far as it would go.

"YOU MADE ME FOR YOU!" he bellowed when I shrank from him. Thunder amplified his anger. *"WE BELONG TO EACH OTHER!"*

I wanted to comfort him somehow, yet I dared not get too close. "I'm sorry," I whispered.

Standing well outside Raphael's reach, Ernst shook his head sadly.

Enraged anew, Raphael looked from the crooked shin of his broken leg, fastened in its iron cuff, to the stub of sword that jutted from his stomach. With an awful yell, he took hold of the nub end of the blade and drew it out of his gut with excruciating slowness.

"Good God," Ernst breathed when he saw what Raphael intended to do. "We must end it. Now!"

As sporadic bursts of light shone through the windows from the thunderbolts outside, he scanned the black corners of the laboratory. Failing to find what he sought, he sprinted out the door into the gloom of the tower's stairwell.

"Ernst?" I peered after him, wondering where he could possibly have gone.

Raphael grunted and roared with triumph as the last of the broken sword slid free from his wound. I sickened when he took the bloodied blade in his fist and hacked at his shackled shin right where the bone had snapped.

Like a wolf that will chew off its own leg to escape from a trap, Raphael meant to free himself at any cost.

"Ernst!" I cried as I saw the blade gradually cleave the foot from the leg. I backed toward the laboratory's exit, ready to fight or flee, glancing around for any weapon close at hand. *"Ernst!"*

Only a thin strip of sinew still strung the foot and leg together. Blood spouted from the open stump. Any ordinary man would have slumped in death long before. Madness alone seemed to sustain Raphael. He slashed the last bit of muscle, then used the swinging chain that held his severed foot to pull himself up onto his right leg. Hanging onto the chain with his left hand for support and bracing himself against the wooden operating slab, Raphael brandished the sword blade in his right hand and smiled.

"I . . . can . . . always get a new leg," he gurgled, swaying drunkenly. "Maybe I'll . . . take one from Herr Doktor. But I *need* you."

He raised the blade as if to dart it at me like a dagger.

Before he could let it fly, though, a thunderclap as loud as the trump of Judgment rocked the tower. The force of it threw me back against the laboratory wall.

A searing white light flared in the room, engulfing Raphael in its aura. Jagged sparks arced from the hanging chains to the tip of the steel blade in Raphael's grasp. He juddered spasmodically, his muscles clenched in a death-grip, his hands unable to let go of either the sword or the chain even as the metal broiled his skin.

A thunderbolt had struck the lightning rod atop the tower. The electricity that had once infused Raphael with life now drained it away.

Then everything went dark, and I thought the Almighty had struck me deaf and blind. I could not hear Raphael's titan body thump to the floor, for my ears still thrummed with the crash of the thunderbolt and all I could see was the ghostly afterimage of Raphael writhing in white radiance, arms flung wide like a wingless angel longing to take flight.

Smell was the first sense that returned to me: the charred odor of crisped skin. The hum in my ears quieted, and I could discern the pop and hiss of steaming meat. Curling vapor rose from behind the operating table where Raphael had fallen.

As the glare of the intense light faded from my vision, I could make out his slumped bulk on the floor. Above him, the chains swayed like slowing pendulums. One still had bits of burned flesh clinging to its links. Raphael lay with his right arm outstretched and did not move.

The strength ran out of my legs, and I slid down the wall until I curled into a trembling heap. Yet I did not take my eyes off Raphael. I needed to know that he was dead but could not bring myself to go near him, so instead I watched for even the slightest movement of his ruined body.

When a flicker of lightning revealed that his right hand had crept forward, I thought it might merely be a figment of my imagination. Then Raphael started to pull himself across the floor toward me, and I shuddered at the thought that somehow my single-minded fear had willed him back to life.

He crawled and mewled like a newborn still bathed in the blood of the womb. His eyes had lost their manic fire and now looked at me with such a frightened, lost confusion that I almost wanted to clasp the hand he lifted toward me.

"*Nana?*" he pleaded.

An ax fell on his neck with a wet clunk. I'd been so intent on Raphael, I hadn't seen that Ernst had returned to the laboratory with a halberd he'd taken from one of the castle's suits of armor. With his good left arm, Ernst held the long-handled weapon high up on its shaft so he could wield it like a hatchet.

Raphael's head rolled away from the blade but the eyes remained open, gazing up at me as if awaiting an answer.

"No," I whispered. "My name is Anna."

Ernst dropped the ax and knelt to hug me.

CHAPTER
25

ANNA AT LAST

Raphael's head rested at the bottom of the small hole I'd dug for it. His red-raw face had purpled to the color of a bruise, and the lidless eyes stared up at me with the same desperate yearning they had during his last moments of life. The white eyes had lost their luminosity, however, the irises dimmed to the gray of the day's overcast sun.

I heaped the blade of my shovel with soil and levered it over the hole but could not bring myself to bury that face forever.

Ernst touched my shoulder with his left hand. "Do it, Anna. It's time you both were free."

I shut my eyes and flipped the blade of the shovel downward. Once the face was covered, I quickly filled in the rest of the hole and packed down the dirt. My arms ached from digging, and I leaned wearily on the spade. With Ernst unable to use his broken arm, I'd had to bury all the dead myself: the pieces of Hans, the headless body stitched together from murdered girls, the abominations Raphael had fashioned from the remains of the Frankenstein heirs. Once the storm had passed, I'd interred them all in the rain-soaked sod beneath the trees that ringed the castle.

I saved Raphael for last. Ernst insisted we cut up the entire body and bury the parts in separate graves.

"A little superstitious of you," I said dryly. "Isn't that what they used to do with suicides? To keep them from coming back as vampires?"

"The men whose corpses we robbed to make him should all have graves of their own," Ernst replied, his splinted arm folded across his chest. He would never admit that, after seeing Raphael survive poison, fire, amputation, and lightning, he feared that even decapitation might not end our misbegotten creation's existence.

We'd set Ernst's broken bones the previous night. He dulled the pain by swilling an entire decanter of cognac he'd found in the castle's front parlor. "To the best medicine . . . and the best doctor . . . I've ever had," he said, lifting the decanter in a toast before guzzling the contents. Then he bit down on a rag, huffing and puffing with muffled screams as I pulled the bones into alignment and lashed them in place with narrow wooden boards and strips of torn linen.

After that, we'd searched the castle until we found the only bedroom that didn't seem to have blood in it—a scullery maid's quarters, by the look of it. I would have thought I'd never sleep again after all the horrors I'd seen that night, but once I lay down alongside Ernst on the chamber's narrow cot, I dropped into unconsciousness almost immediately.

Although I'd cleared the estate of corpses the following morning, there was no way to erase all the blood from the scene of the massacre. Given Castle Frankenstein's remote location and forbidding reputation, it might be days or weeks before anyone discovered the carnage. No doubt it would be attributed to the mysterious killer who'd terrorized the country of late and who would just as mysteriously vanish forever. Ernst and I would be far away by then.

Before we left, though, I had one more act of penance to perform.

I snapped an inch-thick branch off one of the surrounding elms, divided it into two unequal pieces, and lashed them together with twine to form a crude cross. I planted it on the spot where I'd buried Raphael's head—a symbol of the better resurrection I wanted him to have.

"Does he have any hope of Heaven?" I asked softly as I contemplated the marker.

"As much as any of us, I suppose," Ernst replied. "May God forgive us all."

"But if he has no soul . . . then neither do I." I began to weep. The dirt on my fingers smudged my cheeks as I wiped away tears.

Ernst turned me toward him, lifted my face to look into his own. "You have a soul, Anna. I know, because it is the one we share together."

He kissed me, or maybe I kissed him. I cannot remember, and it does not matter. We walked away together and are together still. How long we shall be together and what will become of us is something only the true Creator knows.

STEPHEN WOODWORTH

Stephen Woodworth is the author of the New York Times bestselling Violet Series of paranormal thrillers, including Through Violet Eyes, With Red Hands, In Golden Blood, and From Black Rooms. His short fiction has appeared in such publications as Weird Tales, Realms of Fantasy, Fantasy & Science Fiction, Year's Best Fantasy, Black Wings IV and V, and Midian Unmade. You are welcome to visit him online at-

www.facebook.com/stephen.woodworth2
or at
www.stephenwoodworth.wordpress.com

SHADOWRIDGE PRESS

www.shadowridgepress.com

MAN'S CREATION, MONSTER'S MATE—NOBODY'S SLAVE!

Her fate has become lost in legends. Some say her creator destroyed her; others believe fearful villagers burned her alive. Now, the mate that Victor Frankenstein created for his monster reveals her true story, from her awakening on the slab in the scientist's laboratory, through her tortured initiation into human society, to her desperate quest for a love of her own...even if she has to manufacture the lover she wants.

"As much a gothic romance as it is a horror story, Stephen Woodworth's FRAULEIN FRANKENSTEIN should delight fans of both genres: Unflinchingly dark when it needs to be, but lightened both by a dry wit and an emotionally convincing love story. Our heroine is plucky, resourceful, smart, and alluring. Okay, she's made of old corpse parts, but you'll be surprised by how little that stops you rooting for her. Two transplanted thumbs up!"

— Peter Atkins, author of *Morningstar* and screenwriter of *Hellbound: Hellraiser II* and *Wishmaster*.

Stephen Woodworth is the author of the New York Times bestselling Violet Series of paranormal thrillers, including *Through Violet Eyes*, *With Red Hands*, *In Golden Blood*, and *From Black Rooms*. His short fiction has appeared in such publications as *Weird Tales*, *Realms of Fantasy*, *Fantasy & Science Fiction*, *Year's Best Fantasy*, *Black Wings IV* and V, and *Midian Unmade*.

$14.99 USA

SHADOWRIDGE PRESS

SHADOWRIDGEPRESS.COM